CASTLE IN THE WOODS

ABOUT THE AUTHOR

A former lawyer, Monica Janssens is well qualified to write a book about depression. In the summer of 2005 she was diagnosed with panic disorder and severe clinical depression and admitted to the Priory Hospital in South West London. So, she's 'been there' in every sense of the phrase – both as a personal sufferer who has been to hell and back, and as a sensitive observer of the emotional sufferings of others.

When she regained her health, Monica – a writer and an actress – decided to describe the experience in a novel  which would expose the realities of emotional illness, and explore society's role in creating it. Most of all, she wanted to break down the stigma that still attaches to an illness that by 2020 will be the second most disabling condition in the world after heart disease.

Monica Janssens

CASTLE
IN THE CLOUDS

BUMBURY
PRESS

Copyright © Monica Janssens 2008
First published in 2008 by Bumbury Press
North Den, North Street, Winchelsea, TN36 4HX
www.monicajanssens.com
www.amolibros.com

Distributed by Gardners Books, 1 Whittle Drive, Eastbourne,
East Sussex, BN23 6QH
Tel: +44(0)1323 521555 | Fax: +44(0)1323 521666

British Library Cataloguing in Publication Data
A catalogue record for this book is available from the British Library.

ISBN 978-0-9555657-0-0

Typeset by Amolibros, Milverton, Somerset
This book production has been managed by Amolibros
Printed and bound by T J International Ltd, Padstow, Cornwall, UK

*To Alice for her unstinting support
and encouragement*

FOREWORD

We should be ashamed of ourselves...
we have for years just stood and watched as our
best citizens kept getting this horrid illness,
offering them only blame, contempt and condescension

Dr Tim Cantopher, Depressive Illness: The Curse
of The Strong, 2003

This book is the story of four women and one man
and their battles against a range of depressive illnesses
fought courageously at a rehabilitation clinic just outside
London. Although the characters are not based on real people,
their illnesses are very real indeed. Depression, anxiety and
other mental disorders are biological conditions. When a
person is diagnosed as being depressed, it is their mood
which is depressed. Moods are created by thoughts. All
thoughts are biologically based. They result directly from
the activities of the nerve cells in the brain, meaning anyone
who thinks is vulnerable. Depression is not discriminating
– it affects old and young, rich and poor. In early 2006
Tony Blair's closest friend, the Premier of Western Australia,
Dr Geoff Gallop, resigned on grounds of depression, proving
that no amount of wealth, talent, wisdom or power can

provide immunity. Fame isn't much help, either. In a world where the cult of the celebrity has become almost a religion, those who achieve a god-like status and are idolised in their own time can often fall victim to depressive illness. Overnight success and sudden media attention can prove too intense as the new star struggles – impossibly – to maintain his newfound highs with addictions of all shapes and sizes.

Those who suffer from depressive illness deserve our compassion and should not be ostracised for the enormous pain and anguish they endure. The World Health Organisation is predicting that by 2020 depression will be the number one illness in the developing world. The chances of someone undergoing a major depressive episode at some stage in their life is about one in five. According to the National Institute of Mental Health, more than nineteen million Americans suffer from depression every year, with one in ten committing suicide. In England as many as seven million adults are known to have this illness, with children being equally susceptible. One per cent of under-twelves are thought to suffer while, for the twelve-to-sixteen age group, the figure is three per cent. And these are the cases we know about: around fifty per cent of depressives never seek medical help. Maybe this is because of the stigma attached to the illness, and fears that if the condition were made known, judgements might be made and jobs might be lost. I certainly fell into this category. After I was diagnosed with severe clinical depression and panic disorder, a former colleague put an end to our friendship, while, at work, I was bullied, then fired under the thinly veiled disguise of redundancy.

The cost to our society of failing to recognise the gravity of this illness is both urgent and immense, not least in financial terms. Thirty-three per cent of all sick days taken in the UK are caused by depression and anxiety, costing nine million pounds in terms of treatment, benefits, and lost revenue. An unacceptably high proportion of emotional illnesses is caused by bullying. Around ten million employees in England succumb to bullying in the workplace in the course of a year. Too many sensitive, intelligent people are subjected to intimidating behaviour from colleagues and employers in ways that lead to emotional breakdown. This situation can no longer be tolerated in a just and humane society – if that is what we claim to be.

Perhaps the most common factor linking depressives in today's increasingly anonymous world is a sense of feeling disconnected – be it from community, family or some other closely-knit network. The patient is totally self-absorbed, alienated from everyone and everything around him. During both world wars suicide rates in Britain fell dramatically. Perhaps the strong sense of unity pulling the nation together against a common enemy provided a feeling of belonging not normally experienced by those who take their own life. When writer James Baldwin suggested that the key to contentment is to use individual experience 'to connect me with other people instead of dividing me from them', he hit the nail right on the head.

If anyone is in doubt about the agonising nature of depression, and the physical nature of the pain it inflicts, perhaps the first-hand testimony of a sufferer may prove enlightening. Former President of the Royal College of General Practitioners, Dr John Horder, has experienced renal colic, heart attack and a depressive episode, and has concluded that the last was by far the most excruciating:

> *If I had to choose again, I would prefer to avoid the pain of depression. It is a surprisingly physical sensation, with a surprising semblance to coronary pain, because it too is total. But it cannot be relieved quickly. It even threatens life. It is oneself and not part of one's machinery, a form of total paralysis of desire, hope, capacity to decide what to do, to think, or to feel except pain and misery.*

A radical shift is required to change our culture from one that stigmatises and condemns the emotionally unwell to one that respects and cherishes them – a society that acknowledges its role in promoting depressive illness and takes steps to rethink its priorities. We fail to do so at our peril. What we need is a large dose of emotional intelligence. This book is an attempt to turn that hope into a reality.

Monica Janssens, 2008

MARIANNE

*The way I see it I've got two choices. I can either
turn up for work on Monday—or I can kill myself*

It begins with a nightmare and it goes something like
this. She's driving a car and she can't control the speed.
Every time she pumps the brakes, the car goes faster and
faster. She's on the verge of crashing.

In the midst of her dream she hears screams. They get
louder and louder. More strident. More frightening. Her
eyes blink open. In the first few moments of consciousness,
she's not sure whether the screams are part of her dream
or what's happening around her—each seems to merge into
the other. Placing a hand on either side of the bed to steady
herself, she attempts to stand, her wobbly legs doing their
best to support her frail body. She finally realises that her
sleeping hell has been replaced by a waking one.

She staggers out into the corridor and sees that the door
to one of the bedrooms in the Observation Unit is wide
open. Nurses and patients run in with towels. Figures emerge
with sheets and pillowcases drenched in blood. She can't
help herself. She has to go in.

There's blood everywhere. On the mattress, the lampshade,
the rug, the curtains. A picture she will carry with her always.

The smell is something she will never forget either: rancid, sickly, completely overpowering. Marianne dips her finger in it. Although she's only touched the surface, she feels the blood seep deep within her, permeating her entire being.

'What's happening?' cries a patient from down the hall.

'It's Kalpana,' comes the reply from another. 'She must have got hold of a blade from somewhere. She's slit her wrist.'

Marianne rushes into the kitchen, turns on the tap and thrusts her hands in the sink, scrubbing her fingers with a scouring pad. A voice behind her makes her jump out of her skin. She turns round to face a plump, ruddy-cheeked woman in a faded pink dressing gown leaning against the counter, a half-full mug of tea nestling between her palms. The two patients exchange a few sentences along the lines of 'Boy, what a night!' and 'Christ, I've only been here two days and already…', before a third woman approaches the group and a conversation ensues. Although she's dressed in an oversized, crumpled T-shirt, and has lank, unkempt hair, the bones are unmistakeable.

It's midnight, she's in a nuthouse and one of the inmates has tried to top herself. Just when she's convinced the night can't get much weirder, in walks Cat Green, one of the world's most controversial supermodels. Marianne can just about manage a feeble 'Hi,' shortly followed by a 'Bloody hell!'—her mouth remaining wide open long after the sounds have dropped out.

'Yeah, I know. Mind you, p'raps the experience will come in handy. You know, for your work.'

'Sorry?'

'I heard you're a novelist. Would have thought this was good material for people like you.'

'Well,' laughs Marianne self-consciously, wondering who has told Cat she writes. 'Yeah, well, possibly. Frankly, though, I think I'd prefer not to see people trying to kill themselves. If you know what I mean.'

The woman in the faded pink dressing gown cuts in: 'Hi. Look, I know this is a really stupid thing to say, but you are…I mean…you really are Cat Green, aren't you?'

The girl shrugs her shoulders, 'Yep, that's me. Sometimes I wish I wasn't but…'

As Marianne totters back to her room, she asks herself: 'Christ, what next?' Judging by what has already happened in the space of just a few hours, virtually anything's on the cards. Ten minutes ago she, Lynette and Cat were complete strangers with nothing in common. But with Kalpana's attempted suicide everything seems to have changed.

Marianne falls into a deep sleep as soon as her head hits the pillow—this time succumbing to a new dream. Given the choice, she would have preferred to stick to the same old nightmare. Better the devil you know and all that crap…

Marianne's painfully aware of how dreams have that cruel habit of making you relive the worst experiences of your life—of taking your fears and making them feel like they're all coming true. This time she's reliving a panic attack—the one she had last week. The one that got her admitted. She's at home sitting on the sofa. A phone call has come and gone. She replaces the receiver and starts shaking. Her pulse is racing faster and faster. Thoughts are running wild in her head.

Just don't see it being a long-term relationship that's all

At first, the words make Marianne so fucking angry she could smash something. And she contemplates throwing the carriage clock at the fireplace. Then, the tears come flooding down and she starts sobbing loudly. The fear engulfs her like a thick noxious fog. She's got to escape.

Just don't see it being a long-term relationship that's all

She stands up. But that's no good, either—the fog is everywhere. Wherever she goes it will find her, it will follow her. She goes out into the hall. She opens the door and thinks about going into the garden. Her breathing's getting heavier, faster, more erratic. Now she's choking. What if she stops breathing all together? Her heart's pounding. Her stomach's churning, her head aches and sharp, searing pains are shooting up the back of her neck. She's so hot she's sweating, yet at the same time a cold, tingling sensation is spreading over her skin. Her legs feel like jelly and she's dizzy. She's going to keel over. She's going to faint. She's having palpitations. She's having a heart attack. She can't stay here. She's got to go out. She turns and staggers back to the sitting room. She can't be alone tonight.

She snatches up the phone and calls her mother. 'Mum, it's over, it's over. You see, you see? I knew it. Didn't I tell you this would happen? He's left me. They all leave in the end. It's me. It must be me. Something's wrong with me.

I'm no good. I shouldn't be here. I don't deserve to live. I can't cope anymore. I can't bear life. It's just too painful. Oh, God, help me, help me. I don't want to be alone.' And she collapses to her knees, finding it almost impossible to breathe.

Just don't see it being a long-term relationship that's all

Marianne has no trust in anyone or anything to get her out of this place. This abyss from which there's no escape. The thought of lying down in the darkness is too much for her. She's too scared to close her eyes. Too frightened to sleep. She'll just lie there shaking in blind terror. Why doesn't someone come and put her out of her misery? After all, they'd be doing the world and her a favour. She doesn't want to live if it means feeling like this—that there's no way out, just blackness. It's pathetic, she knows that. And she's so ashamed. She shouldn't be feeling like this. She knows she shouldn't. But she can't help it…

And then she comes to.

Marianne wakes up to the sound of screaming again—this time it's her own screams—and she begins to wonder if she has actually gone mad. Yes, that's it. Mad. Round the bend. Barmy. Nuts. Crazy. Potty. Mental. Screwy. Deranged. Unhinged. Barking. Bonkers. Loony. Psycho. Demented. At least, that's what everyone will say. But they'd be wrong. This isn't madness. It's a physical illness and it hurts like hell.

And that is why Marianne Louisa Evans has been referred to the Cloisters—probably the most famous hospital in the world. She isn't a celebrity suffering from burn-out. She isn't an alcoholic, or one of those down-and-outs with a cocaine dependency. And she certainly isn't one of those women who weigh about five stone because they can't keep their food down. And what about those kids who are supposed to be suffering from text-message addiction? To Marianne, all those illnesses seem self-indulgent and trivial when compared with hers. She's had a breakdown, a genuine breakdown, that's why she's here—for however long it will take her to get better.

Though, now she actually *is* here, the Cloisters is nothing like she'd been led to believe. Nothing at all. And when Marianne arrived two days ago, she was rather shocked. To begin with, there was absolutely no security. She had expected to find the entrance electronically gated, heavily guarded by bouncers the size of Sumo wrestlers, who'd only let you in if you wore dark shades and flashed your bling. But there was no gate or barrier of any kind. There wasn't even a surveillance camera nestling in a tree. Just a slightly built man in a uniform in a hut sitting on a chair. As Marianne's taxi approached his domain, he merely smiled and waved it through. No interrogation to see who its occupants were or what they were doing there. No search to see if they were undercover hacks on the trail of a scoop, with cameras and tape recorders secreted about their clothing. In fact, nothing to protect this secluded sanctuary from the outside, nor, indeed, its inmates from escaping—just one man with a benign grin who didn't speak English but enjoyed smiling and waving a lot.

And then, the patients were all so ordinary-looking. Scruffy individuals dressed in jeans and T-shirts wandering up and down the gardens talking to themselves, while others lay relaxing on the beautifully manicured lawns listening to iPods and chatting, making the most of the weather. Marianne had been expecting something a little different. Straitjacketed celebs running across the grass, hotly pursued by hoards of paparazzi, closely followed by men in white coats, was nearer to what she'd envisaged. And bars on the windows. Not to mention a woman on the roof, with long, straggly hair waving her arms about the battlements screaming and threatening to jump.

Marianne's imagination tends to be a little over-active because most of the time she lives inside her head. She prefers it that way. When anybody challenges her about it, she gets all defensive. 'I'm a writer,' she says, 'and if I weren't able to fantasise, where would that leave my readers?'

At least the building has lived up to Marianne's expectations. When her taxi pulled up outside the large glass doors, flanked on each side by an enormous palm tree, she couldn't help but be impressed by the rambling, forbidding neo-Gothic mansion before her with its turrets and church-like latticed windows all painted creamy-white. It seemed to go on forever—its majestic roof merging in with the sky like a watercolour. 'A castle in the clouds,' thought Marianne. And she jotted down the phrase in case it came in handy later on.

She got out rather awkwardly—her limbs still shaky. She paid the driver and slowly climbed the shiny marble steps into the hall, her small suitcase in her left hand. The man hadn't asked Marianne whether she was a visitor or a patient—he hadn't demonstrated a wish to make conversation of any kind—and Marianne was in no hurry to volunteer the information. He seemed a little bit anxious to leave. Perhaps he thought just being there might contaminate him—or was that Marianne's imagination working overtime again? Catastrophising, as usual. Thinking the absolute worst.

As Marianne's large, hazel eyes took in her surroundings, she couldn't help thinking that it looked more like a hotel than an institution. It was all so plush and grand. An enormous reception area with a swanky shop selling Cloisters' souvenirs, large paintings on the walls, chandeliers on the ceiling, faux-marble pillars, and elegant plants placed at strategic points to create a calming ambiance. Fashionably dressed people were checking in and out with designer luggage. Others were sitting in huge leather armchairs reading the Health section of *The Times,* helping themselves to a cappuccino from the state-of-the-art coffee machine.

Marianne approached the desk, feeling herself grow smaller and the desk get bigger. Flicking a wayward strand of auburn hair away from her eyes, she announced herself. The short, freckle-faced man behind the desk couldn't hear her at first, she was speaking so softly.

'I'm Marianne Evans. Dr Chaudhry's expecting me.'

That was all she could manage before slumping into the nearest available chair. The pleasant-looking receptionist didn't press her. He'd seen hundreds much worse than Marianne. Stunned, shaky, ghostly figures, some unable to speak, others hardly capable of walking.

While Marianne waited, she watched people come and go. A group of nurses brushed past her on their way out for a break, chatting to each other, laughing and joking. It all looked so normal. Nothing remotely 'mental' about the place at all and not a straitjacket to be seen. Not even a museum piece displayed in a padded showcase. Nobody behaving suspiciously, either—no bulges in their clothes concealing flashguns or tape-recorders.

Marianne was forced back to reality when she saw her consultant coming towards her. A short, immaculately dressed man with sleek, black hair and a moustache, Dr Chaudhry welcomed his patient with a smile, his light green eyes twinkling through his silver-rimmed spectacles.

'I'm glad you've come, Marianne. You've had the courage to take the first step. You're in good hands now and we'll do all we can to get you better. Let's find your room and get you settled in.'

Dr Chaudhry took her suitcase and led her through a never-ending labyrinth of nooks and crannies. A long, meandering corridor made up of endless wards, one after the other, broken up by swing doors. Marianne noticed shuffling nomads who could only have been patients. Shadowy figures—like her, wearing jeans and crumpled T-shirts—paced the floor. They looked vacuous, purposeless and numb as they sleepwalked up and down, as though searching for something they had lost. As Marianne stared at each of them, they seemed familiar to her, like she and they had something in common.

The consultant and his patient continued through the endless passageways, turning left, then right, then left again. They passed rows and rows of numbered doors on both sides. Some were open, revealing bedrooms and their confused occupants. Each ward had a lounge in which comatose figures sat doing jigsaw puzzles and newspaper crosswords while sipping camomile tea. There didn't seem to be much talking going on, except from the nurses and orderlies who went about their duties. At long last they came to the end of the hallway marked by an exit sign straight ahead. This was the Quadrangle. A Chinese-looking nurse, with her hair in a bun and dressed in a blue short-sleeved jacket and matching trousers, approached the psychiatrist and his patient from the nurses' station where two women in casual clothes sat writing in notebooks and consulting files.

'Hello, you must be Marianne. Your room's just here,' she said, smiling and pointing to a doorway to the right.

She led them to the open door. Beyond it was a small, primrose-yellow room with a single bed covered in a yellow and white quilted counterpane, a chair and a table. There was a television and an en suite with a shower. You couldn't describe it as luxurious, but it was comfortable and cheerful. There was a small latticed window framed by a Gothic arch covered in yellow curtains which looked out on to the front lawns. It felt safe to Marianne. Well, sort of. As if nobody could get at her. There was the Castle In The Clouds and there was 'out there'. She could be honest here. Herself. She didn't have to hide and nobody could hurt her. She wouldn't have to go 'out there' for a very long time. And she didn't even want to think about that day. Not now, not tomorrow. With any luck, not ever.

Dr Chaudhry departed, leaving Marianne to close the door behind him. She couldn't bolt it—there was no lock. The reason for this had been explained earlier. Privacy was dangerous. The nursing staff had to be able to let themselves in at any time. Just in case. Marianne took off her cardigan. Her fingers searched for a hook on the back of the door to hang it up, but there wasn't one. She carried the jacket to the bed, laid it on her lap and carried on inspecting the room.

The sun poured through the window, casting shadows on the yellow and white counterpane. She felt protected by its warm rays, though it made her blink and she rubbed her eyes. Taking a deep breath, she put her suitcase on the bed and opened it. Then she started to unpack. She took out her pyjamas and placed them under the crisp white pillows at the top of the bed.

There was a brisk knock at the door, which made her start. A nurse came in. She was a tall, plump, black woman—about forty—with broad shoulders and wiry grey hair. Dressed in a well-starched dark blue overall with white piping, she wore a no-nonsense expression on her face. After explaining to Marianne that she was one of the regular Quad nurses, Matilda proceeded to go about her business which was 'to help you with your luggage'.

'It's just a formality,' she said, without smiling, as her long, chubby fingers rummaged through Marianne's paltry belongings, dividing things into different groups. 'For your own safety, sharp objects like razor blades, scissors, nail files, tweezers, needles (crochet and knitting), pins or knives of any kind are not allowed.' The fast, monotonous way in which she reeled off the list as she rifled through Marianne's underwear suggested she'd been through the routine a thousand times.

'No glass bottles either,' she continued, confiscating a pretty bottle of eau de parfum. 'Don't worry,' she said, examining the label and taking the top off to enjoy its floral scent, 'we'll keep everything safe for you and you can have it back when you leave.'

This explained why there weren't any hooks anywhere. All you needed was to tie a towel up to the hook, put your neck though it, and, hey presto, that would be it. Though, to be honest, if people want to hurt themselves or do themselves in, they'll always find a way. No matter how difficult other people might try to make it. Determination coupled with desperation. That's all you needed. The buckle from a belt, a stud earring—the possibilities were endless.

'In case I feel like harming myself, you mean?' said Marianne. 'Not my style,' she reassured the nurse. 'I prefer pills. Much less mess, if you know what I mean.'

The nurse shook her head, bit her lip and frowned at Marianne.

'Don't worry,' Marianne said. 'Only joking.'

The nurse couldn't raise a smile at Marianne's pathetic attempt at black humour. And neither could Marianne.

'Pills aren't allowed either,' Matilda went on, scrutinising the label on a bottle of tablets from Marianne's luggage, 'except as prescribed by Dr Chaudhry and administered by the nursing staff. So, I'll have to take these off you.'

'But,' remonstrated Marianne, 'they're just vitamin pills.'

'As I've already explained, dearie, pills of any kind are not allowed. Doesn't matter what they are. You can have them back when you leave. Now, where are your car keys?'

'Sorry?' asked Marianne, confused.

'Your car keys, dearie. You car's here, isn't it?'

'No, it isn't,' replied Marianne, 'but why…?'

'Just a precaution, love, that's all. Just in case.'

'In case I escape, you mean?'

'As I said, sweetheart, just a precaution for your own protection.'

The dining room's buzzing. The lunatics in the asylum are sharing some animated conversation. There must be at least two hundred people sitting down at the endless rows of wooden tables placed one after another, about ten people at each. As Marianne walks down the centre aisle—feeling groggy and exhausted after last night's nightmare—and studies the people whose bodies lie hunched over their food, she hears Kalpana's name come up a few times. Why all the fuss? It was just another suicide attempt. Nothing out of the ordinary in this place, surely. Why let it affect your appetite? Mind you, she admits, can't be good PR for the hospital, people committing Hari Kari all over the place. Or, at least, trying to. Sort of gives the impression that whatever they're doing here just isn't working. Probably best to keep that sort of thing quiet—if at all possible. Might put people off coming.

Marianne feels someone tug at her sleeve. It's Cat. So she wasn't dreaming last night. Well, not outside the confines of her room, at any rate.

According to the media's image of the place, Cat Green was exactly the kind of person you'd expect to check into the Cloisters. A celebrity. A huge celebrity, in fact. One of the most famous supermodels in the world. And not a tabloid hack to be seen, thought Marianne. Or bodyguard. Not as far as she could see, anyway.

Cat points to the table she's sharing with Lynette. 'We're sitting over there. Come and join us. Everyone's talking about Kalpana and what happened last night.'

Wow! thinks Marianne. A regular girly session. When we get bored with talking about suicide we can bond by swapping views on self-harm. Once patients arrived at the Cloisters it quickly became the norm to start comparing depressive experiences and methods of suicide. That was all anybody was interested in, really. Hardly surprising, when you thought about it. It was the one thing they all had in common.

Marianne looks hard at Cat. Last night she had noticed on the model's left wrist the tell-tale signs which revealed her obvious self-disgust. But what reasons did someone like Cat have for snorting herself into oblivion and lacerating her arms? Known all over the world for her high-profile life and wild partying, every one envied Cat Green. And just look at her: a body to die for with legs up to her armpits. Dressed in a short, tight denim skirt and lacy, low-cut vest, the top of her head is concealed under a white baseball cap, leaving lank, toffee-coloured wisps of hair to flop over her shoulders. She might look a bit pasty—her face is completely devoid of make-up—and Marianne notices the greyish-looking skin is covered with a few blemishes. Must be the detox. All the same, most of the guys in the dining room were ogling her, and with good reason. Cat Green wasn't on the cover of *Vogue* for nothing.

The others are already digging into their food so Marianne gets in the queue, while Cat goes back to her seat. What culinary delights await her, she wonders, helping herself to a brown plastic tray. The aromas which assault her as she waits in line are not very promising. Marianne glides her tray along the counter. First up on the conveyor belt is toad-in-the-hole. She finds the smell of sausages cooked in batter off-putting—it reminds her of school dinners. Lamb curry? No, that doesn't entice her taste buds, either. Looks a bit too fatty for her liking. In the end, she plumps for a baked spud and tuna, with a salad on the side. She can feel the heat coming from the potato and it's kind of comforting. Armed with her meal, she heads for the girls' table. Eyeing up a space next to Lynette and opposite Cat, she goes to claim it. As she sits down, it strikes Marianne how odd Lynette and Cat look together. The one: a twenty-first-century Venus. The other: dowdy, mumsy and unutterably drab in her navy tracksuit bottoms and sloppy grey T-shirt. Unlike Cat, though, Lynette looks healthy beyond belief with her flushed cheeks and bright eyes. Typical, thinks Marianne. Depression's like that; people might think you look great, but underneath you're completely fucked. Cat's fork is pushing her lunch—a few rocket leaves and a cherry tomato—from one side of the plate to the other, hoping to make it disappear. Cat probably never eats anything at all, thinks Marianne. Well, not properly. Not like the rest of us.

No sooner does Marianne sit down, than Cat attacks her with the latest news on Kalpana.

'Nobody knows how she got hold of a blade. It's a real mystery. Anyway, I spoke to one of the nurses and'—Cat leans her head towards her two companions and lowers her voice—'apparently, she got hold of one of those all-in-one razors, broke into it and got the blade out of the plastic. And the rest, as they say, is history. She's gonna be OK, though. They've stitched her up.'

'Thank God for that,' says Marianne, evidently the only one to appreciate the alternative meaning in Cat's last remark.

Lynette, who's been examining Marianne intently throughout Cat's speech, says, 'What are you here for, Marianne? You never said last night.'

Marianne swallows a little bit of potato and tuna and clears her throat. 'Panic disorder,' she confesses, remembering last night's dream with renewed horror.

'Don't talk to me about panic attacks; they're a real fucker,' exclaims Cat, cupping her face in her hands and shaking her head. 'God, do I need a fag. Can we go into the garden when you two have finished your delicious meal? Haven't had any nicotine for a couple of hours. I'm getting withdrawal symptoms.'

Lynette and Marianne look at Cat in bewilderment.

'OK, OK, I know what you're thinking,' barks Cat, glaring at Marianne and Lynette as if they ought to know better. 'No one has a monopoly on depression, you know. It's got nothing to do with how rich or famous you are. And, you shouldn't believe everything you read in the papers. Just because I'm a supermodel and an addict doesn't mean I don't have any feelings.'

A deathly hush falls on the table.

'Sorry, Cat,' says Marianne, 'I didn't mean...'

'Don't worry about it,' snaps Cat, with an air of feigned

indifference. But, her shaky voice betrays the fact that she does worry about it. A lot.

Marianne peers down at her plate. When she finally looks up, her gaze falls on a man sitting two tables away. He has the saddest, most beautiful eyes she has ever seen, grey-black curly hair and soft, bloodless lips. Eager to deflect attention away from Cat, she asks: 'D'you know who that is, guys? Whatever's wrong with him? I've never seen anyone look so…so dead.'

'It's something to do with his job,' answers Lynette, as they all turn to face the melancholy man concentrating on his toad-in-the-hole. 'Bullying or something. I don't know the details but he's really fucked up.' After a brief pause, she added, 'He's got that rabbit in the headlights look, hasn't he?'

'Poor man,' says Marianne. 'He looks so lost. So haunted.' Cat raises her eyebrows at Marianne, but before she can interrogate her about her remark, Marianne turns to Lynette and asks, 'What brings you to the Happy Hotel, Lynette?'

'Emotional paralysis. I think that's what they call it. Anyway, I've got this problem with food. You know, the kind where you just can't leave the stuff alone? Believe it or not, I used to be a stick insect like Cat, but all this emotional crap has turned me into a hamburger and doughnut junkie. Oh, and drinking. That's another one of my problems.'

Then, after putting a generous fork-load of curry in her mouth, she adds, 'Basically, my emotions are fucked.'

Marianne empathises: 'God, I wish I didn't feel anything sometimes. Feelings are so shitty. At least, mine are.'

'Mine too,' nods Cat in agreement. 'Fucking shit.' Standing

up and jogging on the spot, she pleads: 'Please can we go into the garden now. I'm really desperate for a smoke.'

The Quad consisted of two levels. Both ground and first floors contained a number of en suite bedrooms, a kitchen and a nurses' station, staffed by at least three nurses twenty-four/seven. There was also a patients' lounge situated behind the nurses' station equipped with a TV and DVD machine. The TV was usually left on, invariably showing a cartoon or soap instalment. Behind the nurses' desk was the Observation Unit. This consisted of six small rooms each containing items of a very basic standard including an extremely uncomfortable bed, a rudimentary lamp on a bedside table, a basin and a small wooden chair. No windows, of course—that would be asking for trouble—which made the rooms airless and stuffy. The occupants had to share a shower-room located outside. Each of the rooms had a glass wall enabling the staff to maintain a twenty-four hour vigil. Used for potential suicides—usually, though not always, new arrivals—the rooms were spartanly furnished to encourage the occupants to demonstrate that they were no longer high risk and could be moved into cosier, more cheerful accommodation.

The Quad was on the south side of the building with most of the rooms facing the gardens. It was handy for the Therapy Department, too. All you had to do was go through the ground floor lounge at the back of the building, into the garden and through the other side. The Therapy Department consisted of three floors. There were lots of small rooms used for one-to-one counselling plus four or five larger ones for group sessions. There was also a kitchen and an art room. But the largest room in the department— located on the ground floor—was the Stables. It was a large hall with a high roof and two enormous black beams running across the ceiling. It housed a piano and lots and lots of outsize cushions in different colours. It was in this room that Marianne now found herself.

'Welcome to the Experience of Depression and Anxiety,' says the therapist leading the group.

'Is that supposed to be funny?' Marianne asks herself. 'Isn't that why we're here? Because we've had enough of all that? I for one do not want to re-live the experience of depression and anxiety, thank you very much. I want to stamp on it and kick the living daylights out of it once and for all. Jesus Christ!'

Marianne glances round at the other poor buggers in the room. 'What a bunch of losers,' she says to herself, 'sitting on the floor in a circle. Pretty soon we'll all be holding hands and singing "Here we go round the Mulberry bush".'

Marianne's attention is drawn to the man at the far end. His head hangs heavily over his lap while his shoulders— overwhelmed by whatever emotional crap they are carrying—follow suit. He raises his chin a little and Marianne is struck by the frozen look in his dark brown eyes as they stare down at the wooden floor. Dressed in baggy combat trousers and an oversized T-shirt, Marianne estimates he's about fifty, but it's difficult to pin-point a person's real age in this place. Most people seem older than they actually are—depression and anxiety kind of affect you that way.

'What was it Cat had said about James at lunch?' she thinks. 'Oh, yeah. Bullying. What exactly had they done to him to make him look so washed up? So dead? So desperate to curl up into a ball and disappear?'

Marianne's thoughts are interrupted by the therapist who asks everyone to introduce themselves and say a bit about how they are feeling.

'Why do they always ask us that at the beginning of every session?' she thinks. 'How the fuck do they think depressives feel? OK, I thought, I'll enlighten her. Like shit. Like excrement. Like you can't bear the pain of living. Like you want to die. Big time. That's how most of us feel. Only, I haven't got it in me to do THE THING—as they sometimes call it. I've thought about it. Of course I've thought about it. But it's no good. I'm too much of a coward.'

'I'll start,' says a girl three cushions to the right. Pale and drawn, her hands shaking, she looks up and bravely faces the circle. As she pushes back her shoulder-length blonde hair, Marianne catches sight of her face, which wouldn't have looked amiss in one of Leonardo da Vinci's paintings of the Madonna. Foggy with tears, her almond-shaped eyes are crying out for someone to put her out of her misery.

'I'm Susan,' she stammers, 'and the way I see it I've got two choices. I can either turn up for work on Monday or I can kill myself. And right now, from where I'm sitting, the second option is looking really appealing. I thought things were getting better. I thought life was finally picking up. We were going to Spain, my fiancé and I, to start a new life. It's all arranged. He's got a job out there in real estate and we've even found a place to live. But he's blown it all now, he's blown it.'

The sobbing becomes louder, more hysterical. The patients to the left and right of the girl put their arms around her to offer what little comfort they can. And then James moves. Well, just a little. He pushes the box of tissues—always placed in the middle of the circle for easy access—over to Susan to whom he nods pathetically. It's as if he's trying to say, 'I know you're in pain and I feel for you. I'm offering you these tissues as a token of my support. Because right now I can't speak. It's just too much to ask of me.' Susan grabs a couple of tissues, blows her nose and wipes her eyes still dripping with tears. Within seconds the tissue paper is reduced to a tiny sodden ball, and she reaches out for more. She rubs her eyes some more until her face is completely swollen. Most of the women begin to cry in solidarity, but the men hold back and look down at their laps. Even at the Cloisters, getting a man to weep is a tall order. Especially if he's English, and he's not by himself with his therapist.

'He's an alcoholic,' Susan's soft Irish accent continues, the blubbing not showing any signs of subsiding. 'And yesterday he went on a bender. He promised me he wouldn't. He's been clean for over a year. He promised me, he promised me. Yesterday he took out all the money in my bank account and blew it on gambling and drinking. I can't even pay my mortgage now. I can't pay the electricity, the gas or the bloody council tax. All I've got left in the world is ten pounds.' And with that Susan breaks down in a heap of despair.

Marianne's first inclination is to engage in wanton violence. She wants to kill Susan's other half for putting her through all this agony. 'Presumably, he's the reason she's

21

here in the first place. What's he trying to do to her now? Finish her off? It's always a man, isn't it? After all, that's why I'm here.' Then, something makes her revise her thinking. 'Hang on a minute. He's sick. Like I'm sick. So he might be sorry for what he's done, just like I'm sorry for being such a waste of space. But, wait a minute, he can get better. All he's got to do is just not have that drink. OK, OK, so it's not that simple. But it's got to be easier than not knowing when those bastard thoughts telling me I'm a failure are going to get the fuck out of my head. Yes, I envy him. But then I envy anyone in this world who isn't me. Because they don't have to live with these voices shouting at them, telling them it's the end of the world. Or, maybe that's not fair. Maybe they do.'

There she goes again. Another one of her stream-of-consciousness ramblings. Whenever Marianne has one of these internal dialogues, she always thinks of Virginia Woolf. The woman made a career out of that kind of thinking, so it's hardly surprising she suffered from depression and ended up topping herself. 'I mean,' argues Marianne, 'if a person's coming out with streams of consciousness every five minutes, it's an obvious sign they're depressed, isn't it? It's a dead give-away.' Marianne's depressed all right, but she can still tell when someone is having delusions. And right now poor old Susan is having the Mother of all delusions.

'He loves me,' Susan whispers through her tears. But if she really believes what she's saying, she can't muster any volume to back it up. 'And I love him. I know he'll put the money back into my account. And I know we'll go to Spain.'

'And I know I'll get better,' thinks Marianne to herself. 'Dream on.'

Maggie wasn't as Marianne had expected her. Come to think of it, she couldn't remember what she'd expected. But whatever it was, this wasn't it. A tall, matronly looking woman, possibly in her late-fifties, with dark red hair brushed neatly round to frame her face and a determined chin, her piercing green eyes seemed to see straight through Marianne. Marianne looked into those eyes and wondered whether Maggie had the power to get her out of this quagmire. She was supposed to be a relationships expert. Marianne might be her greatest challenge yet.

Maggie was studying the sketch Marianne had completed in Depression and Anxiety. 'Tell me about your drawing, Marianne.'

Marianne shifted nervously in her seat. She felt hot and clammy, and sweat was beginning to dribble down her forehead. She was trembling all over, her stomach was retching and her arms were shaking. She was clearly fighting off a panic attack.

'I'm in a car. Driving. I can't control the speed. The brakes don't work.'

Suddenly, out of nowhere, the lyrics of a Def Leppard song came flooding into her brain:

I'm hanging on the edge and spinning out of control

'I keep pushing my foot down on the pedal but nothing happens. I'm falling into a well. Head first. There's no bottom.

The thick black fog's following me. Suffocating me. I can't breathe.'

That bloody song again:

You're looking down the barrel of a loaded mind

'It's pitch black. The small chink at the top of the well has virtually disappeared. I'm falling deeper and deeper. I can't get out. Oh, shit! I'm crashing. Help me. Help me.'

The car screeches. There's a smell of burning. The tires lock far too late. Far too late.

Does anyone get outta here alive

'I must be losing my mind.'

I'm hanging on the edge and spinning out of control
Choose your medication
It's a generation overload

Marianne's lying on her bed, exhausted after her one-to-one with Maggie, her eyes still wet and stinging from the morning's crying; her throat sore after all the screaming. Maggie has asked Marianne to keep a diary and write *it* down. Once she understands *it*, she can do something about *it*. 'You're a writer,' she says, 'so it shouldn't be difficult for you to put *it* all into words.' Yes, Marianne is a writer. Words are how she earns her living. They're food and drink to her. She's wanted to be around books for as long as she can remember, and they have saved her life again and again.

All those years back they provided an escape route. They offered consolation from a pubescent body plagued by eczema. They soothed her throughout a steady succession of unkind stepmothers. When she buried her nose in her books, she'd run away into a world of adventure, happy families, firm friends and, most of all, love. Everything ended well in the books she devoured and the journey involved in getting there—the actual reading—blocked everything else out. Parents were dependable and constant. People acted heroically. Friends were self-sacrificing and supportive. And love. Love was always accessible in abundance. Yes, there was shit but the good guys overcame it and it brought them closer together. Not like the real world.

Marianne would disappear for hours reading, while all the other children would go out and do normal things like sports, discos, parties. Marianne wasn't interested in any of that; she preferred the company of books. Safe and reliable, books never let you down. This meant she grew up alone, exchanging humans for paper, never learning how to relate to others properly. Especially men. Even her brother was a mystery to her. Simon kept himself to himself and so did she. And as for her father…

With books, it wasn't just the words that enchanted her. It was everything about them. From the fusty smell of old, special editions she would seek out at second-hand bookstores, to the textures and hues of her trusty hardbacks. Marianne couldn't bear the sight or feel of paperbacks. 'They have no spine and no soul,' she would say unashamedly. Hardbacks, however, she adored. Her fingers would caress their jackets, then unwrap them slowly and lovingly to discover what lay within. Books were sensuous, stimulating and intoxicating. Every wall in her flat was adorned with rows and rows of the things from the skirting board to the ceiling—and Marianne's flat had very high ceilings. Like the walls of a castle, they not only protected her, they also kept her locked within a prison of her own making, separating her from people and they from her. But, since Marianne preferred books to people that was OK. Except, of course, it wasn't. As Marianne grew up, the more time she spent with the characters in her books, the harder she found it to be with the characters in her world. Marianne did not come out of her shell until well into her mid-twenties.

Marianne has an ability to make people laugh, in a whacky, sardonic, off-the-wall kind of way. In public, she hides behind the mask of a wag. Though all the time she feels like an outsider. A spare part. Looking mostly at people through a window. It's safer that way. People terrify her, because of what they can do to her, the fact that they will almost certainly judge her. Though, she's not sure why that is. It may have something do with the fact that she never feels OK about herself. And she doesn't take much convincing on that score. She imagines people whispering behind her back all the time, saying bad things about her. She doesn't know why it bothers her so much. But it does.

For Marianne, living in the real world is much like living a bad dream, so Marianne retreats into her world of fiction. One she can control. Writing fiction empowers her to create a world of *her* choosing. One she can cope with. People she can cope with. People she likes. A lot. Who don't freak her out, who don't whisper about her behind her back. Maggie has asked her to write about the real world—her bad dream—and the people around her. As far as she's concerned, that world stinks. That's why she's here. She's written about many things in her life—but the one subject she's always avoided is Marianne. It's just too shitty to commit to paper.

Marianne's filled with fear. Every word she writes is going to stare back at her as she writes it. Large, loud, ugly black words that can't be rubbed out. Usually her friends, the words that she hasn't yet written have already become her enemies. Forcing her to relive what she'd really just rather obliterate from her mind once and for all. But Marianne has no choice. Not if she wants to deal with all the stuff that's inside her head. Not if she wants to move on. Maggie says if she faces up to *it*, and looks *it* straight in the eye, *it* will stop controlling her the way *it* has been doing all these years. For once, she, Marianne, will get control over *it*. That means no more panic attacks. No more nightmares. No more waking up in the middle of the night, breathless, burning up. Or, at least, if they do continue, she will know how to survive. To make it through.

'Yeah, right. I'll believe that when I see it.'

And she has no tranquillisers or booze to dull the pain. She can't even harm herself if it gets too much. And it will. There's nothing she can do to distract from the crappy, horrible feelings that will come to her when she writes *it* all down. OK. So, here goes. And Marianne's pen hits the paper. For twenty-four hours she writes. Through the night and through the day, she just writes and writes and writes. She ignores the clock. She stops going to classes. She misses out meals and resorts to Mars bars and Diet Coke to keep going. The nurses come by and check she's OK. She forgets about the aches and pains in her hand when it's had more than it can take.

'Never mind my fucking hand. What about the pain in my heart?'

Extract from Marianne's Diary

It all started when I was twelve. Well, thereabouts. That's when my parents split up. No, wait a minute. It started long before that. It began whenever the arguments began, and they'd been going on since before I was born. I think that's my earliest memory of my parents. My mum shouting, screaming and sobbing hysterically. My dad standing at the edge of the room on eggshells, not wanting any part of it. He was well out of his comfort zone and it showed. 'Anna, please. Please don't do this,' he would say. I think Dad felt bad that Simon and I were seeing it all, though Mum never seemed bothered. Sometimes, I would put my hand in my pocket and pretend it contained magic dust. I'd take some imaginary particles out of my pocket and throw them over my parents in the forlorn hope that it would make them stop. Everything would be all right then and my parents would never, ever argue again. Children, eh!

Once, there was an accident. I can still see the broken glass on the kitchen floor, though I can't remember how it got there. Mum must have smashed something in a rage. She was dancing about in pain, she'd cut her feet. It was all Dad's fault. She called the police and suddenly there they were in our kitchen. Two men in uniform looking embarrassed. Dad stood on the sidelines as usual, entreating Mum to calm down. Mum yelled at the police, begging them to take Dad away. They didn't. This was a domestic, they said, and they didn't interfere in domestics.

I can honestly say that I have never seen my mother and father share one single tender moment together. I'd give anything for that not to be true. It makes me feel...like I've lost out. Only the other day we were driving and my mum said my dad had never, ever held her hand. Right out of the blue. That really hurts. I know it's not my fault. But—I don't know—I feel as if I must have had *something* to do with it. Anyway, when they finally parted, it didn't come as a surprise. Just a bloody great shock. One that I don't think I've ever really got over. And I'm ashamed of myself for that. It shouldn't be such a big deal. It doesn't seem to be for others. But it is for me.

The marriage started off on a bad foot before it had ever been kicked into touch. The night before the wedding, Dad phoned Mum and told her he couldn't go through with it. Dad didn't give her a reason then and he never has. What was going through his head? If I were going to be purely cynical I'd say that maybe all Dad wanted was a shag, and if marrying her was the only way... . But, when it dawned on him they had nothing in common, and that marrying someone was a bit of an extreme way of getting your leg over... . But, perhaps that's just my imagination and my suspicious mind. Plenty more where that came from.

My parents' marriage was probably the greatest marital mismatch there has ever been. Dad was a young man in his early thirties. Like many young men—and plenty of older ones, too—he was moved by lust. Mum needed shelter and attention. Having lost her father at the age of fourteen, she was on the look-out for a replacement. Dad seemed to offer her all of this—or so she thought. They were emotional opposites. While Mum expressed her emotions big time for all to see, Dad was introverted, repressed, he kept his feelings to himself. Well, that's when he wasn't being what they at the Cloisters call a bipolar. That's manic-depressive to you and me. Bipolars sometimes feel ecstatic. They get so high they believe they can achieve anything they want, no matter how preposterous or unrealistic. Literally the next second, they can sink to an all-time low and retreat into their shell. Soon suicide can look really enticing. I've met one or two of them here. Kalpana, she's a bipolar. And she can really flip. Just like that. Nobody noticed what was happening to my dad. But, then, why would they? I certainly never remember him having one of his highs.

As the whole family were to find out later, my dad's mother suffered from manic depression as a young, married woman and was given a series of electric shocks. That was practically the only known way of dealing with a condition you didn't dare talk about in public. As soon as you uttered the phrase 'mentally ill', people would behave as if you had the plague. At best you'd be marked out for pity and scorn. At worst you'd be written off, discarded, treated like an outcast. It was something to be deeply ashamed about. If you cried in public, people would only ask you why. So you had to keep mum. Say nothing—keep it a dark skeleton in the family closet. Suffer in silence. Mum didn't know anything about Dad's illness. But then Dad didn't know himself. Not then. Not till much later, in fact. And even if he did, he probably wouldn't have told her. It's hardly the kind of thing you blurt out to someone when you fancy them, is it? 'Hello, I'm a manic-depressive. Would you like to come out on a date?' Don't think so. I know that if I met someone tomorrow, and he wasn't from the Cloisters, I don't think I could tell him I was ill. That I was depressed. That I was here. Not yet, anyway. The stigma still exists. I know it does. If somebody tells you they're mentally ill, naturally you're going to be on your guard a bit. And emotionally ill's no better. People just think you're pathetic and need to pull yourself together. They look at you with clouds in their eyes. You can tell what they're thinking, though I could be catastrophising again. Anyway, that's why nobody knows I'm here except my mum and my agent.

Mum felt so desperate when Dad told her he was calling off the wedding. If it'd been me, I think I'd have felt like ending it all there and then. What on earth had she done, for fuck's sake? Why had he changed his mind? She began to panic, to catastrophise. Family trait, which I've inherited big time. She was Lebanese, living in a foreign country, lodging with her fiancé's parents. She felt helpless, hopeless, hideously alone. I know those feelings. I live with them day-in day-out. Like I said, catastrophising's a family trait. Fortunately, or, perhaps, not so fortunately, as things turned out, my uncle managed to calm Dad down and change his mind. Whenever Mum tells me this story, it makes me so fucking angry. Looking at the glossed-up photograph of my parents' wedding, they seem so bloody happy. Both gazing into each other's eyes with apparent adoration. Sometimes, I feel like smashing the photograph to bits. It's just a lie. A sham. I once asked Dad why he married Mum.

He said it was because she was so beautiful. What kind of reason is that? How could two people marry with such little consideration for the future? For their children? It's not fair. Not right. And yet, I don't want to judge either of them. How do you know what you'd do in a particular situation if you've never been there? Especially when you're young. And Ma wasn't much more than a child then. Maybe seventeen, eighteen.

The irony of the whole thing is that Mum's always hated sex. She's never minded telling me that the whole intimacy thing disgusts her and she couldn't bear Dad coming near her. She told me she didn't want children because she never loved my father and she didn't want him. Not in *that* way, anyway. How was that supposed to make me feel? How does it make me feel now? Fucking sad, that's what. Sex was bad. Sex was filthy. That's what my mother instilled in me. And, for a long time I couldn't bear men to touch me, either. For years and years what went on between my legs terrified me so much I couldn't bear to think about it, let alone talk about it. It was like I had a monster squatting down there and there was nothing I could do to get rid of it. Sex was what my father did with bad women. Not a well-brought-up girl like me. Talk about being sexually screwed-up. Freud would have had a field day. He'd have had me lying on his couch practically every day of the week.

I'll never forget the day my periods began. It was a scorchingly hot afternoon. I was on a school trip to Bodiam Castle. Suddenly I became aware of an overpowering smell and then *blood* came pouring down my legs. At first, I thought, 'My God, what's happened? I'm bleeding.' Then it dawned on me.

My dad bought me a negligée. For Christ's sake, I was only twelve. I felt so ashamed, so conscious of my body, my breasts. I just wanted them to disappear so that nobody would notice them. Dad said something mortifying like, 'Well, you're a woman now.' But I wasn't a fucking woman. I was still a little girl who needed her father. I didn't want to be a woman. I wanted to be a daughter, a child doing innocent childish things. I didn't want to have anything to do with sex. Sex scared me shitless.

And I didn't have sex—I mean, the works—until I was twenty-eight. I was just too scared to go the whole way. Before the night I finally did it, every encounter with a man was a complete fucking nightmare. Literally. I just couldn't go through with it. I guess I was frightened of what my mother would think if she knew. She would have said I was a whore, I knew she would. Well, that's what I kept telling myself. I'd be lying there rigid and they'd call me a cock-teaser. Frigid. When I stopped halfway, frozen, unable to go on. Writing that down in black and white makes me feel like shit. To confess in print that I didn't have sex until I was almost thirty makes me feel like I'm abnormal. Like I'm some kind of freak. Like there's something wrong with me. And of course there is. That's why I'm here.

When it finally happened, I went berserk.

'What d'you mean, berserk?' asked Maggie.

'You know,' Marianne stammered, 'I just couldn't get enough. I'd lost contact with my body, hadn't I? I hadn't wanted to have anything to do with it for nearly thirty years. Even when I got undressed and took a bath I found it difficult to look at myself in the mirror. I was just too ashamed. It was like my body didn't belong to me. And then, suddenly, it did. I finally accepted it.'

'So what changed?'

'Falling in love. I mean, thinking I'd fallen in love. Though I found out later I was just infatuated and he didn't return my feelings. Being starved for so long, I guess I was trying to make up for lost time. And I'd been struggling so hard not to recognise sex was an OK part of me, I eventually had to give in. It was too much of a battle. Once I let myself go, I practically exploded. It was so wonderful, so passionate. I lost myself in it, which was…I don't know, the best. But the guy I fell in love with—it was a long time ago, now—he called me a nymphomaniac. He said there was something wrong with me to be so insatiable. And he left. Of course. Like all the others.'

'And you withdrew back into yourself?'

'Yeah. It's like he opened me up and then left me vulnerable and exposed. Dissatisfied. Empty.'

'Marianne, you realise the fact that you're starting to see things clearly means you can now start to do something about it. It's a beginning. The other thing you need to see is that what he did—what he said—reveals a lot about him and his insecurities—not yours. It wasn't you. You do see that, don't you?'

'Yeah, whatever.' Marianne didn't sound very convincing. To herself or anyone else.

It's nine-thirty p.m. and almost time for bed. Marianne,

Lynette and Cat are in the Quad lounge on the first floor, wrapped up nice and cosy in their jim-jams.

'I could really use a drag. Or, failing that, a gin and tonic,' Cat sighs. 'If I'm going to be honest, I'm afraid I have to admit that, well, Horlicks doesn't really do it for me. Still, I suppose it's no use wishing for the impossible while we're holed up in the asylum.' But if Cat were able to get her pretty hands with their elegantly manicured nails on a snort or a G&T, she'd never be able to stop at just the one. And she knows it. Nor would Lynette. Maybe Marianne wouldn't either. Alcohol seems really tempting right now. It promises a kind of oblivion—even if it is only temporary.

Lynette opens her mouth to say something but is stopped in her tracks by the sudden appearance of Kalpana, promptly followed by her minder. Since her aborted attempt to kill herself the other night, Kalpana has to be followed around by a nurse at all times. Marianne wonders what happens when one of them wants to go to the loo. Kalpana walks in mumbling to herself, her long, dark, lustrous hair wet from just being washed. She's wearing a very tight T-shirt with the words 'I walk alone' emblazoned on the front, and a tartan mini-skirt. Her left arm is bandaged from her wrist to her elbow, but it's her eyes the girls can't stop looking at. Kalpana's drugged up to the eyeballs. Her filmy pupils reveal that far-away look that so many patients acquire when they are forced—with the aid of meds—to wind down.

'Hi, Kalpana,' they say. 'How are you?'

'Fucked-up, as usual,' comes the reply, as she flicks her glistening locks behind her ears. Kalpana never makes eye-contact—she doesn't seem to understand the point of conversation. People don't interest her—that's part of the illness. She's too absorbed in herself and what she's doing. Kneeling down in front of the small fridge used to keep a few essentials, and consulting a small pink notebook, she announces the need to do some spring-cleaning. Her tone is professional and brisk.

'Though, frankly,' she goes on, 'I'm beginning to wonder if I've got the energy with all these fucking drugs they're shovelling down my neck.'

Slowly and methodically, Kalpana opens the fridge door and takes out all the miniature jam pots from the bottom shelf. One by one, she wipes each jar with a dishcloth, dusts the shelf meticulously and puts them back, arranging them according to their flavours. Every so often, she consults her notebook. It looks like she's compiled a list, because every so often she takes a pencil from behind her ear and ticks something off. The whole procedure takes about half an hour. Kalpana's in no hurry. It's critical to her that the job is done to perfection. At last she is satisfied with the result. She stands up, brushes down her skirt and turns to go, her minder shuffling off behind her.

'Now that really is bonkers,' says Cat, 'whereas the rest of us—we're just sad bastards.'

Taking a sip of green tea, Marianne relaxes back into her chair. 'I don't think she's mad.'

'Well, I'll tell you one thing' says Cat. 'No matter how crap I felt I don't think I could ever take up housework. There's no way that would ever make *me* feel better. About anything.' After a pause, she adds, 'But you've got to admit, Kalpana does do some really odd things. When Sandy left the other day, did you see what she gave her as a leaving present? She took one of the jigsaw puzzles from under the TV over there, wrapped it up and gave it to her. And if that wasn't crazy enough, she first removed one of the pieces so Sandy would never be able to finish the bloody thing.'

Now, that *is* funny, but perhaps not as amusing as the bottle of Calvin Klein's *Escape* Sandy received from Cat the day she checked out.

Extract From Marianne's diary

Mum divorced Dad on grounds of mental cruelty. And he let her do it. But what about the sex? Or, rather, the complete absence of it. Lust had drawn Dad to Mum in the first place, so it's reasonable that when she proved reluctant to consummate the marriage, she'd drive him into the arms of other, more obliging women. Which is exactly what happened. According to my mum, her so-called friends started queuing up for my father. Mum would never see Dad's side of things, though, and she wouldn't thank me for pointing it out. But, as Maggie keeps telling me, other people's hang-ups are other people's hang-ups. Not mine. Do I blame Mum for pushing Dad away and for turning me into a woman who was terrified of what was going on inside her knickers? I hope not. But I can't be certain.

When my brother was born, Dad wasn't there. Mum says he went shopping. So, nobody was around to help her. To tell her everything was all right. She didn't want to give birth. So, she held her legs together. She must have had the mother of all panic attacks. Eventually, they finally managed to prise her legs apart and the child—a sickly little baby boy—was born. As soon as Mum saw him, she fell in love. But he was blue. He could hardly breathe and wasn't able to speak until he was five. Mind you, since then he's certainly made up for it. He's mega bright. Streets ahead of me, at any rate. Can't understand what he's on about, most of the time.

Mum's always asked me to make allowances for Simon, and I know the guilt is there. In spades. To me he was a little horror who thought plaguing his sister's life was fair game. Whenever he bullied me, hit me, threw me down the stairs or poured boiling water over my toes for a joke, I was consistently fed the same line: 'We must make allowances for Simon, you know that.' Once he really went too far. Well, obviously, judging by my reaction. We were in the kitchen and Mum had got hold of a watermelon. He was trying to take the knife off me so he could cut the blasted thing himself. I was furious after what happened that morning—he'd taken the wheels off my doll's pram to build something with a mate—and I was fed up with him for making my life a misery. We struggled for the knife, I took it off him and stabbed him in the hand. Between his thumb and index finger, if I remember correctly. I still don't regret it. Even now—after all this time.

Truth is I'm not sure I can make allowances for anybody anymore. Not if it hurts. And it still does. Like hell. They teach you to have boundaries here. People aren't allowed to come inside them. Not if you value and cherish yourself. Time and time again I've let people overreach that line and paid the price. It gnaws away at your self-respect and that's shit.

When I was younger, my mum told me she was raped—
by my dad. The idea of my mother being raped by my
father is kind of weird, to put it mildly. It makes me feel a
bit queasy. A bit…I don't know, it's hard to describe. And
writing it down here and now is one of the hardest things
I've ever had to do. It's even harder looking back at it in
print. It feels so disloyal. But disloyal to whom? I'm not
making it up. Why would I? What would be the point?
Anyway, you don't forget things like that, do you?

I remember when the *Forsyte Saga* first appeared on
television, Mum had no objection to me watching it. She
said it was bloody good drama. Except for just one
instalment. The one in which Soames Forsyte rapes his wife
Irene. And when I protested I was put firmly in my place.
I know she watched it, though. On her own, obviously. I
can't see my parents sitting down to watch that together.
The next morning her eyes looked bloodshot. Had the
episode been too close to the truth? I don't know. Maybe
Dad just got a bit amorous.

I was born three years after Simon. Was this another act
of darkness? Again, I'll never know. My dad's got Alzheimer's
now. So, even if he could bear to talk about it, he wouldn't
understand. He's away with the fairies. His head's all over
the place. I know that feeling. My head's all over the place
too. While Simon's birth was a protracted, excruciating affair,
I came to the world in a hurry. Mum says I was in such
an almighty rush there was no pain at all. That's kind of
nice to know. That I didn't hurt her. She says that's why
I'm always so bloody impatient. And it's true. I am. The
story goes that almost as soon as Mum lay down on the
hospital bed, I decided to make my entrance feet first. As

39

the doctor looked at my bottom he declared, 'Look, she's as beautiful as her mother.' Though, how he could tell just by staring at my backside I will never know. Mum fell in love all over again. True to form, Dad wasn't there. He'd taken Simon fishing. Well, again, that's what Mum says.

Mum suffered from post-natal depression, although nobody seemed to know what this was back in the 1950s. The doctor gave her a series of electric shocks without her consent. It was enough for Dad to sign the forms. And he did. Willingly. Without recourse to his wife. She brings it up a lot. She really resents my dad for doing it to her. Think I would too. But perhaps I'm just being a bit melodramatic. They do ECT at the Cloisters—Dr Chaudhry says it can be really effective when people are desperate and don't respond to other forms of treatment. When they work, anti-depressants can take up to a month to start having an effect. Some people are in so much distress they can't wait that long.

When I was five, we moved to a big house in a posh suburb in South West London. Mum was ambitious for her children. She wanted us to be in a good place with good schools. Private schools. Dad didn't agree and refused to foot the bills. He'd gone to grammar school, he argued. So, if it was good enough for him, why wasn't it good enough for his kids? If his wife wanted her children to go to a fee-paying school, she'd have to pay the fees. So Mum did longer hours at work to get the money together.

Marianne was desperate for a break. She'd had enough of writing. Well, that kind of writing, anyway. All she wanted was to lie down on the grass in a quiet, sunny spot and go to sleep. With any luck, she thought, she might not wake up. She staggered out on to the front lawns with her iPod, her notebook and pen. The words of the song she was listening to, 'When your day is long and the night is yours alone', were doing their best to drown out the memories. Unfortunately, she could still think through the noise. For Marianne and so many others who occupy the same space the ability to think, to come up with one thought after another, can be such a curse. If people lacked the ability to think, they would certainly never get depressed, and for those who think a lot, well, that's a recipe for disaster. When they first met, Dr Chaudhry told Marianne that creative types, especially writers, artists and comedians, tend to be more prone to depression and anxiety than other people. Because of their propensity to think, over-think and then think again. Too much bloody thinking. Too much analysing.

'Great,' she thought. 'Why did I have to be born a writer with an over-active imagination? Why couldn't it have been an over-active thyroid? Surely, that would have been easier to treat?'

Marianne collapsed on to the grass, breathed in deeply and lay back, her hands supporting her neck. There were others sharing the lawn, but they were far enough away not to trouble her. And with her iPod, she couldn't hear them properly anyway. She could smell cigarette smoke quite near but that didn't seem to bother her either. Marianne looked up at the sky and followed the slow pilgrimage of the clouds above her, trying to make out recognisable shapes. Becoming aware of a voice, she opened her eyes, took the plugs out of her ears and sat up. It was James. He was sitting down next to her, cross-legged, playing with the grass.

'Hi,' she said, surprised and pleased at the same time.

'Is it OK if I sit here?' he enquired apprehensively. Dressed in the same combat trousers to which he seemed permanently attached, a white T-shirt and a striped jacket she'd never seen him wear before, he waited for permission.

'Of course, James. No need to ask.'

'I've never seen a four-leaf clover before. Have you?'

'Er…no…I don't think I have,' she stuttered, slightly taken aback by his choice of subject matter.

'They're very rare,' he added, thoughtfully.

'So, they do really exist? It's not just a myth, then?'

'Oh, yes, they do. They really exist,' he nodded earnestly, totally absorbed by his task and the apparent seriousness of it.

'A rarity. A bit like a sane person in this place?' Marianne's pathetic attempt at trying to make her companion laugh seemed, much to her surprise, to have a positive effect. James chuckled nervously and rather self-consciously. She joined in.

'Sorry, that was really stupid,' she apologised.

'No, no,' he replied, looking up at her, the fear in his eyes still very much there. 'It's fine. Don't laugh much these days, that's all. Feels a bit strange. Unnatural somehow. Look, I'm sorry, I don't know your name.'

'Marianne.'

'Sometimes I need to sit with someone. Quietly. Not talking or anything. Hope you understand.'

Marianne could feel the tears welling up inside her but these were good tears. The best tears. 'Yes, it's OK. It's really OK just to sit quietly.'

There were so many things Marianne wanted to know about this man. But there was a great wall keeping her out. A wall he'd constructed to stop anyone on the Outside getting in. To protect himself. He'd been hurt enough, thank you, and Marianne—like everyone else in this place—was still part of the Outside. For all she knew maybe she'd never be anything else.

As they sat together in silence, James carried on looking down. Marianne searched for his eyes—she wanted him to return her gaze—but maybe that was too much to ask. Too direct. Too intrusive. So intently did he fix his eyes on the grass below him, it was as if his recovery depended on finding that elusive four-leaf clover.

'If only it were that simple,' she thought.

Marianne took her iPod and handed it to James. She wanted him to hear the next track. He accepted her offer and put the plugs in his ears. Though she couldn't hear the lyrics, she knew them by heart and started to sing them silently to herself.

Ain't it good to know that you've got a friend
When people can be so cold.
They'll hurt you and desert you
And take your soul if you let them.
Oh, but don't you let them

For just one tiny second their eyes met and Marianne felt what she could only describe as a very gentle electric current pass through her. It was exhilarating but it was also fucking scary.

Extract From Marianne's Diary

Religion has always been kind of important to Mum. She's a Muslim. Not one of those fundamentalist extremists. Christ, no. She thinks they're all crackpots and if you really press her you'll find she agrees with the *Daily Mail*. Take all that stuff about virgins in heaven just waiting for the next suicide bomber to check in—as far as she's concerned, that's all a complete load of bollocks. Mum's the kind of Muslim the *Daily Mail* thinks is just about OK—she seems to believe passionately in the Koran and the C of E at the same time—and prays quietly on her own, without bothering anyone. No mats on the ground (she's got two new knees so genuflecting would be a bit much at her age), no facing Mecca, no scarf round her head, no Ramadan. Oh, and she likes the odd glass of wine. But she does pray a lot. A lot. Sometimes, when I'm driving her in the car, I can hear her mumbling under her breath. I never ask what she's saying. She's probably asking God to make sure I don't crash.

Mum's never once tried to force her faith on to Simon or me, either. I'm completely ignorant about Islam and wouldn't know where to start. When Mum emigrated to England to marry an Englishman she became English. And she didn't see how it would benefit her children, being born and living in England, if they grew up confused about their identity. I went to a Church of England school and occasionally to Mass with my once-Catholic father. What does that make me, religiously-speaking? Confused, I guess. Mum says that when they married, Dad promised to convert to Islam. If he did actually make my mum this promise— probably another ruse to get her into bed, I reckon—he never did anything about it. Every Sunday morning Dad would traipse off to Mass, sometimes taking me with him. I'm not sure why I went, really. I guess I looked on it as a kind of outing. Maybe it was something he and I could share. Sometimes I think it was a way of getting away from the intense atmosphere at home. Anyway, it wasn't to last. And it all came to a head one day when my brother returned from Sunday School.

There had been omens before that fateful day that something was brewing. When my mum became pregnant with Simon, the Pope brought out an edict—or whatever you call it—which really made her fume. His Holiness ordained that when it came to a tricky birth, and there was a toss-up between saving the mother and the child, it was always more important to save the child. After all, the father could marry again and it would be a sin to take away a new life. This became official Church doctrine and every God-fearing Roman Catholic had to abide by it. My mother asked my dad if he went along with this and, to her horror, he said he did. If the proclamation had emerged from the Pope's arse he'd have to take it as gospel—though he didn't put it quite like that, of course. Mum became hysterical and denounced his terrible religion. 'What kind of God d'you call that?' she cried. 'Allah is supposed to be merciful. And intelligent. It says so in the Koran. Where's the humanity in your Godforsaken religion?'

On the fateful Sunday in question Mum was in the kitchen getting the roast ready when my eight year-old brother breezed in with my father.

'Mummy,' announces Simon cheerfully, like it was some kind of holiday, 'you're going to hell.'

My mother is so taken aback she stops peeling the potatoes and stares at her young son who has just told her she is going to burn in the everlasting flames of Hades.

'What did you say?' she asks, while my father looks on in disbelief.

Simon repeats it with relish, obviously unaware of the implications of what he is saying. 'The priest says you're going to go to hell because you're not a Catholic. You're a…you're a…heath…heathen. Yes, that's right. Everyone who's not a Catholic is going straight to hell when they die.' And, as if to give the statement even more authenticity, 'That's what the priest says.'

My mother shifts her gaze from her son to her husband. Shaking with rage and sobbing with tears, she tells Dad in no uncertain terms that if he ever goes back to his precious Church, she will divorce him on the spot. And this seemed to do the trick. From that day onwards, my father never went back to Church and Simon never returned to Sunday School. And that was the end of the family's relationship with Roman Catholicism. Dad could have let Mum divorce him if he felt that strongly about it. But he didn't. Did he finally accept he couldn't live with the hypocrisy? Or did he feel that he didn't want to be separated from my mum? That he loved her? Maybe he didn't want a divorce because of the stigma. It's just something else I will never know. Him being away with the fairies and all that.

The girls can't wait for the Salsa class to begin. Part of their recovery programme once a week, it's intended to help patients express themselves and release some of the baggage that's been holding them back. It might be a bit of a laugh, too—a commodity that's a little thin on the ground when you're in the depths of despair. Even so, that's not why this is the most popular class at the hospital. And it's certainly not why Marianne, Cat and Lynette have turned up. They knocked on Kalpana's door, but she waved them away saying she had far more important things to do. The girls have heard the gossip about Damien, the Gym and Dance instructor, and they want to see for themselves. The story goes that Damien is an ex-stripper and possesses an amazing body. But, will the rumours stand up to reality?

It's three-thirty p.m. and, as Lynette, Cat and Marianne saunter into the Stables, they can't believe their eyes. Damien—who can't be more than five-feet-seven tall—is wearing (if you can call it that) the briefest of yellow silk shorts containing the tiniest bottom the girls have ever seen on anyone—man, woman or child. Athletic and highly toned, his upper torso is, arguably, impressive. Talk about a six-pack. His muscular arms are covered in elaborate tattoos and on his head he sports a white bandana with red spots. He hasn't started the lesson yet, but his face and body are already sweating profusely. The veins in his face stand out beneath the perspiration, giving him a rather pained expression. Latin American music booms out of a ghetto blaster as Damien proceeds to march up and down with his back to the class so he can admire his reflection in the mirror—his pert little bottom swaying from left to right in time with the pulsating beat. He opens his mouth and begins to yell at the group in a sharply nasal accent that can only hail from Manhattan.

47

'OK, you pathetic bunch of psychos. Start marching. And if you think you gonna get away without putting any work in, you got another think coming.'

Cat, Lynette and Marianne exchange bemused glances and immediately start laughing. Damien turns round to face his victims and glares at Marianne aggressively. 'I can see you, Marianne. Don't think you lunatics are gonna pull me into your psycho world. I'm untouchable. Now, start dancing, and no talking in my class. That includes any psycho-babble you're into.' And with that, he turns round again to give the girls (surprise, surprise, there are no men in Damien's class) his back. Lynette looks as if she's undergoing a seizure as she loses control of her body. She's certainly in no state to concentrate on complicated dance steps. Damien turns on the hysterical Lynette, tears streaming down her face. 'You're not auditioning for the cavalry,' he bellows, 'you're meant to be dancing the Salsa. Now, pay attention, loonies. Watch my feet and my aaaaasssss.' But if he wants his pupils to try and re-establish some control the word 'aaaaasssss' is a very bad choice. Marianne is now laughing so much, she's gripping her stomach from both the agony and the ecstasy. Within a few seconds, she keels over and collapses in a heap. It's not long before Cat and Lynette join her, all three bent double in fits of hilarity. Damien turns on the trio, smiling for the first time. His magic is definitely working. Now that's what Marianne calls therapy.

Extract From Marianne's Diary

Every Christmas without fail my father would take the whole family—including our disapproving Catholic cousins (that was before they excommunicated us, of course)—to the panto. And we'd always go out for a meal afterwards. Which I dreaded. Dad would say something. Mum would take it the wrong way and end up with a bone stuck in her throat. Or, she'd feel sick. Whatever it was, it would always be his fault. Dad worked so damn hard all the time. Usually, he never came out with us. It was always just my mum, Simon and me. I have this picture of my dad bent over his typewriter in his study, transcribing some technical text or other into English. He was a linguist and made a good living as a translator. He was really gifted at languages. Not any more, of course. Now, he can hardly even speak English. Well, not in any way that makes any sense.

Did my dad and I ever spend any real time together back in those early days? Apart from church? Just by ourselves, chatting, chilling out? I remember the odd outing to the local swimming pool with friends. And, apparently, he took me to a pop concert once. He told me later but I don't remember it. To be honest, I always felt uncomfortable around him. Perhaps awkward is a better word. I always wanted the encounter to end. I never knew what to say. What to do. He always seemed a stranger to me. My mum says that when I was tiny—just a toddler—he would hold me in his left hand. Raising me high above his head, he'd say with immense pride, 'This is my daughter.' But I can't remember that. Obviously. I was only a baby. The thought of my dad doing that makes me really emotional, but whenever the picture comes into my head, that baby isn't me. How could it be? I can't relate to my dad like that. Except perhaps the last time I saw him. In his wheelchair. When the roles were dramatically reversed.

It's his eighty-sixth birthday. He's at the old people's home where he's been for the past four years. He looks tiny and shrivelled, a shadow of his former self. What's left of his hair is white and baby-fine. His chiselled cheeks stick out of his thin, hollow face, and when he smiles, he opens his mouth to reveal a toothless cavern. The medication's so strong it's rotted his teeth.

'Hello, Molly.' He's always confused his sister's name with mine.

He goes on in the same way, each one of his words meaningful and intelligent on its own but, when strung together in endless sentences, complete gibberish. A flash of inspiration comes to him and he asks me about my 'relationships'. Amid all the confusion inside his head, how does he remember my Achilles heel? Now *he* is the child, the helpless, frail child. And I am the parent. How can I be angry, resentful, bitter? He's a harmless innocent— interested only in his next meal, sleep or visit to the toilet. For him, that's what life has been reduced to. Except for the odd joke. He's still retained a flavour of the old sense of humour for which he was so well-known, and which I seem to have inherited. When a visitor asks him, 'Say my name,' he replies disingenuously, his face beaming, 'My name.' Then he turns to us and says crossly but with a wink, 'Can't you be quiet for ten minutes?'

After a few moments' staring into space, he says, 'This morning I went to an AGM.'

Yesterday, he went hand-gliding, so at least he's having a jam-packed retirement—if only in his head.

'Really,' I ask. 'Whose?'

'The Fairies.'

Like I say, Dad's on a different planet. One inhabited by pixies and goblins, by the sound of things. A sort of *Midsummer Night's Dream*. Except, of course, Alzheimer's is more like a nightmare.

I remain numb, untouched. There's such a gulf between us. We hardly know each other. I know I'm not to blame, though I often feel I am. And there's certainly no point in cursing him for it. Not anymore, anyway. Not in his condition.

I feel ready for the eventual loss that I will have to bear because, let's face it, the thing I stand to lose was never mine in the first place.

When I was about twelve my dad lost his job and then got offered a better one. Abroad. He had to move to Rome. After seventeen years of marriage. Dad suggested putting Simon and me in boarding schools while Mum moved to Italy with him. Coming from someone who didn't actually believe in the public school system, that was quite something. She refused. No child of hers would ever go to boarding school. Over her dead body. She had been put through it herself. And that was enough. More than enough. My mum saw her chance and took it. She would divorce him and start a new life. She had already rejected his love in the only way he had known how to give it. Now, she was telling him she didn't want to live with him—to be with him

51

on any level. First it was his body she was chucking out—now it was the whole fucking works.

So, Dad went to Italy, taking his freedom with him.

The first time Dad came back from Rome he arrived at the house in a small, dirty Fiat with an Italian number plate. It soon became clear that it belonged to his 'floozy', as my mother insisted on referring to her. My mother swears blind she found the woman's frilly knickers on the passenger seat. I never quite worked out what Mum was doing nosing around in the car. I mean, if it had been me, I wouldn't have waded in looking for things that would break me. I mean, that's wantonly self-destructive. Really masochistic. Asking for trouble. Big time. But perhaps she just couldn't stop herself.

The discovery of the Roman floozy's knickers was a gift to my dad. Mum has never liked sexy underwear, he knew that. It made her feel dirty and reminded her of what can happen to a woman when she takes it off. Mum likes sensible cotton briefs with no hint of sensuality, or even femininity. Mum launders her knickers with prestigious care. She starches them and irons them. Then she folds them in half and places them neatly in the top drawer of her dressing table. Knickers are to be kept on at all times, according to my mother. As a child, she used to insist I wear knickers to bed—I think she felt they were the next best thing to a chastity belt—and to this day I have difficulty sleeping without them. Dad took those knickers and rubbed Mum's nose in them. Well, metaphorically speaking. 'Look at me,' he was saying to her, 'you may have chucked me out but I'm happy now. I've got a woman who loves me, who wants me. Who enjoys having sex with me. I've even taken her to see my family.' He was referring to his Catholic family, of course. They may have excommunicated my mother, my brother and I, but Dad was miraculously accepted back into the fold after the divorce. He must have gone to confession. To me, my dad seemed to be saying, 'I don't need you either. You would only get in the way of my happiness. My freedom. You come second, last even, in my list of priorities right now. I'll give you money. That's easy. But not love. You'll have to make do without.'

I grew up thinking it would always be like that with men, measuring everything they did for me in terms of how much they spent. I was scared shitless of them—of what they could do to me; how they could hurt me. And, what I feared most I began to attract. I became so needy and desperate, I'd respond to any man who showed the slightest interest in me. I craved attention like a drug and I'd put up with anything, no matter how badly I was treated. I'd set potential partners stupid little tests. We'd be in the car and I'd say to myself he must look at me within the next three minutes; if he doesn't, it means he doesn't love me. And, when he didn't, I'd have a panic attack—though I didn't realise it at the time. I'd be thrown into despair, paralysed with dread. A wave of despondency would pass through me and I'd convince myself the relationship was doomed. I'd push and push till I sabotaged every potential relationship that came my way. I applied so much pressure that it had to fail, just like my parents' marriage. I was a suicide-terrorist. I'd place a bomb under each of my potential partnerships and blow both them and my emotions to smithereens. And then I'd say to the world and myself, 'See, I told you so.'

Maggie has read it all. Every word. She congratulates Marianne on completing what must have been one of the hardest things she's ever had to do.

'You do understand where the neediness comes from, don't you, Marianne?'

'The absent father thing?'

'Yes, but not just physically absent. The two men you started off with were emotionally unavailable to you. You were starved of male attention so you grew up with an insatiable hunger for it. Desperate for men's approval, yet terrified of rejection, you'd rush into relationships choosing the wrong man and believing, on the basis of past experience, things could only go one way.'

Maggie studied Marianne's silent, nodding reaction, then added, 'Relationships—do they still scare you?'

'I guess I sometimes still think I'll end up on my own. But, somehow—I don't know—it doesn't frighten me as much as before. It's OK. I don't feel the need to put such a lot of emphasis on it any more. Not make my life depend on it.'

'Why, do you think you'll end up alone? Because you feel you don't deserve someone?'

'I don't know. The prospect of me being in a permanent relationship sometimes just seems like it isn't for me. It's not something I can relate to easily because of what's gone before. And yet…'

'And yet?'

'I don't always think that. Not all the time.'

'What d'you think has changed to make you feel like that?'

'Being here. Knowing that actually, even if I get frightened again, I might be able to cope. That I'm OK on my own.'

Maggie smiled at Marianne and then said: 'Great, I'll see you on Thursday. And keep doing the CBT, OK?'

Marianne's in a class full of friendly faces that are all looking at her. And she's neither embarrassed nor shy. She's between the devil and the deep blue C. CBT actually. Cognitive Behavioural Therapy. She's been doing her homework for days now and it seems to be having a positive effect on her mood. How does it work?

The therapist explains: when we get depressed it's because we're thinking depressing thoughts. OK, OK, that's obvious. But if our thoughts are influenced by our moods—which they are—it makes sense to look at them. What is happening to our thoughts at a given moment when we're experiencing a depressed mood? Answer: we're distorting and twisting them to reflect our mood, even if those thoughts are completely unrealistic—

Example: I've lost my job which means I'm useless and will never find another one. That makes me a loser and I might as well top myself.

If you can get a depressed patient to see that those thought patterns are distorted and there's as much truth in them as there is in saying that bananas are pink, you might get somewhere—over time. Then you replace the distorted thoughts with something more realistic, more positive:

Example: I've lost my job but my employer's gone bust and they've just made half the workforce redundant. So, the job loss doesn't mean I'm a waste of space. It makes me sad and anxious but there's no reason why I can't find another job. I'm not a loser because, actually, I've got quite a good skillbase.

Today, surrounded by a class of other anxiety-anoraks, Marianne is trying this CBT malarkey out for herself. In front of people. Slowly, she articulates the cancerous thoughts that can chew away at her brain and make her feel like shit. Here she goes. First, she takes a deep breath and then says out loud:

'Every man I've ever known has left me. That means I'm repulsive, ugly, hideous to be with. Not worthwhile. Not capable of staying in a long-term relationship.'

That leads her to what practitioners call the 'hot' thought. Because it's so hot it burns:

'I will end up alone, unloved, desperate.' And when things are bad Marianne believes it with a vengeance. Let's see, on a scale of one to one hundred per cent, she might give it one hundred and fifty per cent. Today, though, it's more like eighty per cent. That's progress. Little steps, as they say at the Cloisters.

The therapist calls on the group to come up with reasons why what Marianne has just pronounced is a load of bollocks. Logically, that is, not emotionally. The fact that CBT is vaguely rational gives Marianne confidence. Well, a little.

'She's fortune-telling, she's using distorted thinking,' suggests one kind soul. It's a man. How reassuring, thinks

Marianne. 'How can she know that every man she meets is going to reject her? She can't predict the future, can she?'

'She's catastrophising,' adds another.

'Well, of course I'm catastrophising,' she says. 'That's what I do. I have a history of using distorted thinking. It's a family trait and one I find extremely difficult to let go of. Anyway, whoever said depression and anxiety were logical? That's the whole point. They're not.'

'She's discounting the positive and labelling herself a failure,' shouts another. 'That's not realistic. She's not looking at the facts.'

No, it's not realistic, objectively speaking. But, subjectively speaking, it can sometimes feel bloody realistic to Marianne. Though perhaps not today. Things may have begun to change.

The class works on alternative, more reasonable possibilities to counteract her catastrophising. They need to be plausible so she can really start believing in them.

'She's hot,' shouts out one guy who Marianne feels like kissing. Though, at the same time, she feels that maybe he needs to go to the opticians.

He goes on: 'Why would any man in his right mind not fancy her?'

'Yes, this man really needs glasses,' thinks Marianne. 'Badly. Though, maybe he could get away with contact lenses. He really does have rather a nice face and it would be a shame to hide those lovely, sensitive eyes behind specs.'

'She's sexy,' shouts another. Looks like this guy is overdue for an eye test too.

'She's funny.' Another male voice. Marianne can buy into that one. She likes to think she can make people laugh.

And then:

Cat: 'She's great company.'

Lynette: 'She's a wonderful friend.'

By now Marianne's in tears. Good tears. Great tears. The bestest tears in the whole damn universe. No pain attached to these ones, either.

And then from James: 'She…she's…special…v…very special.'

This time James is looking straight into her eyes. And she's bursting with happiness and hope. Marianne's future has been brought back from the dead. She would quite like to run round the grounds naked, punching the air, and she isn't high, drunk or on any kind of hallucinogenic. But someone might mistake her for a bipolar and, in any case, she doesn't want to startle the patients.

Marianne stands up and shouts, 'I'm OK. I'm OK. Tomorrow I might have a relapse but today I'm OK.'

And that's what matters. That she can know what it feels like to be OK so she can hold on to the feeling for the next time things get bad. She's at the beginning of a long, difficult journey, but she's going to make damn sure she enjoys the scenery along the way.

The class is over and the therapist opens the door. Music blasts in from the radio in the Day Patients' Lounge across the hall:

Yeah, she caught my eye
As we walked on by
She could see from my face that I was
Fucking high

And I don't think that I'll see her again
But we shared a moment that will last till the end
You're beautiful You're beautiful
You're beautiful, it's true

LYNETTE

The reason we're in here is to protect us from the people out there. If they were in here it would be safe for us to be out there

Pete drives slowly without saying a word. Lynette sits next to him in matching silence. Their two-year-old daughter, Lily, is strapped into the back seat and even she seems to realise the need for absolute stillness.

In her sobriety—Lynette hasn't had a drink for at least two days—her senses are more alert than usual. For instance, she's never really noticed that her husband's car has its own distinct aroma, but today the smell of its leather seats and shiny dashboard invade her nostrils. And then there's the scent of their tiny daughter—a mixture of baby talc and nappy cream—as she sits in her chair, taking in the trees and the buildings that pass her by. They ought to soothe her, she thinks to herself, these comforting, mundane smells, but they don't.

Lynette stares straight ahead. It's pouring outside and, as the wipers move monotonously from side to side, she just keeps on staring, blinking only occasionally. She avoids looking at Pete and he avoids looking at her. He pretends to be completely wrapped up in navigating the journey. In reality, he just doesn't know what to say. Lynette feels nauseous—she's shaking and sweating. And that's not just fear; Lynette's experiencing withdrawal symptoms. The drive's not helping much, either, even if they are going at a snail's pace. It's only five miles between the house and the hospital, but it seems to take forever. The morbid slowness with which her husband is driving reminds Lynette of a funeral procession and, God knows, she been in a few of those in her time. But today it feels like it's *her* funeral. Like she's the one who's going to be buried. Alive. She knows no one's actually going to lay her in the ground and cover her with earth. But, it feels like she's being got rid of, thrown away. Her husband's had enough, she thinks, so he's throwing her away, taking her to a place for dead people. Emotionally dead people. Dumping her like a black bin bag full of garbage because he can't bear her around him or Lily anymore, contaminating them. He goes on about how he's doing this for all of them. How he wants her to get better so she can come home—when she's well. But Lynette doesn't buy it. Why would he want her around any more, after all she's put him through? She's failed him as a wife and she's failed Lily as a mother. And she rests her case.

That's why she drinks, she tells herself. It helps. When she's wiped out with booze—blacked-out—she gets a break. Her memories evaporate, though she knows it's not forever. The really shitty ones, they're never very far away. They take a perverse pleasure in hanging around and smacking her in the face when she could really do without it. And when she's trashed and she decides she'll get trashed again, there are always those horrid moments in between. The interludes of shit between oblivion and oblivion, when the blackest of the black memories come flooding back. And what about the hallucinations? She's had plenty of those too—and they terrify the crap out of her.

What are these memories that Lynette's always trying to escape? Well, for a start, there's her wedding day. She had every reason to be happy, too. The man she was marrying loved her and she loved him. She should have been swinging from one chandelier to the next in a state of rapture, but her emotions were all fucked up. To be honest, Lynette can't remember the last time she felt, well, anything really deeply. She just goes through the motions. She does things, she goes places, but she can't *feel* things—not properly. She doesn't know how to, not since…

Imagine going through your own wedding day—the day you've dreamed of since you were a little girl—without feeling anything. Smiling at everyone mechanically with no emotion—no emotion at all. She remembers walking down the aisle. Yeah, she remembers that all right. The happy-clappy music, the flowers and the frocks. All her friends and family were there. Well, not quite all—there were a couple of people who should have been there, but they couldn't make it. She'd lost them. Lynette believes that eventually she will lose everyone she loves. Time has bolstered that belief, and the belief is so strong, it's unshakeable. It has a life of its own.

What's wrong with Lynette? She doesn't want to be like this, but there's nothing she can do about it. Nothing Pete can do about it, either—not without help. She feels like a big hollow, a ZERO, lots of 00000000000s strung together. If they were to cut her open and look into her heart—maybe they'll do that here—she thinks they'll find absolutely nothing. Nothing at all, just an empty shell.

'Christ,' she says to herself, 'I could murder a vodka. That's a bottle I'm talking about, not a glass.'

Lynette recalls her wedding night too, though she wishes she couldn't. After all the guests had gone, when she and Pete were alone in the honeymoon suite. Huge vases of flowers filled the room with their heady scents. She can recollect the overpowering smell of lilies as if it were yesterday. Surely, lilies were for funerals, not weddings?

She remembers Pete holding her really tight. She didn't object to him actually touching her flesh—but she felt nothing. A passive response was about all she could offer him. As he caressed her mouth with his lips, she still felt nothing. He put his hand on her breast and still she continued to feel nothing. NOTHING, NOTHING, NOTHING. What kind of word is that, anyway? NO THING, NOT A THING, NOTHING.

He asked her what was wrong. 'Nothing,' she said, both lying and telling the truth. Just a little tiredness at the end of the big day. He led her to the bed, whispering how much he loved her, proceeding to show her with his hands, his tongue and with every part of him, just how much he wanted her. Lynette played along. While she might feel nothing, she couldn't deny him her body. After all, it was the only thing she was able to give him. There wasn't anything else.

'If our child is conceived tonight,' she remembers saying to herself, 'it will be born to a woman who cannot feel.'

And she couldn't even cry about it, she couldn't even manage that. Why couldn't she fucking cry about it, for God's sake?

Pete fell asleep eventually. Lynette lay awake all night, hoping she hadn't spoilt his wedding night. She didn't think she had, though from her side it was shit. All Lynette could think about was (1) 'Where did I hide that bloody bottle?' and (2) 'Why have I got chronic diarrhoea?' Another side effect of all the booze.

Ten months later she was in hospital giving birth to their daughter. The nurse handed Lynette her baby while Pete sat on the bed, looking on with pride, weeping tears of joy. He was weeping for both of them because the baby's mother couldn't. It was eleven in the morning, she'd just given birth and all she could think of was having a drink. As Lynette looked at her beautiful, perfect, healthy baby, she was seriously considering swapping her for a bottle of Smirnoff.

Lynette and Pete arrive at the hospital. Neither one of them looks at the other. He takes a big, deep breath and gets out of the car. He walks over to his wife's side and opens the door. He helps her out. She stands there, unable to do or say anything. She has a husband and a child, that's indisputable, but, right now, she's reduced to feeling unutterably alone. Isolated. Discarded. Most of all, she's disgusted with herself. This is all her fault. She's let this happen—her—she's done this, caused all this pain to her husband, to her child, to anyone who has the bloody misfortune of coming across this pathetic excuse for a human being. What does her life add up to? Nothing. And there she is, back to NOTHING again. But, she's in pain too, she hurts like hell. Doesn't that count for something? Lynette doesn't think so right now.

Pete unstraps Lily and takes her in his arms. The infant absorbs her new surroundings placidly and thoughtfully.

Lynette looks up at the enormous white building that confronts her with its massive Gothic arches and turrets. It seems to go on for miles. This is to be her prison for the next five weeks. Her new home. She's signed a declaration that if she tries to escape, she won't be able to come back. Pete would never forgive her so she has to stay behind bars—even if they're not real bars. And she's allowed visitors. At least that's something. But Lynette can't see that far ahead, she's overwhelmed and filled with dread. Her body's weak all over and she's beginning to tremble. There's a sinking feeling in her stomach. She forgets the obese lump she usually feels, and instead cowers, tiny and insignificant, beneath the vast whiteness. As if she doesn't matter. And she doesn't—she knows that.

Pete puts his free arm round his wife and together they climb the few steps to whatever lies beyond. How will she survive and what will happen to her in the end? Or is this already it?

They arrive at the front door. It's open. People come and go about their business. Others lie sprawled out across the vast lawns chilling out, listening to iPods and smoking. Like it's summer term at university.

'Why are they acting as if everything's normal?' she asks herself. 'Nothing's normal. Nothing's right. Don't they realise

I'm dying inside? Don't they realise I'm about to be buried?' She grabs hold of Pete. She wraps her husband and her daughter in her arms as tightly as she can and starts wailing like a banshee. 'Well, if I'm mad,' she thinks, 'and I'm being incarcerated in a mad place, I might as well act like it.' The whole experience feels surreal, like she's in some kind of parallel universe. She falls down to her knees and implores her husband to take her home, promising him she'll change. She'll do whatever he wants. She pleads, she begs, she screams: 'I'm sorry, Pete. I'm sorry, Lily. I'm so, so sorry. Please forgive me. Don't leave me here. Please take me home. Please. Please. Please.'

'How pathetic,' she says to herself, later that evening, her first night at the Cloisters. 'Talk about making a scene. I don't know how many people it took to force me to go inside. I mean, there's quite a lot of me (all that drinking and stuffing doughnuts down my neck have taken their toll) and I'm quite strong. But they managed somehow. The whole thing was so unreal, like something out of a dream, like it was all happening in slow motion. I felt like I'd stepped out of myself and was watching it all, helpless. The next thing I remember was Dr Chaudhry giving me a sedative, and waking up in this pretty yellow bedroom with the lovely view of the lawns.'

Nurses stop by every fifteen minutes to check up on her. Sometimes, they don't even come in. They just look through the flap on the door. She'll be dropping off to sleep when suddenly she'll hear a noise. It's the flap sliding across the door from left to right. She tries to go back to sleep again but she can't for long and has to make do with catnaps. At least she feels safe and quiet.

Pete's left a photo by the bed. Pete, Lily and Lynette all together. She holds it in her hands. 'Christ,' she thinks, 'Lily's wearing that gorgeous pink frock I bought her on one of my outrageous sprees, when I'd go out and spend a small fortune. I'd come back and Pete would go berserk. I once worked my way through eight thousand pounds in just one afternoon. They say that's part of the illness—I do it to try and feel alive. I think. Whatever. It works for about ten minutes, then I have to have a drink (or three) to try and maintain it. But it never lasts and I just keep drinking.'

Lynette looked at her watch. It was about ten-fifteen and, though she was really tired, she couldn't sleep. The Quad kitchen was just down the corridor. Perhaps she could make herself some toast and have a hot chocolate. It might make her drop off once and for all. The next time the nurse came to check on her, Lynette asked for permission. The nurse said, 'No problem,' so Lynette put on her slippers and dressing gown and made her way down the corridor to the kitchen. She noticed a figure dressed in combat trousers and a baggy white T-shirt walk down the corridor and go into one of the rooms with quick, shuffling steps, shoulders hunched forward, head bowed. It looked like James, the really shy chap who'd checked in yesterday.

Someone had definitely been in the kitchen in the past half hour or so. The smell of recently grilled toast was overpowering. Perhaps James had been helping himself to a snack. And there was another easily recognisable aroma invading the air. Someone had been raiding the Horlicks supplies in order to get their nightly fix. The malted smell was unmistakeable.

The large Quad kitchen was certainly well stocked. In addition to a cooker, a microwave and a large sink, there were lots of cupboards containing different types of tea, coffee and drinking chocolate. In the end, Lynette decided to have a Camomile. She put the kettle on and helped herself to a teabag from the box. Then, she looked for the fridge. Ah, there it was. Inside were copious supplies of white and brown bread. She took out two slices of brown from the wrapper and popped them in the toaster. She grabbed some butter and searched for a knife and a plate.

She was all set. Apart from the whistling of the kettle, all was quiet and peaceful—nobody else around except for the sound of the night-nurses rustling papers at the desk down the corridor.

Suddenly, out of nowhere, came the most terrifying noise Lynette had ever heard. She couldn't work out what it was to begin with—it was like something out of a Hammer Horror film. Someone—a girl, she thought—was screaming at the top of her voice. Where was it coming from? The Quad leaped to life in a matter of moments. Nurses and patients rushed here and there. Lynette recognised a few faces from classes she'd been to, most of them still half asleep.

'Kalpana's tried to kill herself,' someone cried.

Lynette was on the phone to her husband: 'Pete, I can't stay here. The place is full of psychos. You'll never guess what's just happened. This Asian girl, Kalpana, she tried to top herself. Apparently, she tries to kill herself a lot. And when she's not doing that, she washes her hair. I mean, like every two hours. And, that's not all. Whenever she sees a man, she lifts up her skirt and asks him what he thinks of her knickers.'

'Bloody hell. Is she gonna be OK?'

'Well, it looks like they got to her in time. She's been taken down to surgery to be stitched up. And you'll never guess who else has checked in. Cat Green. Yes, Cat Green. The papers said she'd gone to the States. But that's rubbish. She's here. The woman's got slashes all the way up her arms. She cuts herself, for Christ's sake! They all cut themselves. I don't do that. I just drink. Well, OK, I drink quite a lot and I know it's not good. But she takes drugs. I don't take drugs. I wouldn't dream of taking drugs. Pete, I can't stay here. They're all nuts.'

'Now, darling, you promised. You said you'd give it the full six weeks. Lily and I will come and see you this weekend. By the way, what's Cat Green like?'

Lynette did her best to ignore her husband's last, intensely irritating question and continued regardless, 'And there's this guy. James. Apparently, he's been bullied at work and he wanders around like a zombie. He can hardly speak.'

'Poor chap,' said her husband. 'Bullying at work seems to be spiralling out of control. It's all over the papers.'

Lynette continued, breathless and impatient, 'I'm telling you, Pete, I can't stay here. It's a madhouse.'

'Now, Lynette. You know you're in the best possible place. They're going to get you better. And then you can come home. That's what we want, isn't it?'

'Yes, I s'pose so. But, Pete, I feel such a failure. Such a

waste of space. I mean, I've got you. And I've got Lily. I shouldn't be like this.'

'Now, listen, you silly thing. Have a nice hot bath, drink some cocoa and get an early night.'

'If you think I'm going out of my room again tonight, you've got another thing coming. Not after what happened earlier.'

'You've got your first EMDR session in the morning, haven't you? Try and get some sleep. You need an early night so you're fresh.'

'Yeah, and I'm not looking forward to it. The whole idea frightens the life out of me.'

'Sweetheart, it's going to help you. Dr Chaudhry said it's the best thing for you.'

'I know, I know. But that doesn't stop me being scared. Of what it's going to do to me.'

'Lynette, I love you. Just remember that. You're not doing this on your own. I might not be with you there in the room. But Lily and I, we're always, always thinking of you, willing you to get better so you can come home soon.'

She's in bed looking at the photograph, shaking. Thinking about what tomorrow will bring. She knows it's going to be hell, and she can't even have a drink. If she could just have *one* she could have a bloody good stab at blocking out her fears. A real bastard of a memory keeps coming into her head, too. It just won't give her a break. It happened only a few weeks ago. It was Lily's second birthday and Pete had taken the day off work to organise a party for her and her friends.

And—without any attempt to consider the evidence—Lynette proceeds to pronounce herself guilty as charged. 'Well, Pete could hardly rely on me, could he? All I could manage was to go to the office. While I was there—out of the house—I didn't have to face the fact that I was an out-and-out failure as a wife and a mother. Well—let's be honest—as a human being.'

That afternoon Lynette had left work earlier than usual—but not to go home and help Pete get ready. 'Oh, no, I went to the pub, didn't I, to get rat-arsed. Home was the last place I wanted to be—not sober, anyhow. All I'd see is happy families, something I just couldn't be part of. The loving, responsible father and husband and my gorgeous little daughter begging me to become a wife and a mother again. To be all jolly and join in the party. To feel what I should be feeling but can't. I couldn't face that—well, certainly not without a drink or two. So, I went to the pub and, after a bottle or two of vodka, I staggered into a cab and headed home.'

As soon as she walked through the front door she could see she was in big trouble. 'Pete's face was a picture—not a very nice one, I grant you. Well, not from where I was standing, at any rate. I'd never seen him look so angry before. He left the nanny in charge of the mad hatter's tea party and dragged me off to the sitting room.'

'What the hell d'you think you're playing at, Lynette? This is your daughter's second birthday. And she's having a party. You, her mother—the most important person in her life—gets home an hour and a half late, and you're as pissed as a newt. What's the matter with you, for Christ's sake? Don't you care about your own daughter? About me? What's going on in that head of yours? We can't go on like this, Lynette. We just can't. It's killing us. It's destroying our marriage. And what about Lily?'

Pete moved closer to Lynette and lay his hand on her right shoulder.

'I love you, Lynette, you must know that. But you're miles away from Lily and me. You're in some kind of bubble all on your own. And the drinking. It's just got to stop. It's just got to.'

He sighed heavily, shook his head, then moved towards the door to return to the party. Before he disappeared he gave his wife an ultimatum.

'Either you sort yourself out or we're through. I want my wife back and Lily needs her mother. That's you, in case you'd forgotten.'

And, for the first time in years, Lynette burst into tears. Falling down to her knees, she sobbed and sobbed for what seemed like hours. She wailed and howled in anguish. At last, at last she could feel something. But it had taken the terrible thought that she might lose everything that mattered to her. Maybe, just maybe, she thought, her emotions weren't completely fucked, after all.

And now she's got to go through this EMDR treatment. Dr Chaudhry hasn't told her much about it, but the little he has mentioned is enough to make her want to dive straight for the bottle, only she can't, of course.

According to Dr Chaudhry, the reason she's in such a mess is because she's buried her memories of a number of 'adverse life events'—that's what they call them at the Cloisters—without ever trying to 'process' them.

Adverse. Lynette thinks that's an interesting way to describe what she's been through. Losing her sister in a motorbike accident. Being nearly strangled by her fiancé (after he admitted sleeping with all her girlfriends). And then her brother's girlfriend topping herself. Anyway, the long and the short of it is she's buried all this crap deep inside without ever dealing with it. Pretending it hasn't happened. Out of sight, out of mind. Well, out of sight, maybe. But, certainly not out of mind.

Dr Chaudhry says it's like getting a letter that brings you bad news. You know you've got to deal with the bad news, but you procrastinate. You throw the letter away, or maybe you stuff it under the sofa. At any rate, you do nothing about it. You just hope it'll go away. But it won't go away, and if you don't deal with it pretty soon, it'll just zap you between the eyes when you're least expecting it. And it'll be much worse than if you'd dealt with it there and then, 'cos you've left it festering like a sore. The sore gets worse, uglier and meaner till it kills you—well, that's what it feels like. Like a cancer growing inside till it gets so big it explodes, and you're left to clean up the mess.

Lynette's left this cancer growing for so long, it's taken her over, so it needs to be removed—now. To stop her feeling stuck, to enable her to move forward. So she can claim her life back from the dead.

Dr Chaudhry says that sometimes memories are so bad they just don't get processed. They get stuck on one side of the brain; they never make it to the other side. It's like there's a barrier between them and ne'er the twain shall meet. That's what's happened to Lynette, apparently. This American woman Lynette's read up on (Francis, or Francine, something-or-other) came up with the idea of how you can successfully smash through the barrier.[1] Apparently, it's like driving a car through a tunnel very fast—the tunnel being the journey you need to take to get better. EMDR's supposed to get you through to the other side quicker than any other way. Faster than pills, electric shocks or counselling.

'They've got hold of this specialist chap from America to help me with processing the memories that are really fucking me up,' Lynette told Pete. And she's already chosen what she's going to start with—her sister's death. While she focuses all her thoughts on this, her eyes have to try and follow the therapist's fingers as he moves them from left to right. Apparently, this Francine woman found that once a patient's eyes begin to track the therapist's hand movements, it becomes very difficult to concentrate on the horrible memory. And once the memory's been taken out of cold storage, getting the eyes to track the therapist's hand movements enables the memory to be processed—or resolved—on a deeper, more subconscious level. Dr Chaudhry has told Lynette that if all goes according to plan, these sessions will enable her to resolve all her bad memories once and for all.

'Both sides of the brain will link up,' she says to herself, repeating what she's been told, 'and we'll all live happily ever after. Yeah, right. Despite Dr Chaudhry's deeply rational analysis of what is going to go through my mind and my heart, it is, after all, my mind and my heart which are about to be pulverised. I mean, don't get me wrong I like rational argument, and what the good doctor has come up with is

1 Francine Shapiro PhD, 1989

convincing. In objective, cold-light-of-day terms, that is, but not in terms of emotions—my emotions. And, let's face it, we're dealing with my emotions here, are we not? Having lived with them (or, I suppose, some might argue, without them) for so long, I'm the best person to judge what they're like. And I just know that when I relive these memories it's not going to be very pretty. Just a warning, really, to anyone who comes within a mile of that explosion.'

'All these years,' she thinks, 'I fooled myself that I was in control. I mean, by refusing to face my emotions, I stupidly thought I controlled the bastards. But what happens is they end up controlling you. You can kid yourself all you like. You can get fucking angry at them. You can drown them in booze. Bury them knee-high in drugs. Wrap them inside an extra-deep pizza. But you can't get rid of them. Not for ever. They'll be good and patient for a while, but time and time again, with alarming regularity, they'll rise up and smack you in the face. Then you'd better run for cover. Except there isn't any. Cover, I mean. No hiding place. Truth is, I've never really been in any kind of control. I've got a responsible job that I've managed to keep on top of. But so bloody what? That means nothing when compared to not being able to call yourself alive. Compared to not being able to feel anything. Well, not without getting paralytic on vodka. And that's lying to yourself. Or, at least hiding from yourself—your real self. Hiding from the pain and the raw emotion of being alive.'

His name's Matt. He's supposed to be the best money can buy.

'Thank God for private medical insurance,' thinks Lynette, beginning to shiver. 'How on earth are people supposed to get this on the NHS?'

Matt looks quite benign for a sadist. He's dressed in a camel-coloured, v-neck sweater—not the kind of thing you'd expect a sadist to wear—and jeans. This confuses Lynette. She'd been expecting someone more sharp-suited, less rounded at the edges. He's softly spoken, too. Maybe he wasn't out to get her, after all.

Matt asks Lynette if she's ready to begin.

'Oh, yeah, simply rearing to go.' She keeps this thought to herself and asks a question instead.

'How long will it take?'

Matt folds his arms, scratches his forehead and says, 'Well, Lynette, that depends on a number of things. You've chosen to focus on the memory of your sister's death. Now, it depends on how long it takes you to process that memory. If it gets too traumatic, and I have warned you that's quite likely, you only have to hold your hand up and I will stop at once. You've never focused on these emotions before, so it's bound to be overwhelming. Nobody can say just how overwhelming it will be until we actually begin the session. D'you have any other questions?'

'I just call up the image in my mind, right? I don't start talking about it out loud?'

'Yes, that's correct. Concentrate all your efforts on the picture that comes into your head as well as any smells, sounds or thoughts, feelings and bodily sensations it conjures up. Just let me know when you're ready to begin.'

Lynette takes a deep breath and starts travelling back in time.

Emma was just eighteen; she'd been going steady with Paul for over a year. She'd gone out for a ride with him on his motorbike.

She never came home again.

Lynette can see Paul standing at the doorway, her sister's helmet in his right hand, and she can recall the strong aroma of baking in the air. Her mother had been making lemon meringue pie and the smell was everywhere in the house. She was getting ready to go to university, she'd got a place at Oxford.... She just couldn't stop talking about it. She'd been rushing about here and there doing this and that. Emma was like that, she just never stopped, she was so full of life.

Lynette notices Matt moving his pen from left to right. He carries on for what seems a few seconds, then he pauses.

Lynette remembers her parents rushing in, staring at Paul in disbelief as if they somehow knew what had happened, but were too scared to say it out loud. Why was Paul standing there with Emma's helmet in his hand? Where was she? Where was their daughter—their beloved eighteen-year-old daughter?

Matt moves his hand and Lynette's eyes track the pen from left to right. Again and again. Momentarily, she abandons the image of her grieving parents, but her eyes are beginning to well up. Lynette's heart has been smashed to pieces—that's if it was ever whole in the first place, which she doubts.

She loses sight of the pen and goes back to her parents. She can see her mother breaking down, collapsing before her eyes, her hands wringing her apron over and over again. Lynette hears her screaming and sobbing louder and louder. Uncontrollably. In anguish. There's a new smell too. It pervades the atmosphere, completely drowning out the baking aroma, making her feel sick. It's an unmistakable stench—putrid, suffocating, horribly familiar.

Motorbikes.

Lynette hates motorbikes with a vengeance. The screeching noise they make as they tear down the road with malicious intent. The black foggy excrement pouring out of them. Their oppressive, brooding, menacing presence.

The presence of an assassin.

'Emma would have been at my wedding and at the birth of my daughter had it not been for that fucking motorbike.'

There it is, the pen again. And as it continues to move from side to side, so do Lynette's eyes. But it's too much. She raises her hand and screams at the top of her voice, 'Stop! Stop! For fuck's sake, stop!'

Afterwards, Lynette is exhausted. She sleeps for hours. When she wakes up, the first thing she's aware of is the terrible soreness of her eyes, the way they're all puffed up from crying. And the heavy thudding inside her head. Then she remembers she's supposed to be going to the Day Support Group. She pulls on her tracksuit bottoms and a crumpled sweatshirt and closes the door behind her. On her way she goes past the Day Patients' Lounge. As usual, the radio is blaring out all the hits. Given the state of Lynette's head, the loud booming of the music is the last thing she needs. This small lump of metal and chrome is the sole reminder of what is going on 'out there'. It doesn't seem to worry the patients—this jarring remembrance of a world they'd rather forget, and the regular news updates. All that belongs 'out there' and it can't harm them while they're protected within the thick walls of the Cloisters. When tubes get bombed and people get murdered, it doesn't touch them. It is part of another world, after all, which is far, far away. Out of reach. Everything 'out there' is chaos, whereas 'in here' there's order, structure, security. Of a kind.

Lynette is the last to arrive, and when she sits down and studies the afternoon's circle of woe, she's really sorry she's come. There are about ten in the group. One pretty, wet-faced girl dabs at her eyes silently with her handkerchief. A teenager with hunched shoulders and pimples coughs nervously. A thin, tall guy shuffles in his seat uncomfortably. An older woman stares desperately into the distance. Most of them have the marks to show why they are here. The cigarette-lighter and match burns lie grouped on wrists in circular clusters like bullet holes—no skin to cover that excruciatingly raw tissue now exposed to the punishing air. Further up, the arms are rows and rows of pink slashes. If Lynette didn't known better, she might have thought someone had dragged a red felt tip pen across the helpless flesh. But the culprits are far more likely to be dirty razor blades and rusty penknives held by unsteady fingers. One girl's arm is bandaged from the bottom of her wrist to her elbow. No need to guess what lies beneath the bandages—no one in the group needs to be shown what many of them have all seen before and lived with (if you can call it living) for so long. And then, there is the smell—a sweet, sickly aroma that Lynette can't put into words and which is everywhere in the Cloisters.

A disembodied voice emerges from the circle. 'My name is Sarah,' it says, 'and I'm a therapist here at the Cloisters.'

'Well,' thinks Lynette to herself, 'she has to be, doesn't she? She's the only one amongst us without incriminating marks on her arms; the only one who doesn't have a face like a wet Monday; the only one capable of getting her words out without breaking down.' Dressed in a long, floaty skirt and a T-shirt, her long auburn hair swept back tidily and professionally into a pony tail, Sarah gives off an aura of normality. Of sanity. Well, normal and sane compared to Lynette and the rest of the psychos in the room.

Sarah scrutinises the sea of lost souls surrounding her. 'This is the Day Support Group which takes place every afternoon at four-thirty p.m. Here you are free to share your feelings and thoughts with other members of the group. The idea is that by describing your emotions, however painful and upsetting, others here can empathise with what you are going through and maybe share a similar experience they have had. Perhaps we can offer support and suggest coping strategies.

'I need to stress that everything you hear and see in this room needs to remain confidential to ensure that people feel it's a safe environment. As it says on the wall, whatever you are told here please leave here. I may share things we discuss with the therapy team, but that's only if I feel it would be of help in aiding your recovery. Please make sure your mobile phones are switched off; it can be so disconcerting if one goes off in the middle of a session. We begin now and have forty-five minutes.'

Sarah fixes her kindly gaze on Lynette—her eyes daring her to explain her reason for being allowed to join this exclusive bunch of saddos. But if Lynette is to begin speaking—and that's a big if—how will she ever be able to stop?

'Lynette, would you like to begin by introducing yourself and telling us how you're feeling today?'

Lynette looks up slowly. As she does so, she can feel her head shaking. Her hands are sweaty, her feet shuffle from left to right. She feels like she's on the verge of throwing up and her head's on fire. During the morning's EMDR session she rediscovered a part of her that had remained closed for years—her tear ducts. Her clammy hand stretches out for a tissue from the box on the table beside her. Packs and packs of tissues can be found in every room at the Cloisters. A stupid thought passes through Lynette's head— how many boxes do they get through here a week? They must be able to keep Kleenex afloat single-handedly. As Lynette's hand moves to mop up the tears, she becomes conscious of how awful she must look. Her eyes are red and blotchy, the skin just below smeared with mascara and sore from the countless times she has been rubbing it. But Lynette doesn't care. Her whole world has come crumbling down on top of her. Nothing matters any more, least of all her appearance.

Lynette stares helplessly at Sarah, as if Sarah can somehow rescue her from her torture—the thoughts and memories that are invading her brain, reminding her of the worthless piece of shit she undoubtedly is. Her cheeks are ablaze and there's a strange hissing noise in her ears. She moves her tongue inside her mouth and manages to part her lips slightly. She tries to begin. But a huge lump in her throat— it feels like her stomach—tells her that whatever words lie trapped within her, she will never get them out of her mouth.

'Some people say having a lump in your throat is a sign of poor communication,' says Lynette to herself. 'Are they trying to be funny, or what? Do they know what it's like to feel this way?'

Just then the door is flung open and a glamorous Asian woman in her late thirties breezes in, followed by a black nurse. Wearing a green sundress with a baby-pink bra over the top, the woman is carrying a city gent's umbrella in her left hand and a colander in the other. At least, it looks like a colander. It's metal, has a handle on each side and lots of small holes. The woman's long, jet black hair looks like it had just been washed, and she behaves as if there is nothing peculiar about her appearance. She collapses into the chair next to Sarah, takes out a small pink notebook from her pocket and begins to read it silently to herself. She makes no attempt to say 'hello' and refrains from making eye contact with anybody.

'Come in, Kalpana,' Sarah says softly. 'I didn't know you were attending the group, but you're very welcome.'

Lynette returns to her room and collapses on her bed. She feels much worse than she did when she woke up this morning. She was emotionally wrecked at the end of her EMDR session. And then having to sit with a group of suicidally inclined self-harmers for an hour was excruciating. It hasn't exactly had a positive effect on her mood.

Most of all she feels guilty.

'Guilt. That's what I've been running away from. The

shame I felt because Emma went and I stayed. The look on my parents' faces—I'll never forget it as long as I live. They didn't say anything, but I knew it, I just knew it. It should have been me, not Emma, who went. After all, Emma was the beautiful, brainy one, the one who was going to Oxford, the golden girl. And now there's just me. What's the point of that? Of me, I mean, of me? Thinking about myself that way makes me feel even more ashamed, because I should be thinking about Emma. What we lost in her, not what's happening to me, how *I* feel. Why should anyone care about me?'

Dr Chaudhry says she should feel proud of herself, having gone through such an ordeal. He says she was brave. 'Proud of myself? I don't think so. Guilty, yes. Ashamed, yes. Not proud. I want to drink myself into a coma, to black out just one more time. But I can't—I'm not allowed. In that case, where did I put that giant Toblerone?'

On the phone that night Lynette tells Pete about her harrowing day and how she ended up in the lunch queue next to Cat Green. 'Christ! Talk about little and large, I felt like a beached whale. She only weighs about five stone—well, maybe that's a bit of an exaggeration. No secret why she's in here, of course. I blame that low-life boyfriend of hers, or, maybe he's an ex now. She's stuck in here and he's off doing one of his gigs. Scumbag. She's surprisingly normal, though and quite chatty. Not a prima donna, at all. Doesn't come across as spoilt or bitchy. Really down to earth in some ways. Strong sense of vulnerability about her. Nervous too—smokes about fifty a day, as far as I can make out. Must be the withdrawal symptoms. Or the detox. Or both. I'm sorry for Kalpana, though. I thought at first she was faking it. I mean, there are always those who pretend, who milk the system, aren't there? But she's not like that, I can tell.'

Marianne, Lynette and Cat had just finished lunch. Cat was desperate for a fag so they all went outside into the gardens. A cluster of inmates had gathered around the ping-pong table while two guys enjoyed a game. Others were sitting on the opposite side of the garden, puffing away, discussing their respective illnesses and comparing burns and cuts. The girls took up residence on a garden seat just big enough for the three of them. Cat lit up a cigarette with her lighter, inhaled and looked up at the sky. It was one of those illogical rules they had at the Cloisters. While matches were forbidden, you could have as many cigarette lighters as you liked.

It was a lovely day—warm, dry, balmy even. Nearby, there were a few tubs of miserable-looking flowers doing their best to survive underneath enormous mounds of fag ends.

Thanks to Kalpana's aborted attempt to turn out the lights the other night, and her rather unusual behaviour, neither Cat nor Marianne were paying much attention to Lynette, for which she was grateful. Talking about Lily was OK, though. If she kept going on about her two-year-old daughter, she thought she could avoid having to delve into all that shit she was going through, especially now the EMDR therapy had begun.

All of a sudden, Cat burst into tears.

'God, what is it, Cat?' asked Marianne, putting her arm round her newfound friend.

'It's Os, my son. I haven't seen him for over a month.

They won't let me. I know, I've been bad, I've been irresponsible and I'm a crap mother, but it's doing my head in.'

Lynette swore at herself under her breath. Moving to Cat's other side, she put her arm round her.

'Christ, Cat, me and my big mouth. If it's any consolation, I've not been around for Lily that much. I've been a much worse mother. A real waste of space. And I've seen so many pictures of you with Os holding him, cuddling him, making such a fuss of him. It's obvious to everyone you're nuts about him.'

Lynette was drowning and fast. Marianne came to her rescue.

'Cat, you're a fabulous mother. Lynette's right, you care heaps about Os. If you didn't, you wouldn't be crying now, would you? And, anyway, you're ill, we're all ill. We can't be any good to anyone when we're no good for ourselves, can we? That's why we're here. We need help and we're getting it. We just have to be a little patient, that's all.'

'But nobody's come to be with me, to help me while I'm in this shit. No one wants to be mixed up with Cat Green, not now I've been caught. Look at Dave, for fuck's sake—he's the one who got me started on coke in the first place. Where the fuck's he?'

'*We're* here, Cat, and we're not leaving,' Lynette reassured her.

'Yeah,' said Cat, wiping the tears from her eyes. 'But you *can't* leave, can you? You haven't got any choice. You're stuck with me whether you like it or not. And I'm stuck with you.'

They all laughed. Well, they did the best they could.

Looking down, Lynette noticed that Cat had had her nails painted recently. Bright pink, too. 'Wow!' she said. 'They look great. When did you have them done?'

Cat sniffed a couple of times and replied casually, 'This morning. The agency arranged for someone to come in and do it.' For Cat, getting someone in to perform a manicure was hardly a big deal. It was like getting Waitrose to deliver your groceries.

Rubbing her right hand over the marks and bruises that adorned her left arm, she added, 'I know it seems odd. Getting my nails done when my arms are smashed up. I thought it might take attention away from the cuts. Maybe. You know?'

But the incompatibility between the beautifully painted talons and the ripped arms was startling. The wantonly, savagely butchered skin was winning the competition for attention hands down.

Marianne bugs Lynette because she's always on the verge of tears while Lynette finds it so hard to cry, to let go. To Lynette, Marianne seems so in touch with her emotions, so unafraid of letting them out. Not like Lynette. She's petrified of what they can do to her. Dr Chaudhry tries to impress on all his patients the fact that their emotions are the only thing they can really trust, because they never lie. So there is no need to fear them.

'Yeah, right,' says Lynette. 'Don't think I'm quite there yet.'

It was time for Lynette's second EMDR session. Matt was about to make her go through yet more hoops. This time— joy of joy—it was to be Stuart. Good old Stuart, her ex-boyfriend of fourteen years ago.

Lynette was just twenty and, though she'd never have admitted it at the time, desperate for someone to tell her she was OK. That was all she wanted, that it was enough to be OK, that she was good enough. Unfortunately, she picked the wrong guy.

It had been four years since Emma's death and Lynette was at college studying law. She was cramming so hard, she wanted to make up to her parents for Emma. She thought if she could do well at college, get a career and have the right kind of boyfriend (the kind Emma would have had and therefore the kind they'd approve of), she might get them to tell her she could stop feeling guilty. That she didn't have to try any more, that she was enough. Why she thought she wasn't enough for them, she didn't know. They never said so. In fact, they never said anything much at all. Since Emma's death, they had lost touch with Lynette. Emotionally. And she with them. This made her feel unworthy, inferior, unlovable. Cheated of love and misunderstood, she buried herself in her career.

Stuart was tall, good-looking, with arresting blue eyes. He had an infectious sense of fun too. When he was on form he made you feel on top of the world. Stuart was an achiever. It was written all over his face and in the self-confident way he held himself. He was going to be a barrister and, undoubtedly, one day, a judge. A success story from beginning to end. Charming. Self-assured. Clever. He really knew how to make people around him have a good time.

Lynette's parents liked Stuart enormously. But when he and Lynette were alone together, he showed a completely different side to his character. He put Lynette down all the time. She was useless. She didn't wear the right clothes. She wasn't slim enough. She couldn't cook. Her tennis needed to improve. The list went on and on. So what did she do? Stuart chose her clothes, he made her go on one diet after another. He made her go to cookery classes and have private tennis lessons.

Since Emma died, Lynette had no trouble believing that, if things were going badly, it had to be her fault, that it was up to her to put them right. So that's what she did. Or, at least, that's what she tried to do. Once they had a dinner party for twelve of their friends. Well, his friends, mostly—he didn't give her much choice about the guest list. Though the dinner party was Stuart's idea, Lynette had to do the cooking, the shopping and all the preparations. All Stuart did was to turn up late and tell her off for not doing a good enough job. The highlight of the evening was when the two of them were in the kitchen together just before the main course. Grabbing the serving dish with the potatoes in it, he said, 'These aren't cooked properly. We can't possibly eat them.' Then he proceeded to empty the contents over the kitchen floor.

Stuart went even further, telling her she wasn't good enough in bed. Instead of suggesting she take lessons, he went out and slept with every one of her friends. Stuart took the utmost satisfaction in confessing all this to Lynette one Sunday morning. In filling in every detail from beginning to end. In rubbing her nose in all of it. They'd been lying in bed, and he'd been upbraiding her for her lack of sexual know-how. 'If only you were more like Mandy,' he boasted. 'She really knows how to please a man. The way she delivers a blow job has to be seen to be believed.' To tell the woman you're going to marry that you've slept with her best friend, and then to tell her, without any remorse or shame whatsoever, that you've slept with all her other friends… . Something just snapped inside Lynette—all the rage and the resentment that had been building up came out and she went for him. She moved over to his side of the bed and beat her arms against his chest. She screamed, 'You bastard! You bastard!' at the top of her voice. 'Why? For God's sake, why?'

Stuart had no idea why Lynette was getting so het up. How dare she behave like this. In one swift, smooth movement he grabbed the tie he had placed on the chair next to the bed. He stretched it taut with his hands and, before Lynette could guess what was about to happen, tied it round his girlfriend's neck, pulling tighter and tighter. Lynette could feel her breath failing and she was virtually paralysed with fear. Her throat had become puce from the pressure Stuart was applying with his fingers. She tried to pull at the tie and get it off her neck, but it was no good. Her strength had faded, and all she could do was to stare into Stuart's cold eyes as he proceeded to kill her. Suddenly, a quiver went through Stuart's body and he began to take stock of what he was doing. He pulled the tie away from Lynette's neck and got off the bed. Silently and quickly, he took his clothes from the chair and got dressed. Then he left.

Lynette never saw him again. She didn't call the police and she didn't have the guts to tell her relations or friends what had happened. She was so full of shame for what Stuart had done, she didn't want anyone to know. Like everything else that went wrong, she felt it was her fault. She didn't think her parents would believe her if she told them that Stuart—their beloved Stuart—was a potential murderer, not to mention a serial womaniser. And she wasn't sure whether she had any friends left, either. Or, at least, people she was now prepared to call friends.

It had been so long since Lynette had thought about Stuart properly. Really allowed herself to relive all that shit, take it out of cold storage and heat it up. Now, all she wanted to do was sleep, for days, months, years. And she didn't give a fuck whether she'd 'processed' that memory or not.

It was eleven-thirty p.m. and all the patients were tucked up in the Land of Nod. Except for Lynette. There seemed no danger of falling asleep, so she thought she might as well get up. As usual, there were two night-nurses at the desk. Matilda and Trish were on duty tonight. It looked like they were sharing a private joke as they sipped their milky coffee and filled in their time sheets. Lynette whispered that she was having trouble getting to sleep, so they let her stay in the lounge. They could keep an eye on her there. It was only just round the corner.

'Just for a bit, mind.'

As hospital lounges went, it was OK. Two expansive pink sofas, coffee tables, pretty pictures on the wall and a big plasma TV. Sort of homely with a safe feel about it. Lots of magazines, too. Helping herself to an old issue of *Hello!*, Lynette flicked through its pages, hoping and praying that they would do the trick and send her off to sleep. Among the glossy pics she caught sight of Cat doing a fashion shoot. Two or three pages later, there was another photo of Cat and that waste of space, on-off boyfriend, Dave Hackett. What on earth did Cat see in a loser like him, for God's sake? Perhaps she just didn't rate herself very highly. Difficult to believe, the way she looked.

Just then, the woman herself slouched into the lounge. Dressed in a baggy designer T-shirt, which would have been tight when stretched around Lynette's generous proportions, and some cute bunny-rabbit slippers, she had that little-girl-lost look. She looked kind of ordinary, too, with no make-up and her hair all over the place.

'Can't you sleep, Goldilocks?' Lynette enquired, rather obviously.

'No, I fucking can't,' replied Cat as she collapsed into the vacant sofa with a huge sigh. 'I can't sleep unless I take something. And I'm sure you know what I mean, Lynette Forrester.'

'I'm sure I don't, Cat Green,' said Lynette disingenuously.

'Coming from a woman who could drink for the entire Southern Hemisphere, I don't think you're in a position to cast stones.'

And they laughed.

'What were you looking at when I so rudely interrupted you?' Cat asked, catching sight of the name of the magazine.

'You, actually.'

And with that Cat bounced on to Lynette's sofa and grabbed hold of the offending article. 'Shove up, then.'

'Oh, yeah,' she said, with a studied air of nonchalance in her voice. 'They were taken months ago. God, what a bore it all was. And there's that useless shithead. Boy, I hope I never see him again. Yeah…'

From Cat's hesitation Lynette could tell there was still an attraction. And, before she could stop herself, she waded straight in:

'D'you mind me asking, Cat? What was it about…I mean…?'

'You mean, why would I be interested in a junkie who's done time, whose friends are East End smack dealers and who smashes up apartments for kicks? Why would I want him messing with my head?'

'Well, now you put it like that, yeah,' said Lynette.

'Well, basically, because he was—is—a bloody good shag.' And then, pausing to think about what she had just said: 'Actually, I'm not really sure whether the sex was good because of him or because of the drugs. Or, maybe, because of one of the others. I mean, I might be shocking you here, Lynette, but it wasn't always just the two of us, if you know what I'm saying.'

Cat looked at Lynette to try and gauge her reaction. She didn't think Lynette seemed too traumatised, so she went on:

'Anyway, Dave has this dark side to him which, for some masochistic reason, I found…I think I still find it really sexy. Well, sexy and repulsive at the same time, if I'm honest. God, that shows you how screwed up I am, doesn't it?'

Lynette was thinking of Stuart and she didn't feel shocked at all.

'Not really,' said Lynette. 'I know what it's like to be under a man's thumb to the extent that you don't…you can't exist as a person in your own right. Yeah, I know what that's like. And it's good enough reason to be in here. That's for sure.'

Then she added, looking pensive, 'As far as threesomes are concerned, I don't think it would ever be *my* cup of tea, but that doesn't mean I would judge anyone for it. Just wouldn't fancy it myself, that's all.'

Cat sighed. 'Thank God for that,' she said, laughing. 'Thought I'd just pulled the plug on a beautiful friendship. I think you're right, though. I mean, about being here. I think it helps, not having to be responsible for anything, not having any decisions to make. Though, at first, I didn't want to come at all—my agency forced me into it. Damage limitation exercise, they said. I'd messed up so many modelling contracts. When they discovered those photos of me at that cocaine party they practically threw me in here on the back of a wheelbarrow.'

Cat pulled her legs up to her chest and rocked from side to side.

'The thing is, before I came here, I felt I was the only one in the world feeling like this. Like I was bad. Like I was the worst person in the world. The worst person in the world,' she repeated. 'But here, so many people here are in the same boat. It makes you feel kind of…well…as if it's not your fault. Well, not all of it, anyway. And it's OK to be yourself.'

'Yeah,' agreed Lynette. 'Out there you feel like nobody could be as bad as this. No one could feel this desperate. And then, when you come in here, you realise, yes, they could. They do. That's the really great thing about being here. The thing that helps most. The other thing is it teaches you not to judge other people so much. I mean, before, if I'd heard someone was off sick with depression, I don't think I'd have been very sympathetic, but now…'

Lynette leant over towards Cat and said, 'D'you know what? I think I've worked it out. It's them out there.'

'What?' said Cat, looking puzzled.

'Don't you see? It's them out there, they're the ones who ought to be in here. They're the ones who've messed everything up for us. All the insensitive types, the bastards. I mean, if they were in here, it'd be safe for us to be out there, wouldn't it?'

Cat laughed and nodded her head. 'Yeah, you've got a point there. They're the ones who've landed us in here. So, by rights…'

Lynette was all fired up. 'Sometimes, when I'm lying in bed, I imagine all of them standing up in a line. All the bastards. All the people who've fucked things up for me. Who make me so fucking angry. Lined up in a firing squad. I go up to them and smash each of their shitty faces in.' And she punched into the air with her arms, her fists clenched. 'There's never any blood or anything. They don't collapse or fall down. I don't know, it just makes me feel better. God, the amount of people in that line, it just gets longer and longer. Every night, it grows and grows until there are so many people in it, it takes ages to get through them all. D'you ever feel like that?'

'Yeah,' agreed Cat forcefully, 'I bloody do. Though, I guess I've never thought about it quite in that way before.' After a pause, she added, 'I do miss having something to take…if you know what I mean. It's such a crutch. Trying to deal with all the shit on your own, it's so hard.'

'I know, I know,' empathised Lynette. 'I feel like that about drink. I've relied on it for so long, it's so hard doing without it. And this detoxing crap is shite.'

'Yeah,' agreed Cat. 'You know, given the choice, I'd still go back to the drugs. And, you know what, you don't put weight on with cocaine. You don't have to go on a diet. It's brilliant.'

'Well,' mused Lynette, patting her stomach, 'p'raps I should try it then.'

They both laughed.

After a pause, Lynette asked, 'What's it like, anyway? I mean, what does it actually feel like when you take it? What does it do to you? God, Pete would kill me if he knew we were having this conversation.'

'It's fucking bliss,' said Cat, enthusiastically. 'If you're at a party, it makes you feel full of energy. You can talk for hours. You can sort out all the problems of the world, solve the mystery of world peace and talk bollocks all at the same time. You feel...well, like you're on top of the world. Confident, you know. Great. And the sex. God, it's awesome. You just *feel* it more, if you know what I mean. You're so much more aware of it. And it frees you. Completely. You're just so uninhibited. So relaxed. So open. Christ, I wish you hadn't asked me. Just talking about it makes me want some. Even though I know it'll kill me if I don't give up.'

'Sorry, Cat,' said Lynette. Changing the subject, she asked her what she thought of Marianne.

'I think she's cool. Yeah. Great sense of humour, too. Really cynical. Even when she feels like shit she can say something funny—even about this place. That's a real talent. And her imagination. No wonder she's a writer. I've told her she should write a story about the Cloisters. About us. I don't mind if she puts me in it. I've told her.'

'Yeah,' said Lynette, 'but think about it, Cat. Some people might find it a bit weird reading about themselves and all their crazy little ways, don't you think? Just imagine if you were Kalpana and you read about yourself lifting your skirt up every time you saw a man. I mean, it's a really sensitive area, isn't it? It's like washing people's smalls in public. Things they're ashamed of, I mean.'

'I know, but people ought to know about this place. About these illnesses. That we aren't faking it. That it's *well* serious. There's such a stigma attached to depression. I mean, tell me something. How many people in your life know you've checked into the Cloisters?'

Lynette thought about this and said: 'I haven't told anyone. I mean, Pete knows, of course, and my boss—I had to tell him. But apart from them, nobody. God, I'd die if I thought my parents or friends knew I was here.'

'But why?' Cat pressed her for the answer she already knew.

'Because they'd judge me. They'd think I was nuts. Or lazy. Or a complete loser. Or all three. Oh, I don't know. Anyway, they'd tell me to pull myself together.' And, raising her voice, she exclaimed, 'If I could fucking pull myself together I'd have done it by now, wouldn't I?'

'Well, what about me?' said Cat. 'Everyone knows I'm in rehab. The whole bloody world knows about me, thanks to the media. OK, they might think I'm in Arizona or California. But so what?'

'Yeah,' said Lynette, 'and it shouldn't be like that. People don't realise this is more than just mental—though, God

96

knows that's bad enough. And it's such an ugly word. Mental. It has such awful connotations. People start thinking of asylums and straitjackets. And men in white coats. It's physical, our depression, anxiety, whatever it is we have. Our addictions, our obsessions. They all make us physically ill. Which means we hurt physically. Why can't people see that? If we broke our leg or cut our heads open, that'd be different, wouldn't it? Because people would see. It'd be obvious. Our wounds would be on show. They could see the pain. But breaking a leg or cutting your head, once it's mended, the pain is gone. It doesn't cock up your life. Threaten your relationships. Your work. Your heart. You don't feel like topping yourself when you break your leg. Do you?'

Cat didn't answer. Silent tears were trickling down her face.

It was twelve-thirty. Lynette had gone back to bed but she still couldn't sleep. Her conversation with Cat had made her feel very angry. Angry that it was almost impossible to explain to people on the outside how people like her felt. And virtually impossible not to feel stigmatised because of it. People in here had serious illnesses which made them wish they were dead, for Christ's sake. For some—like Kalpana—it was so grim they actually tried to kill themselves. Again and again. 'Well,' she said, with a deep sigh, 'I'll have to stay here, then. This'll be my new home. And I'll just visit the outside from time to time. I don't have to explain myself here. People understand. They've seen it so many times. They don't judge. They don't try to make me feel ashamed and they don't tell me to pull myself together.

They empathise. And I don't have to be perfect. Just me. I might as well face it, I'm too scared to go back out there.'

Lynette began to think about Stuart for the umpteenth time that day—Stuart, Emma and her parents. She had decided she would call her mother and father. She would tell them that she wasn't what they wanted her to be, perfect. She was just her, Lynette, and that that was enough. She wanted to tell them the truth about Stuart, too. She had been living a lie all these years and she couldn't—not any longer.

While she was thinking, Lynette became aware of noises coming from the room next door. Somebody had moved in the previous day but no one seemed to know who it was. It was definitely a woman, though. Earlier on, Lynette had seen a figure wearing a floor-length, hooded cloak and carrying three Prada cases glide into the room. As far as the girls were aware, she hadn't emerged since. Though, staff had been seen going in and out at various times. As Lynette continued to listen, she could make out a number of voices, though she wasn't sure how many. It soon became clear that one of these voices belonged to none other than Dr Chaudhry. As far as Lynette could tell, he seemed to be telling someone off. 'Perhaps I misheard,' said Lynette, as she moved closer to the wall. Putting her ear up against it, she listened as hard as she could. No, she hadn't made a mistake—it was definitely her consultant.

'Miss McFarlane,' said Dr Chaudhry, 'this is a hospital. The people who are here need peace and quiet, especially at night. As you well know, patients are not allowed to go out, except as directed by their consultant and at appropriate times. And they certainly aren't permitted to bring alcohol on to the premises. If you remember, it was explained to you when you were admitted yesterday morning; alcohol is banned in the interests of the patients, some of whom are in here because they are trying to fight their addiction to it.'

'Oh, my God!' whispered Lynette excitedly. 'It's Cherry McFarlane.'

The dressing-down was followed by a succession of loud hiccups, and then a deafening and rather protracted belch— but not from the psychiatrist. Once this had subsided, Lynette heard the soap-star deliver her defence in her trademark estuary accent.

'Oh, come on, darlin.' You can't expect me to stay cooped up in here all night. It's not right. A fun-loving girl like me having to do without her jollies. Anyway, don't forget, mate, I'm paying *you*. Not the other way round. And I want room service.' Pause for a dirty laugh from Cherry. 'All I did was go out for a boogie with my boyfriend. Just went clubbing, that's all, and brought back a bit a' fizz. What's wrong with that, darlin'?'

But the hiccups had resumed, making it impossible for the television star to go on.

'Miss McFarlane,' continued Dr Chaudhry, raising his voice a little to be heard over the tirade of hiccups and intermittent burps, 'I'm afraid you will have to leave the hospital. We can't have this sort of thing going on. You have flouted a number of rules that have to be adhered to if the hospital is to run smoothly. This is a place for seriously ill people. I do not believe you are seriously ill. Therefore, you, your boyfriend, and your alcohol, must leave. And immediately, please.'

After a few seconds of silence, Lynette heard the door close. This was followed closely by hoots of raucous laughter.

Lynette studied the blank piece of paper in front of her and wondered what on earth she was going to do with it. As she'd be the first to admit, she possessed absolutely no artistic talent whatsoever. She wasn't the only one being asked to draw a picture of her mood—the way she was feeling right now. There were about eleven of them in the Stables, sitting in a circle, as usual. On the floor on big, brightly-coloured cushions. This is what they called Art Therapy. It was supposed to be cathartic and help people come to terms with themselves and what was troubling them.

On the trestle table at the end of the room were lots of drawing and colouring implements. Thick crayons, felt pens and pencils in all the different hues of the rainbow. Assorted shapes and sizes of paper, too. Pieces of A4 and A3 in pink, white, green and blue. But Lynette didn't see the colours, Lynette only saw black. She helped herself to a thick black marker and a piece of white A4 and returned to her cushion. She took the top off the pen and placed the paper in front of her on the floor. She inhaled the glue-like smell coming from the nib, its powerful smell making her feel slightly nauseous.

She led the pen to the middle of the page and drew a black line from the top to the bottom. When she got to the end, she went over the line again, exerting more pressure. It was important that it was really thick and there were no breaks. On the left-hand side of the paper she drew a large black circle, once again, going over the edge several times to make it dense. Inside the circle she put a stick figure. It was clearly meant to be female because Lynette had given it a skirt. Above the top of the circle she made a thick black squiggle that was possibly meant to resemble a cloud, then she filled it in with the black marker. It looked a bit more like a cloud, now. A really angry cloud. Next she turned to the right-hand side of the picture and drew two more figures: a man and a tiny person wearing a skirt. Lynette joined the two figures up in the middle, suggesting they were holding hands. Lynette then added a few miniscule circles below the faces of each of the two figures on the right. Were these supposed to be tears? Finally, the artist inserted a bubble with a caption above the small figure on the right. It read: 'Mummy, we love you and miss you. Please come back.'

From the second they get into the taxi they can't stop giggling.

Cat: 'Escape from Alcatraz. Yippee!'

Lynette: 'Retail therapy, here we come!'

Marianne: 'Freedom!'

Look out, London: the girls are going shopping. At the Cloisters patients are always being told to pamper and treat themselves. So, that's exactly what Marianne, Cat and Lynette are doing. Sod the bank manager. Not that Cat has to worry, of course. They've been at the Cloisters more than two weeks so they're allowed out for a short while. When they get back their bags will be searched, just in case one of them tries to smuggle in something sharp, poisonous or made of glass. Since the girls are concentrating on shoes, that shouldn't pose a problem. They'll have to sign themselves out and if they're not back by the agreed deadline, they'll be for it. One patient who went out the other day was an hour late getting back and got about ten calls on her mobile. She came back soon after that. But, if they don't get you to come back that way, they'll probably send out an ambulance. At the end of the day, if you disobey the rules you'll get thrown out—that's the ultimate penalty—and you won't be able to get back in, either. They won't take you back. There's no such thing as heavies or physical pressure to coerce you into doing anything at the Cloisters. It's your decision. All of it. Here, each man and woman is encouraged to be responsible for themselves.

Cat is heavily in disguise. The last thing she wants or needs is to be recognised. If the paparazzi get on to her, that will be that and she'll be thrown out. The Cloisters won't stand for anything that threatens patients' privacy and her agency wouldn't exactly be over the moon, either. Not to mention the fashion houses who have provided her gear for the outing. She's wearing a short brunette wig, a pink mac, knee-high boots and dark glasses. She really does look amazing; Cat's got such style, such charisma—she could never look what Marianne calls *vin ordinaire*. Well, she might not get recognised—hopefully not, anyway—but she'll certainly get looked at.

Lynette's got dressed up too. The others have never seen her look so glam. Pressed jeans and a tailored jacket. She's brushed her hair and she's put a lot of scent on. Eau de parfum. Hermès. The nurses have let her get some from her locker. Cat and Marianne won't be able to lose her— they'll be able to smell her miles away.

Even Marianne's made an effort, so she must be getting better. She's painted on some slap, combed her hair and put some heels on. Not exactly Jimmy Choos, but she doesn't care. They're already beginning to work their magic and she's starting to feel like a woman again. A half-attractive woman, even. And she's wearing a dress—Marianne wants to feel flirty, frilly and flouncy. It's been such a long time since she felt that way. And it feels good. The girls are trying to reclaim something they've lost, and maybe, just maybe, they're beginning to find it. Well, almost.

On the way back from the shops, they drop into a bar for a reminder of what the outside world feels like. It's strictly off limits, but the temptation is just too strong. Funnily enough, it's not the drink that's brought them in—what they really want is a flirt.

Kevin's a plumber. Dressed in a loud, short-sleeved Hawaiian shirt, worn over his trousers to conceal his beer-gut, he's very, very chatty and is particularly interested in Cat. He keeps offering to buy the girls a real drink, but they hold fast and stick to cranberry juice. Cat finds all this abstinence a bit trying and chain-smokes to compensate.

'How did you three meet?' he enquires.

For obvious reasons (except to Kevin) the girls find this highly amusing and begin to snigger.

Poor Kevin thinks they're laughing at him. When he adds, 'Was it bad luck?' this is too much and they fall into hysterics. Yes, three people meeting in a hospital because one's an alcoholic with emotional paralysis, another's a drug addict, and the third suffers from panic disorder, might be regarded as a bit of bad luck.

Kevin stares down at his shoes while the three girls giggle away.

Cat thinks this is a real hoot. Tapping Kevin's wrist, she whispers in a serious tone, 'Actually we met at choir practice,' which only make things worse. By now, Lynette, Cat and Marianne are practically on their knees, tears streaming down their faces.

'I'm not stupid, you know. Just because you three are obviously very hoity-toity, you think it's funny to laugh at me because I'm…I don't know, because I'm a plumber or something.'

Marianne feels sorry for Kevin so she decides to level with him. 'Sorry, Kevin, we didn't mean to laugh. It's just a silly private joke, that's all. You really wouldn't find it very funny. You see, the thing is, the three of us, we…we've escaped from a mental hospital.'

Cat and Lynette stare at Marianne, unable to believe what she has just said.

'It's just down the road. I'm sure you've heard of it. The Cloisters?'

And with that Kevin is off faster than a bat out of hell.

Lynette's sitting on her bed looking at her drawing. She's crying quietly to herself and paying attention to what this is telling her. As much as she wants to get to the right-hand side of the picture, and as much as the two figures want her to join them, she can't. Not just because of the thick black cloud above her, but also because of that thick black wall in the middle. The blackness is outside her and it's also inside her. She *is* the blackness. The blackness *is*

her. Sometimes, it becomes so overpowering and so oppressive she feels she will implode.

But, doesn't she have any power to change things? She looks down, sees that she's still got the felt pen in her hand, and she squeezes it. Maybe she does have some control—she can edit the drawing. As her tears fall on to the paper, she removes the top of the pen and draws another figure on the right-hand side next to the tiny figure. It's Lynette. So, now, she's on the left and the right, but that's OK. All this shit she has to deal with, it might be her shit, but that doesn't mean she can't get support when she needs it from those she loves and who love her. Why didn't she see that before? It doesn't matter, she does now and that's all that counts. Though, in this game, she can't be certain if she'll still be seeing it that way tomorrow. Lynette grabs her mobile and sends her husband a text message:

ANY CHANCE OF CUDDLES IN NXT FEW HRS? BRING LILY'S BK SO CAN READ HER STORY. MISS U BOTH. XXX

A reply comes back within three minutes:

ON OUR WAY
XXX

The prospect of a two-and-a-half-hour creative writing session did not fill Lynette with unmitigated glee. She'd had a brilliant afternoon with Pete and Lily yesterday and for a change was feeling quite good. Anyway, she didn't

know how to write—creatively or otherwise. She looked at the clock in the dining room. It was one-fifty p.m. Ten minutes to finish her coffee and psyche herself up. She'd agreed to meet Cat and Marianne at the class. They'd gone up to their rooms to make some calls.

As she strolled down the corridor to the Seminar Room on the other side of the building, Lynette wondered what they were going to ask her to do. She thought about skipping the class but something told her to go.

When she arrived there weren't many patients. Punctuality was not in abundance at the Cloisters, at least, not when it came to patients. Whatever the excuse, lateness was always accepted, as long as you arrived within the first ten minutes. If you were later than that, the rule was for those already there to decide if the latecomers could be admitted.

The Seminar Room was probably the most impressive part of the Cloisters. It was a vast hall with a high ceiling and a massive stone fireplace. The ceiling was intricately carved and painted soft cream in keeping with the overall style of the building. From the centre hung an elaborate chandelier. Lynette nodded hello to the therapists and the patients, and then sat down. Opposite her was a young American girl called Veronica, probably no more than twenty. Her skeletal body was dressed in a faded yellow tank top and a pair of threadbare jeans. Practically every part of those jeans had been autographed or doodled on by the wearer and, even now, Veronica was adding further contributions. In the clinic Veronica was known as the 'chick with the scars'. Her bare arms were embellished by endless slashes that in some macabre way harmonised with the artwork on the jeans. On her right wrist was a large black cross made up of a number of individual burns. Wherever she was, Veronica would be scribbling or drawing on her jeans with a thick felt pen. It was clear the jeans hadn't seen the inside of a washing machine in a long time—the writing and sketches looked as fresh as the day they were printed. Veronica's long, greasy black hair can't have made contact with the contents of a shampoo bottle for weeks either. It hung down in limp, stringy strands as she concentrated hard on her work.

Veronica had a haunting face—on the rare occasions that her hair wasn't obscuring it and you could actually get a look. Dark brown, velvety eyes, whiter-than-white skin and hollow cheeks. She didn't smile a lot, but when she did she looked beautiful—in an unconventional, pale-and-interesting kind of way. Her passion was philosophy which, given that it required copious amounts of thinking, was enough to land her in the Cloisters. She liked getting to 'the root of all existence', she said, though it troubled her deeply. Veronica never shied away from awkward questions, but she asked them, not to unnerve or expose people, but because she couldn't stop thinking. That was her blessing and her curse. What mattered to Veronica was people and what made them tick. So, it was typical of the girl that when she was asked to introduce herself at the beginning of the session and say how she was feeling, she responded with a question:

'Can you tell me what we're supposed to get out of creative writing classes?' It wasn't a criticism, just a search for truth.

Veronica suffered from panic attacks. She was also recovering from drug addiction and self-harm. She'd been paranoid about ending up on the streets and that's exactly what happened. As Veronica would say, 'Don't we always attract the things we fear?' She was bright, intensely sensitive and a deep, deep thinker. This was Veronica's last day at the Cloisters. She'd been there for five weeks and was going back to her life as a philosophy student at Oxford. The prospect unnerved her.

Lynette's thoughts about Veronica were interrupted by the therapists telling the patients what they were expected to do. At one end of the room on a big table lay scores of colour copies of paintings. Some featured old masterpieces, others new. Some were really famous works, others completely obscure. Everyone in the group was invited to go up to the table and select a picture. They were then asked to return to their chair and compose a piece of writing based upon what they saw in it.

Lynette trawled through the stacks of images that lay before her. It wasn't long before she found one which pulled her towards it like a magnet. It must have been the most dismal picture in the whole pile. A woman, whose face we cannot see, sits in the foreground of a room staring at a fire on the opposite side. The room is dark and gloomy except for the firelight in the corner. But even that is beginning to lose its glow as its sparks are threatened by a black fog coming down the chimney. At the back of the room, to the right, is a closed door. Next to the door is a chair. On the wall to the other side of the door is a violin. The woman has her back to the viewer and holds her face in her hands. Next to her is a table upon which stands a vase of violets.

Lynette looked at the painting. It repelled and attracted

her at the same time. She picked it out of the pile, returned to her seat and sat down. The words flowed out of her quickly and effortlessly without the need for thought. Within ten minutes she had put down her biro.

As the black fog envelops me I make no effort to avoid it but sit there waiting for the inevitable. It grips my body and my mind and I struggle to breathe. Once upon a time the firelight was cosy and welcoming. Now, the black fog threatens to extinguish whatever warmth and cheer it once offered. I'm waiting for someone or something to come through the door and rescue me, but the door stays firmly shut. I've left a chair by the door, but it remains empty. Once music was played in this room by the glow of the fire, but now the violin remains on the wall gathering dust. The sickly smell of fear is all around me as I cup my face in my hands. The oppressive darkness embraces me. It reminds me that I'm totally alone. But I'm staying with whatever troubling thoughts invade my head. I know they'll eventually pass and that I will emerge strong.

It's a very painful journey—the one that I must make—and it requires patience and tenacity, but I'm clinging on to whatever is inside me to see me through. I placed the violets in the vase this morning. They remind me that something beautiful can come out of something dark and austere. I'm waiting for courage and love—because I need stacks of both. One day soon I'll have the belief and the strength to open that door and walk out into whatever is waiting for me. Out there. I'm strong enough to do it on my own and to stand up and be counted. Right now, though, I am still afraid. I keep looking at the violets. They have a fresh, clean scent that struggles to force its presence on the hostile fog, and reminds me that something in this room is alive. Like a small candle in a big, bad world. I'm like that candle. The flame is fragile and risks being blown out all the time, but it fights on—stubborn, angry and resolute.

That night Lynette found it hard to sleep. She kept on thinking about the picture she had written about. She'd had such a good time with Pete and Lily the other day and yet now she was feeling really low. How could things change so quickly? She began to shiver and experience a strong desire to drink.

Lynette was scared.

Dr Chaudhry led the way into his office. It was small but elegantly furnished. With its elaborately upholstered sofa and chairs, framed botanical prints, graceful vases and ornaments—and no psychiatrist's couch—the room looked more like something out of *House and Garden* than a consultation room in a hospital.

Pete sat down in one of the two armchairs. Nervously, he took a sip of coffee, then began to speak.

'Thanks for seeing me, Dr Chaudhry. I just wanted to ask you how Lynette was getting on. She seems so much better. It feels like she wants to come back to me and Lily. It's such a transformation. It's amazing.'

Dr Chaudhry, sitting in his favourite red armchair in

the corner of the room, adjusted his silver-rimmed spectacles and coughed. He was impeccably dressed in a conservative, dark blue suit, a starched white shirt and a red tie.

'She is undoubtedly improving,' said the psychiatrist, leaning back. 'But, she is still very fragile. The piece she completed in the Creative Writing class yesterday, for example, indicates how vulnerable she is. If she were to return home at this stage, it would not be a good idea. She needs to stay until we can be as certain as possible that she will not go back to drinking. And we also need to continue the EMDR treatment to be sure that she has resolved all the memories that have been holding her back.'

'I see,' said Pete. The smile on his small mouth disappeared and, as he swallowed from disappointment, his Adam's apple became more prominent. His eyes looked down at Dr Chaudhry's richly coloured Persian rug and then up again at a brass lamp that was casting light on to the opposite wall. 'That's a bit of a blow. You see, I'd hoped...'

'The signs are very reassuring,' interrupted Dr Chaudhry, putting his hands together and bringing them up to below his chin. 'She is responding well to treatment but we don't want to risk anything. She is beginning to re-establish her bond with you and your daughter and that is excellent progress. But depression is a relapsing illness. It can recur if the patient does not continue treatment for a good few months. To allow her to leave now and interrupt the pattern of treatment she has been receiving may well make her susceptible to a setback.' And then, he added, 'But she could certainly go home for the odd night. That would be a very good idea.'

The smile returned to Pete's thin face. There was at long

last something to be hopeful about. Though he knew there was always a risk…

They walk to the car arm in arm. Lynette opens the back door and straps Lily into her chair on the back seat. Pete waits until she has finished, then helps his wife into the passenger's seat. He walks round to the driver's side, opens the door and climbs in. Pete looks at Lynette and then at Lily. His wife is singing *The wheels of the bus go round and round* while his two-and-a-half-year-old daughter does her best to join in. Lynette is patting her thighs with her hands in time with the music. Turning round to smile at her daughter, she catches sight of her husband's face. She's been allowed to go home for the night and is beginning to get excited. She can't wait until she and Pete are in bed. Nor can Pete.

KALPANA

Here's the thing. If they don't get me off the booze and drugs I'll die. And if they do, I'll probably kill myself anyway

Natalia let herself in through the main door, then climbed the three flights of stairs to the apartment. Fishing out the keys from the bottom of her bag, she put the Chubb into the top lock and turned it to the right, making a creaking noise. It wasn't locked. That's odd, she thought. Kalpana was normally out at this time—at her office in Chelsea. Maybe she was working from home today. Natalia cleaned Kalpana's flat every week, but they hadn't been in contact for over a month—Natalia had been in Warsaw seeing her family. This was her first visit to the flat since she got back.

Natalia tapped gently on the door. There was no answer. She fumbled with the second key and placed it in the bottom lock, then let herself in. Before she had time to shout hello, she was hit by an overpowering smell. It was coming from a candle on the table at the back of the room. 'Hmm,' murmured Natalia, breathing in the exotic perfume of Egyptian Jasmine. Kalpana was into scented candles in a big way and went for those exquisite-looking ones you get in glass jars. The kind of thing you find on the ground floor of Harvey Nichols—Kalpana's favourite store. This one must have been burning for a few hours. The fragrance was really strong and there was a thick layer of liquid wax at the top.

Natalia called out 'Kalpana?', then looked round the room for signs of life. As usual, everything was in its proper place. Kalpana was a neat-freak, obsessed with order and cleanliness. She filed all her possessions in tidy, methodical rows, sections and piles. Each row, section and pile had a schedule describing its contents. Kalpana completed schedules for virtually everything—from her clothes and make-up to the packets of washing powder and bleach she kept in the kitchen. There were short schedules. Long schedules. Schedules about schedules. Schedules that cross-referenced other schedules. All bullet-pointed and laid out in great detail. Natalia—who put this extremist behaviour down to English eccentricity—waded across the plush cream carpet up to the table where she found an immaculate pile of crisp twenty-pound notes (they looked like they'd been ironed), some coins placed one on top of the other (the widest at the bottom), keys, a wallet, a comb, a bottle of *Poison*, a small make-up bag and a packet of clean tissues. In fact, the entire contents of Kalpana's handbag organised in perfect order and, where possible, in line with the table edge. Next to the money was a note in Kalpana's handwriting. Natalia's English had definitely improved, but she still found it harder to read than have a chat with someone. And, when it came to making out Kalpana's flourishes and swirls, forget it. Beautiful, yes, but hard for anyone, let alone a foreigner, to decipher. She picked up the note and screwed up her eyes to try and work out the writing. She couldn't make head nor tail of it so she gave up.

An empty magnum of champagne lay on the table on its side. Next to it was a champagne flute, also on its side. There were a few drops of liquid on the table—probably the last dregs that had seeped out from the glass or the bottle. Veuve Cliquot was Kalpana's favourite brand—the woman seemed to live on the stuff. Every time she came to clean the flat, there would be at least three used bottles lined up by the dustbin like foot-soldiers on parade. When Natalia started working for Kalpana she'd been curious about the champagne. Surely, Veuve Cliquot was very expensive? One day she popped into her local wine store, just to get an idea. The poor girl nearly fainted when she saw the price. Odd, thought Natalia, that this stray should be laying haphazardly on the dining table, not standing in its assigned place by the kitchen bin.

It looked like Kalpana had been sorting out her medicine cabinet. Kalpana was always cleaning out drawers and cupboards. Natalia often wondered why she bothered having a cleaner at all. Sometimes, she'd turn up and there'd be very little to do. Everything would be dusted, wiped and vacuumed to a faultless standard. On the table next to the champagne bottle stood a couple of empty paracetamol bottles turned upside down, together with some used tablet strips—the ones she took every morning. Kalpana took a lot of pills. She suffered from migraines and seemed to get depressed a lot. As far as Natalia could make out, it was usually about her family or her boyfriend. Natalia read out the unpronounceable name *Paroxetine* with difficulty, before noticing all the tablets had been removed. She stared in front of her, transfixed by the empty bottle of bubbly and the discarded bottles and packs. Her stomach was churning and she could feel her heart beating faster and faster. Her whole body began to shudder and she felt physically sick. She rushed down the passageway that led to Kalpana's bedroom, both compelled and terrified by what she might find. She glanced inside rather furtively as she held on to the doorframe to steady herself.

Kalpana lay stretched out on the bed, her toes pointing up towards the ceiling. She would have been in complete darkness had it not been for the candles on the bedside table casting flickering light and deep shadows over Kalpana's striking features, her closed, deep-set eyes and soft brown skin. Dressed in her favourite sari of light blue silk, she wore a necklace of wooden beads and a garland of marigolds. Her long, jet-black hair was wet and she smelt of sandalwood. All around her—upon the bed and on the richly coloured rugs that covered the floor—lay masses and masses of marigold heads in different shades of ochre and sienna.

What Natalia was looking at resembled a shrine, though it was really a kind of human sacrifice. And it shocked her to her core. It was a situation in which nobody wished nor expected to find themselves, let alone a nineteen-year-old girl from Poland. Natalia shook her employer again and again, but Kalpana did not respond. She cried out in desperation: 'Wake, Kalpana. Please, you wake. Now.' Still no response. Natalia stepped back from the bed and ran into the next room, clutching her head with her hands. Where was her handbag? She looked round the room hurriedly and tried to remember where she'd left it. She couldn't think straight but then she saw it. She had thrown it on the sofa. She grabbed her mobile and dialled. In a few seconds she was connected.

'Hurry, please,' she stuttered in her broken English. 'Lady ill. She take pill. She try kill herself. Please. You come now.'

Natalia threw the phone down and was immediately sick all over the cream carpet.

Kalpana is stretched out on the bed in the Quad Observation Unit, unaware she's being scrutinised through the glass wall like a goldfish in a bowl. It's her third afternoon at the hospital and she's struggling to keep her eyes open. The medication's making her drowsy. Her brain feels like it's floating and thinking's not an option. Given what she's been through in the past forty-eight hours—the aborted suicide, the rush to A&E and her trip here—that's probably a blessing.

Kalpana's chest is sore. Her throat is raw and tender, having had all that plastic tubing shoved down it. Her stomach is in agony from the pills and booze the doctors pumped out of her. Fortunately, there's no irreparable damage. Her kidneys are still OK, the tests they ran for signs of brain damage proved negative, and her body temperature's back to normal. Kalpana looks as grim as she feels. Her eyes resemble needle slits and the lids are heavy and puffy, making it difficult for her to see. Her skin has turned a greyish kind of yellow. Her cheeks feel delicate and damp. Her body's emaciated. She only managed to grab an hour or two's sleep last night. Although exhausted, she was too restless and spent most of the time tossing and turning from one side to the other. A thought would come into her head, then another wholly disconnected to the first, and then another. They kept whizzing round in her brain in never-ending circles.

Kalpana longs to stay horizontal, but the staff have asked her to go and watch a cake being made. They say it'll be good for her. Soothing. Baking classes at the Cloisters are reserved for the most desperate patients—many of the new recruits and a few old timers. Those who need to be handled with kid gloves because their wounds are so raw. People like Kalpana.

She arrives late because she's had to wash her hair again. Grace—her minder—does it for her. Kalpana can't quite find the strength. But it's got to be done. Her hair has to be washed repeatedly. It's important. To Kalpana, that is. The only objection the hospital has to her washing her hair so frequently is the condition of her scalp. It's become macerated from the constant scrubbings, so Dr Chaudhry has prescribed some special cream. Kalpana must be watched while she washes her hair. Just in case she tries to drown herself in the basin, or strangle herself with the plug chain. It might sound preposterous, but you can't rule anything out, not with patients this fragile, this deep in despair. Other hospitals might adopt a tough love approach and take her shampoo away—force her to leave her hair at is. But not here. At the Cloisters patients have to be ready to change themselves, not have it forced upon them, so it's more likely to last.

It's taken her ages to decide what to wear. It has to be a skirt, of course, not trousers or jeans. Some of the butter or flour might land on her and it would be a lot easier to clean her flesh than it would to remove a stain from the fabric. But which skirt? After much deliberation, Kalpana pulls on a denim mini with an embroidered hem and a gold-coloured T-shirt. She tries to make out her silhouette through the glass wall. Mirrors aren't allowed in the Observation Unit; they're far too dangerous and an unnecessary extravagance in a room intended as a temporary stop-gap. Then she exits stage right. Grace chugs along behind her like a steam train, breathing heavily as she tries to keep up. Short and dumpy, with inflated ankles covered in flesh-coloured pop socks that plop over her off-white trainers, Grace is wearing a clean white coat, too tight to button up over her enormous chest. Beneath it is a blue dress with large cerise flowers.

Kalpana takes with her a black city gent's umbrella, a stainless steel colander and her small pink notebook which she puts inside her pocket. As she walks through the garden, she talks to herself and, after a few seconds, turns on her heels to go back to her room. Two guys playing ping-pong turn to talk to her. Kalpana's already intimately acquainted with one of them, having shared a shower with him earlier on. It's a habit of hers, another one of her compulsions— bursting into men's rooms while they're taking a shower. Some of the guys are OK about it; others get a bit pissed off. At the Cloisters there are no locks to stop her.

'Nice skirt, Kalpana,' says the one who's showered with her, fully aware of the response this remark will provoke.

'You haven't seen my knickers yet,' Kalpana responds obligingly, lifting up her skirt to reveal a pair of flouncy pink briefs that are virtually see-through.

The other guy asks Kalpana how many times she's changed her clothes.

'Oh,' she replies absent-mindedly, as she walks back to

her room, waving her umbrella in the air, 'I can't remember things like that. And, anyway,' shaking the umbrella to make the point, 'the weather keeps changing. I have to be prepared.'

She returns to her room, followed by the sluggish Grace, chatting to herself the whole time. She takes off her skirt and replaces it with an even shorter one. But this time it's green, which means she has to change her undies too.

She makes the same journey back through the garden, not forgetting the umbrella and the colander, past the boys playing ping-pong. But, when she arrives at the kitchen door, she shakes her head, turns round and goes back to her room. This procedure is repeated a couple more times until finally Tilly manages to cajole her into staying.

Tilly is in charge of the baking class. A gentle, softly spoken woman, she is probably in her early forties. She has light grey, shoulder-length hair, a warm, welcoming smile and a kindly expression. She loves all the patients, sees their discomfort and wants them to get well. In the art room— she takes Art Therapy sometimes—several of her students' paintings hang on the walls, many of which have been dedicated to Tilly. One reads:

> *To Tilly, my guardian angel. Thank you so much for everything. You have helped me get better. I will always remember you.*

She's a superb cook, too, and even before the cake is ready to come out, the sugary-lemony smell is bewitching. They were right about it being soothing. Kalpana finds watching Tilly hypnotic. As the therapist's fingers knead the flour in with the butter, she starts to feel drowsy. Kalpana isn't really part of what's going on. She's having an out-of-body experience. Like the person sitting down in the green skirt and gold-coloured T-shirt isn't really her. Like she's standing beside herself observing everything she does. A bit like a cat examining the world through a window. From time to time, she glances at her small pink notebook and jots something down or crosses something out.

So, who are all these desperados—Kalpana's new friends? Some people call them the catatonics but that's not fair—they've all been to hell and back a few times. Some of them are probably still there. They can manage nothing more demanding than watching a cake being baked, making a wonky mug out of clay, doing a simple crossword puzzle or sitting through a dozen episodes of *Neighbours* one after the other. Perhaps with *Classic FM* on in the background and a cup of hot chocolate. Something they can get lost in without getting involved.

Edna's here, of course. Nobody really knows how long the old lady's been at the Cloisters. But it's definitely a good few years. They say she's actually bought herself a room here. A bit like a time-share, except that Edna doesn't share it with anyone. She never leaves, she's here year-in year-out. Christmas, Easter, the works. She never really talks about why she's here. Not to the other patients, anyway. And, of course, the staff would never spill the beans. It would be more than their jobs are worth. All she will say is that she doesn't like being 'out there' and that she feels much safer and happier here in the hospital.

Edna likes to invite people to her room for afternoon tea. Here, on her favourite green velvet armchair, she holds court as fellow patients come to pay their respects to the old veteran. Edna's a bit like a frail bird—tiny, anxious and chirrupy with a shrill voice—and she likes to chat. Since it's her room, she feels free to decorate it in whichever way she chooses. And there's been no holding back on that score. She's had a mahogany four-poster bed delivered, as well as a green velvet suite, two chandeliers from Harrods and some Laura Ashley curtains. She's even installed brass taps in the en suite. When you go in, you can't help whiffing this old-fashioned perfume. Edna's been wearing 4711 Cologne for over forty years and she doesn't stint herself when she splashes it on. The room is littered with photographs of herself as a young woman. She used to tread the boards in musicals back in the fifties. The story goes that a very wealthy man came to see one of her shows, fell hook, line and sinker and married her. He died about ten years ago, leaving his old lady dripping in gold. Very big in shipping, apparently. Just as well, too, or she'd never have been able to purchase a bit of real estate at the Cloisters. Not the worst place to spend your twilight years, either.

In the photos you get a glimpse of what Edna looked like in her heyday. Tight, curly blonde hair, dazzling smile and great pins. Bursting with vitality and hope. Her face is now lined with crow's feet, her chin saggy and limp, her body shrunken and weak. Her mind's gone the same way too. Someone only has to mention the word 'outside' and she starts to shiver. But nobody—except perhaps her shrink—knows why.

Next to Edna is a young man. He can't be more than about twenty-five, but he spends all his time shaking. His hands quiver, his head shudders from side to side and he shifts his weight from one leg to the other incessantly. His name is Gregg and he's an Iraqi war veteran. He says very little and is in a really bad way. They used to call combat-related stress shell shock. Now it's known as PTSD—post-traumatic stress disorder. Except for the nervous twitch, Gregg's a good-looking young man. Tall, slim, broad shoulders, he works out a lot. Or, at least, he used to. His face is thin, taut and stretched. His light grey eyes look haunted. They say Gregg saw something in Iraq that changed him. Lots of young men have been plunged into that pointless theatre of war and it's screwed them up for keeps. In Gregg's case, it was a little boy who had his leg blown off. Of course, it was an accident. It wasn't meant to happen, but that doesn't make any difference to Gregg. The boy's screams went on forever and Gregg can't get them out of his head. He can't sleep at night, but he refuses to take sleeping pills. He's scared if he sleeps the nightmares will come back. But even if the nightmares were to go away—which they won't—there are always the flashbacks to keep him company. Gregg's only been at the Cloisters a week. They're trying to get him off the drugs and the booze. If they don't, he'll probably die. And if they do, he'll probably still die. The idea of topping himself appeals to Gregg a lot. For him, it means no more nightmares.

Tilly's heard a rumour about a multi-million-pound deal between the Ministry of Defence and the hospital to get people like Gregg well again. 'It'll take more than a few months,' she tells her husband. 'They'll probably end up moving in for good like Edna.'

Luella's on the other side of Gregg. Compared to the rest of the baking class, she's relatively talkative. She's a heavy, big-boned girl in a dark blue tracksuit and wearing prescription glasses, one of many referred by the NHS. A black single mother of thirty-three with two daughters under twelve from different fathers, Luella lives on a council estate in Brixton. She's been in trouble with the police for taking drugs. Now, she's vowed to give up for her children's sake. And hers. Luella turned to drugs because it seemed like there was no one and nothing else to turn to. She's been at the Cloisters for nearly two weeks now, but is still very traumatised by recent events. After losing her mother to cancer six months ago, she travelled to America to find her father, who she hadn't seen since she was five when he walked out on her and her mother. When she arrived with her two children on her father's doorstep, he turned them away. He's married again and has a new family. He doesn't want his past bothering him. Getting in the way. Messing up his life. Even if it means turning his back on his daughter and his granddaughters.

Olivia's here, too. Twenty-six, tall, slim and blonde. Beautiful girl—those legs of hers just go on and on. A touch of the Marilyn Monroes about her—creamy white complexion with plump rosebud lips and radiant pink cheeks. Baby blue eyes too. When things get really bad—and it's usually to do with a man—she takes the iron to her arms and…burn, burn, burn. She says it reminds her she's alive, because, most of the time she feels dead—numb. She's got so many scald marks—large, circular, scabby scars full of angry pus—there's no room left. So she just piles them on, one on top of the other, till they look a bit like pancakes.

And lastly there's James. James neither says nor does anything. Wearing his trademark T-shirt and combat trousers, he just looks down at his lap. Unaffected by the smell of the freshly baked cake, he just wants to fade away, to dissolve.

Kalpana's not interested in any of them. She doesn't even acknowledge their presence. She's too wrapped up in her own world to notice. Too busy worrying about her lists and her hair, as she talks to herself incessantly.

Opening the oven door, Tilly scoops out the cake, its hauntingly sweet aroma wafting out of the door and down the corridor. Turning to the group, she smiles and says:

'Well, everyone, it's ready. Who'd like a piece of cake?'

After the class Kalpana returns to her room in the Observation Unit, collapses on to her bed and lies down. Unable to stay still, she bounces back upright and opens one of the pages inside her small pink notebook. She sighs, then gets up and walks towards the sink.

'I've got to wash my hair,' she says, looking distractedly into the air, ignoring her companion. She's not inviting Grace to engage in conversation, merely making an announcement.

Although Kalpana's in the Observation Unit, she still has to have a minder with her. Just in case the nurses get busy at the desk or are called away. With someone like Kalpana, they just can't take the risk. Grace—who's sitting in a chair by the door—clicks her yellowing teeth and crosses her saggy arms. Grace has worked at the hospital a long time and has seen some very strange things, but Kalpana takes the biscuit. She's so stubborn and can be really rude. She resents been followed around all the time and doesn't hide the fact. Grace has to grin and bear it. Say nothing, just watch, click her teeth, fold her arms and listen.

As Kalpana walks up to the basin and turns on the tap, there's a knock at the door. Kalpana ignores it and starts washing her hair. Grace opens the door to Dr Chaudhry. Kalpana has being moaning to her captors about the need to have a constant bodyguard and the amount of medication she's taking. She's demanded to see her consultant to register a formal complaint.

Dr Chaudhry walks in and greets Grace with his usual smile. Seeing that his patient's occupied, he says he'll wait and sits down in the armchair. Dr Chaudhry asks Grace about her family and a brief conversation ensues about her children. Occasionally, they're forced to raise their voices an octave in order to be heard over the swishing of the water.

After about ten minutes, Kalpana turns off the taps and wraps a towel round her head. She doesn't apologise for keeping Dr Chaudhry waiting. The thought would never occur to her. With a detached air, and making no attempt to engage eye contact, she states, 'I've been washing my hair.'

Dr Chaudhry asks Kalpana to sit down while he whispers to Grace that it's OK for her to leave them. He will come out and get her when he's ready to go.

Kalpana sits down, removes the towel from her head and begins to dry her hair with it. Dr Chaudhry pulls his chair closer to the bed to face his patient.

'How are you feeling, Kalpana?'

'Like shit.' Kalpana's in a belligerent mood. 'These pills you're giving me, they're making me feel so...so...out of it. I can't think straight. And,' pointing to the door with her finger and her voice raised a notch or two, asks, 'why do I have to be followed around all the time by that…that lump?'

'Kalpana,' says Dr Chaudhry in a soft, calming voice, 'let me tell you what is wrong and what we are doing to address it.' He joins his hands together and places them under his chin. Then he adjusts his spectacles. 'You suffer from an illness called bipolar disorder.'

'Bi what?' says Kalpana, combing her hair as it lies cold down her back. 'What on earth are you going on about?'

'Manic depression,' the doctor continues. 'Nobody's sure where it comes from and it's not curable. But we can treat the symptoms.'

'Which are?' she demands, continuing to comb out her hair.

'Mood swings. With this sickness one minute you can feel elated. Literally, the next second your mood can go to the opposite extreme for no reason at all, making you feel desperate. At the moment, you're at the lower end. That's why you tried to kill yourself. This is a very dangerous time for you. We want to protect you, which is why Grace is here.'

'But I don't want to be protected. I tried to kill myself because I wanted to die—get it? And *you* bloody stopped me,' she snaps, still averting her eyes from the object of her hatred while continuing to comb furiously.

'That's part of the sickness, Kalpana. The way you feel. Not wanting to be here.'

But Kalpana is not prepared to leave it there. Throwing down her comb on the bed, she says, 'Why on earth would I want to hang around? My family's abandoned me. My boyfriend's fucked off. They're all out to get me. You're all

127

out to get me. And I'm here in this glass prison with my own personal warder.'

'Kalpana, these thoughts, the paranoia, it's all part of your illness. You're not in prison and Grace is not your jailor. She's a nurse who is here to watch out for you, see you don't come to any harm.'

'And what about all this crap you're forcing down my throat? I don't want it. It's turning me into a zombie.'

Dr Chaudhry continues to speak as softly and as directly as he can. He doesn't want to enrage his patient any further. 'Lithium, that's what we're giving you. I mentioned that the intense lows you are currently experiencing are highly dangerous, but so are the periods of elation that come with the illness. The Lithium will stabilise your mood. It will stop you having these extreme highs and lows. I warn you, though, it won't happen overnight. It might take as long as a fortnight to take effect. We'll have to monitor your blood from time to time, too, to make sure the amounts we're giving you are correct.'

'I don't want all these chemicals in my body,' says Kalpana, like a spoilt child refusing to do her homework. 'I'm already taking anti-depressants. Christ knows I've tried to come off them, but the withdrawal symptoms were shit.'

'Yes, and you need to carry on taking them. Because of your second illness.'

'My second illness?' asks Kalpana, with obvious annoyance, as if this is somehow Dr Chaudhry's fault. 'Isn't one enough?'

'Again, we're not sure where the illness comes from but when you start your counselling sessions, you will, hopefully, get to the bottom of it. It's called OCD. Obsessive-compulsive disorder. And it causes you a lot of distress, which the anti-depressants can help keep to more manageable levels.'

Kalpana finally turns to look at her psychiatrist in the face, her eyes on fire. 'What on earth d'you mean?'

'Washing your hair repeatedly, changing your clothes several times a day, all the lists and schedules you keep. These are symptoms of OCD—your excessive devotion to repetitive tasks. You need to take something which will help with that, so I've increased your daily dose of Paroxetine from twenty grams to forty.'

But Kalpana isn't in the mood to be reasonable—or polite. 'Fuck sake,' she cries, standing up. 'So, now I'm a junkie.'

Dr Chaudhry breathes in, straightens his jacket and purses his lips. He gets up, walks over to his patient and puts his arm round her shoulder protectively. 'Please, Kalpana, sit down. We're doing everything in our power to get you better with the most effective means at our disposal. One of these is psychological counselling which you're beginning tomorrow. But you need medicine as well. You have a chemical imbalance, a biological condition. You have a shortage of serotonin in your brain. The medicine we are giving you will restore the balance, that's all.'

'So, I'm not going crazy?' asks Kalpana, sitting down again. She pulls her knees up to her chest and places her hands down by her side.

'Not at all,' replies Dr Chaudhry. 'Like most people who are suffering from these illnesses, you set yourself impossibly high standards. You're a perfectionist. You don't accept yourself as you are and when you inevitably fall short of these standards, you feel guilty and decide to punish yourself. Your attempted suicide was an expression of guilt because you feel you've let your family down. You have tried so hard to please other people. At best, that leads to disappointment. At worst, despair. But one thing is certain, you are very far from being crazy.

'You have traditions and high standards about family and family honour. You have to remember, though, that you are, first and foremost, you. An individual. If that individual isn't happy, it's very difficult for her to make others happy. Try not to be so hard on yourself.'

There is no reaction as Kalpana stares blankly into the distance.

Dr Chaudhry rises to his feet and walks towards the door to call Grace back in. Before leaving, he turns to Kalpana and smiles. 'Make sure you have a nourishing meal tonight, Kalpana. That's very important. And try to get some sleep. I will see you tomorrow. Goodnight.'

Kalpana didn't have much of an appetite that evening, so it was difficult for her to take Dr Chaudhry's advice. She played with a bit of green salad, and finished off with a handful of black grapes. That was all she could manage as she listened to the same old tape going round in her head:

You feel you've let your family down You feel you've let your family down.

The meal over, Kalpana returned to her room to wash her hair and change her clothes. All of a sudden, she began to feel intensely energetic and inexplicably enthusiastic. She put on a black and white polka-dot skirt and a tight white T-shirt. Then she slipped on a pair of bright red stilettos. All the time, she talked to herself non-stop.

Grace looked at her with a worried expression. She scratched the top of her head and thought, 'Oh, oh, I think we're in for a mood swing.' And she proceeded to watch Kalpana unfold like a wound-up coil.

First, she started to sing. Grace couldn't make out what it was, but it sounded vaguely religious. As if she was chanting. Then, it turned into a sort of aria from one of those melodramatic Italian opera. Next, she started ranting, though Grace found it impossible to tell what she was saying. Finally, she knelt down and started praying. Well, that's what it looked like to Grace. And, before Grace knew what was happening, Kalpana had got up off the floor and flown out of the door. She fled down the corridors and into the gardens, shouting and laughing hysterically, her scarlet stilettos sailing through the air behind her.

Kalpana was in a state of euphoria when she got outside. It was about eight-thirty, still fairly light—except for a few early evening shadows—and quite warm. A number of patients were sitting on the grass smoking a cigarette and chatting about their day. She ran up and down the lawns in her stilettos. Her thoughts were racing and she was talking ten to the dozen, telling everyone she met how wonderful life was. Patients stood and watched. Some laughed, others remained speechless. Her head was buzzing with masses and masses of ideas—most of them completely disconnected. She ran faster and faster, her body trying to keep up with the pace of her thoughts. Everything had become urgent and deeply intense, and this became reflected in her movements, as she ran faster and faster round the perimeters. The more rapidly her thoughts took shape, the faster she ran. Soon she was out of breath and her cheeks were flushed. She kicked off her shoes and threw them into the distance. Laughing, singing and shouting in turns at the top of her voice, she ran in her bare feet, as if she were trying to catch the wind. Each time she passed a man, she would lift up her polka-dot skirt, show them her knickers, throw back her head and laugh. She even managed to coax one into taking her for a piggyback ride. As she climbed on to his back, she slapped him on the arm, shouting, 'Faster, faster, Jake.' Then she whispered something in his ear and, within a few seconds, they were out of sight.

Grace arrived with other members of the nursing staff seconds afterwards. They ran up and down the gardens looking for the lost patients, but nobody seemed to know where Kalpana or Jake had gone. It was no good trying to get her on the mobile either. She hadn't taken it with her.

There was method in Kalpana's madness. She'd only been at the Cloisters for four days but one thing was really beginning to bug her. She'd written it down in her small pink notebook and she badly needed to tick it off. There it was in large capital letters, taking up almost the whole page:

A R M P I T S

Kalpana's armpits were hairy and badly needed a shave. For someone as obsessed with cleanliness and hygiene as her, this was a really big deal. And, since patients weren't allowed to bring razors into the hospital, there was nothing she could do about it. Until now. Kalpana had been told about the parade of shops nearby that could be reached through a shortcut from the back of the hospital. There had been a fence there once, but it had been taken down and not replaced. There was a mini-market in the parade that sold all manner of things and stayed open late. Kalpana was sure she could find a razor there and then she could say goodbye to all those irritating little black worms. With Jake's help it would only take about five minutes to get there. Fortunately, Jake was game. She was lucky when she got to the shop, too. On a plastic hook behind the till was a pack of those all-in-one jobs for sensitive skin. The last pack on the shelf.

Kalpana knew she'd be searched when she got back to the hospital, so she gave the razors to Jake and told him to hide them in his room. He could pop one in later on when the coast was clear. She was right. They did search her, and they were so preoccupied with what Kalpana might be smuggling in, they forgot to frisk Jake who had stashed the razors down one of his trouser legs.

When they asked her about the 'escape'—which had lasted no more than twenty minutes—Kalpana had the perfect repost. 'I'm a bipolar and I got elated. I can't help it if I get a mood swing, can I? Anyway, I don't feel high anymore. I feel like shit. OK?' Kalpana certainly did feel like shit. The pendulum had swung right the other way and she was at rock bottom.

From now on, Grace and the entire nursing contingent were instructed to watch their charge like a hawk. Locking the girl in was not an option. Not unless they wanted to section her under the Mental Health Act on the grounds that she was a threat to herself. Which, of course, she was, really. But nobody wanted to resort to those extremes. Not yet, anyway.

It's about ten o'clock. Everyone's in bed unless they're walking the corridors, unable to sleep. Grace is no longer around. She clocked off about an hour ago. The nurses at the desk take it in turns to stare at Kalpana through the glass. Like a monkey at the zoo. They can't afford to make another mistake. Not with someone like Kalpana.

It's nearly ten-thirty. Kalpana gets out of bed, opens the door, and says to the nurse at the desk, 'Just thought I'd come and tell you I'm going into the shower-room to wash my hair.'

'That's fine, dearie. Just leave the door ajar, will you?' This seems to satisfy the night nurses who don't ask Kalpana why she can't wash her hair in the basin in her room. They don't want Kalpana having one of her tantrums. They know what a handful she can be. Anyway, they can see the shower-room door from where they sit, though, naturally, they can't see through it.

It's ten-forty. Kalpana gets herself together and glides into the shower-room, taking with her shampoo, conditioner, face flannel and towel. The nurses see her do this. They watch her pick up her toiletries and go out of her room into the shower cubicle. They repeat, 'Leave the door ajar, dearie.'

'OK,' replies Kalpana, who does what she's told.

She takes off her dressing gown and climbs into the shower. She turns on the water until it jets noisily and powerfully down to the bottom. She wets her hair thoroughly, then opens the top of the shampoo bottle and pours a little into her left hand. She returns the bottle to the shower ledge and rubs the sticky substance between her two moist palms until it turns into suds. She massages it into her scalp for a few minutes, wincing as the soap stings the cuts, then rinses it off. She does the same with the conditioner. Then she takes some soap from the dispenser on the wall and lathers it up in her wet hands. She grabs her flannel and washes every inch of her body from behind her ears downwards to in between her toes. She bends down and stretches to reach for her towel. Inside, she finds one of the razors she purchased at the shop. As per instructions, Jake had slipped it into her room earlier, concealing it inside a shampoo bottle.

Kalpana stands up and begins to shave. Raising her arms, she moves the razor up and down smoothly and steadily. She does the same with her legs and finishes off by doing her bikini line. All the time, she studies her actions closely, making sure she does a thorough job. Once she is satisfied with the results, she runs the razor under the water until it runs clean and begins to sparkle. Then, she takes the showerhead and rinses away until all the hairs have disappeared down the plughole.

She sits down on the floor of the shower. She notices she's nicked herself on the leg. She places her finger on top of the cut, then puts it in the mouth and licks the blood. It's so distinct, the flavour of human blood, and it leaves a strange aftertaste in her mouth. The blood continues to flow down her leg and she watches it obsessively.

She jumps as the sound of a disembodied voice accosts her from outside.

'Are you OK, Kalpana?'

'Yeah.'

Kalpana is inexorably drawn to the blade inside the razor and, after managing to force it out of its plastic coating on one side—covering it with the towel to muffle the sound—it emerges gleaming. She places it in her mouth. The metal has a strange rusty taste—a bit like the blood—and saliva forms. She removes the blade from her mouth and guides it gently towards her left arm, staring at it. It makes contact with her goose-pimpled skin and the fine hairs on her arm tingle as they are stroked.

After a sharp intake of breath, she drags the shiny blade from the crease on the inside of her wrist up to the elbow, exerting more and more pressure as it travels up her arm. The motion is carried out slowly and calmly. Her arm doesn't shake and the rest of her stays absolutely still. The blood spouts out thick and fast. The incision itself—clean, sharp and smooth—does not unnerve her. In fact, it gives her a kind of thrill. But the smell of the dark red juice and its velvety richness shocks her. With a powerful, uncontrollable will of its own, it pours down the side of the shower lip and along the floor like a river whose dam has just burst. Panicking, she jumps to her feet and grabs her towel. She wraps it round her arm, no longer able to look. She runs back into her room, screaming at the top of her voice. Within minutes she has fainted, but not before leaving indelible stains in every part of the room.

'Oh, well,' said Kalpana, an unmistakable air of defiance in her voice, 'if you're going to cross-examine me.' She was looking straight out into the distance, refusing to make eye contact.

'I'm not cross-examining you, Kalpana, really I'm not,' said the woman sitting opposite her. 'Just trying to get you to talk about last night. And why you tried to kill yourself. It's not the first time, is it?'

'You tell me,' snapped Kalpana as she took out her small pink notebook from her pocket. 'You're the expert. Haven't you read my notes?'

'Well, it would help if you tried to put it into words.'

Kalpana closed her eyes and pursed her lips. She obviously had no interest in that suggestion. She just sat there, one knee crossed over the other, looking at her small pink notebook. When she wasn't writing something down or crossing something out, she massaged her bandaged arm with her right hand. The night doctors had done their stuff. Acting swiftly to stitch up the cut—which had not been as deep as first thought—there had been no need for her to go to A&E.

Finally, she looked up and said, 'Look, don't push me. I don't want to talk and you can't make me.'

A pleasant-looking woman with hazel eyes and a placid expression, Marisa scratched her head. She was a highly experienced psychological counsellor. She had been doing this job for over fifteen years and she'd had a lifetime of complicated cases. But there was no getting away from it, Kalpana was hard work. It was going to require patience. A lot of patience and perseverance.

'Would you like to tell me a little bit about your family?'

Silence.

'OK, then, what about your boyfriend, Dominic?'

Secrecy.

Marisa took a deep breath. 'Is there anything you would like to talk about?'

Evasion.

Just the mechanical movement of a plastic cup of water raised from table to lips, a sip, then the return of the cup to the table. Next, the closing of the eyes proclaiming the shutting down of the face and the solidifying of the wall made of silence, secrecy and evasion. Marisa knew she was skating on perilously thin ice. One carelessly chosen word, one unwelcome gesture and the wall would stay up for a long, long time. Maybe Marisa had already gone too far. Seeing a counsellor—a specialist, an expert in her field— or at least going through the motions, was bringing no relief, no respite to Kalpana. That much was clear. But it was still early days.

What now?

Kalpana was the eldest of her parents' four children—all of them girls. It was bad enough for her father—a strict Hindu—that he had no sons, but for the eldest, the first-born, to be a girl, that was nothing short of a catastrophe which made him feel deeply ashamed. Sanjay was seriously disappointed and did not conceal the fact from Kalpana while she was growing up. His frustration manifested itself in a number of physical attacks, which resulted in Kalpana the toddler having to be rushed to hospital. At meal times, her mother would make a point of giving her younger daughters the best cuts of meat while Kalpana, consigned to a table on her own at the far end of the dining room, was handed the scrag ends and sent to Coventry. She grew up knowing that she could never seem to earn her parents' approval. Her very existence made that impossible.

But still she sought it. Desperately. For her parents' last wedding anniversary she spent almost ten thousand pounds on a party to end all parties. A marquee in the garden, private caterers, endless supplies of Veuve Cliquot. And still there were no thank-yous, no acceptance of her existence, of the path she had chosen. It might have been different if she could have submitted to their will and married a good Indian doctor or accountant chosen by her parents. If she could have apologised to them, not only for being a woman, but also for not having let herself be governed by them. Her mother would have gone into raptures every time her daughter admitted how undeserving she was and, dressed in her best sari, kneeled down by her father's feet, craving pardon. She would be their little girl again, no will of her own, a pawn in their hands. That was what they wanted.

Kalpana sits on her bed, her small pink notebook open on her lap. She has entered today's date and put the word URGENT on the left-hand side. Kalpana is climbing steadily towards new heights of exhilaration. And it starts with a cough.

Grace—sitting on the chair by the door—coughs, and Kalpana begins to write.

> THERES A WOMAN IN MY ROOM AND
> SHE WANTS TO KILL ME I THINK SHES
> BEEN PAID TO KILL ME BY MY FAMILY
> OR MAYBE THE PEOPLE HERE SHE HAS
> TRIED TO POISON ME BY GIVING ME
> PILLS BUT I HAVE FOOLED HER BY
> SPITTING THEM OUT WHEN SHES NOT
> LOOKING SOMETIMES AT NIGHT I SEE
> HER STANDING IN THE GARDEN
> LEANING UP AGAINST A TREE TRYING
> TO UNNERVE ME WAITING FOR ME TO
> DIE

And she goes on writing. She seems to be in some kind of trance. There are voices inside her head telling her that Grace is trying to murder her, that she should make a run for it as soon as possible. A potent, irresistible force is driving her; a terrifying sense of exultation she cannot control. She puts the small pink notebook in her pocket, stands up and announces her decision to call on Jake.

Grace stands up, studies her charge and says calmly, 'OK, I'll come with you.'

Kalpana combs her hair and glams herself up. She applies a little pink gloss to her lips and some mascara to her eyelashes. She charges out of the room, omitting to hold the door open for Grace. Within moments she is out of the Observation Unit, down the corridor and at Jake's door. She doesn't bother knocking, just opens the door and walks in. Grace is just behind her but Kalpana closes the door in her face, with the following dismissal:

'You can watch if you like, but somehow I don't think it's your cup of tea.'

Grace stands still, dithering, perplexed. She has to think on her feet. While sexual relations between patients at the Cloisters are not encouraged, it is practically very difficult to do anything to prevent them. So, she'll wait outside Jake's door for however long it takes and knock every fifteen minutes. Who knows? She and Jake may have made a suicide pact. Such things did happen.

Jake is lying on the bed listening to his iPod. A successful music producer, he's dressed in a purple vest and tight black jeans. His naturally mousy hair has been bleached blonde and he looks the business.

'Heh, babe,' he says, casually, 'come and join me,' and he gestures to her. 'We can listen to the music together.'

While Jake was giving Kalpana a piggyback ride to the shops the other day, she thought he was OK. Nothing to write home about—just OK. Now, in her heightened sense of euphoria, the initial attraction has propelled itself into an obsessive compulsion, and one that has to be satisfied. At once. Like Kalpana, Jake is a bipolar, so maybe they have reached the same high, the same peak. If this is true, it could be dangerous. They might kill each other.

Kalpana rips off her clothes and throws herself on top of him, not giving Jake a chance to undress himself. She tears off his vest and then his trousers, then yanks at his thong. Quickly and urgently, the two wrap themselves into a 69 and she begins to suck him off. Jake's tongue soon finds her spot and they lick, suck, nibble and thrust at each other for a good forty minutes. Every quarter of an hour, Grace taps on the door and receives a grunt in response.

Her hunger abated, Kalpana climbs off the bed, puts her clothes back on and leaves the room without any words. Jake gets back to his music.

Continuing to ignore Grace, Kalpana walks back to her room and shuts the door in her minder's face.

The Prasads were holding a family conference. Gurinder, Kalpana's mother, a tall, striking woman with black piercing eyes and greying black hair cut to just below her ears, sat at one end of the dining table. Dressed in a gold silk kameez consisting of a tunic and trousers, she looked composed and purposeful. At the opposite end of the table was her husband, Sanjay. Smartly casual in a cashmere sweater and jeans, Sanjay was good-looking for his sixty-two years, his eyes as black as his wife's, his sleek black hair distinguished by the occasional peppering of silver strands. While his sizeable moustache lent him a kind of authority, there was something hard about his face. You noticed it in the tautness around the jaw, suggesting flexibility wasn't his strongest suit. Sanjay didn't look the approachable sort.

And then there were Kalpana's three younger sisters. The eldest, Parminder, was about twenty-nine. She had been married for over four years to a doctor. The match had been arranged by her parents. Parminder was her mother's favourite. She never argued with what her parents said or did and she respected their judgement in all things. Her marriage to Ashok had, unfortunately, not turned out well. He was hard-hearted and cold towards her. Occasionally, he hit her. But she would never admit this to her parents, convincing herself that it was her lot to be married to a man she feared. Mira was twenty-seven and engaged to an accountant. While the marriage had not been arranged— in the strict meaning of the word—it had received her parents' blessing. Mira told her father she had met an Indian boy from a good Hindu family and begged her parents to put him on their 'list'. Sanjay and Gurinder checked him out, made extensive enquires within the community and liked what they heard. Then they interviewed him and that was that. While Parminder adhered rigidly to her parents' rules and regulations, Mira was more interested in being happy, in being herself. But she knew how to use her wits and her cunning to achieve her ends. An enchanting girl with sleek black hair, doe eyes and plumped-up lips, she had always been able to wrap her father round her little finger.

Lastly, there was Yasmin. Just twenty, Yasmin was training to be a doctor. Blessed with a studious, serious face and not terribly interested in clothes or boys, she didn't want to be part of her parents' marriage game. Not so long ago, they used to show her photographs of prospective candidates and propitious horoscopes, but she managed to ward them off, saying, 'I'm working so hard trying to become a doctor. I haven't got time for marriage now. I need to concentrate on my exams. If I don't, I'll fail. You don't want that, do you?'

Sanjay and Gurinder could think of nothing worse than their daughter *not* qualifying to be a doctor. They were so proud when she told them, they just had to pass the good news on to everybody. How humiliating it would be for them if she flunked. So, they agreed to leave her alone. But only till she qualified.

The remaining family member present was Ashok, Parminder's doctor husband. Tall and broad-shouldered with a moustache like his father-in-law, and wearing a sharp grey suit, his expression was stern and uncompromising. He sat with folded arms between his wife and his sister-in-law, Mira. Ashok made no attempt to conceal his determination to dominate the discussions and to influence the outcome.

'There is no doubt at all,' he began, placing both hands firmly upon the table in front of him, 'that Kalpana has disgraced this family. First, she undutifully refuses every man she is introduced to. Good, professional, successful Indian men from respectable families. Accountants. Lawyers. Surgeons. Then she lives with a succession of boyfriends—Englishmen, too—when she knows no self-respecting Indian woman would ever think of having a boyfriend, let alone living with him.'

After taking a deep breath, he continued, 'Finally, she tries to kill herself and gets herself admitted to a mental hospital. She has brought dishonour to our family. How can we hold our heads up in the community? What will happen when Yasmin'—turning to look at his sister-in-law and adopting a sarcastic note in his voice—'decides that the time has come for her to consider a husband. Will she, too, turn round and say she wants to shack up with an Englishman?'

Kalpana's father looked straight at his wife and nodded his head gravely. 'I have to agree with Ashok. Kalpana has shamed us with her contempt for duty and her disrespect for her own honour and that of her family. In my eyes, she might as well be dead. We should have sent her to India years ago, when all this trouble began, and taken away her passport. She could have stayed there until she changed her mind and submitted to her parents' wisdom.'

Suddenly, as if from nowhere, a small, shaky voice began to speak. Everyone turned to look at Yasmin.

'Dad, Mum. We're Indian. Of course, we are. And I'm proud of my roots. I know Kalpana is too. But we've been brought up here. In England. We have a British way of life. Don't you see how hard that is for us? To be Indian and carry on living here completely as Indians? You've sent us to English schools. We live in an English city. We work with English people. We are English as well as Indian. We have to be.'

But the last remark had gone too far for Ashok. He stood up and, pointing a figure at the youngest of his sisters-in-law, said, 'That is enough. You have insulted your family and your religion. Go to your room.'

Yasmin looked at her mother and then at her father, praying that one of them would intercede. But there was no dissent. Their silence confirmed it. She got up, left the room and went upstairs.

Then, for the first time, Gurinder spoke. Her face showed she was very upset.

'What did we do that was so wrong, Sanjay? We brought them all up as good Hindu girls. We didn't let them have boyfriends. We didn't even let them *discuss* boys. If they got friendly with the wrong sort of girls who we thought might introduce them to boys, we put a stop to it at once.

We worked so hard for them. We worked day and night to make a success of everything.'

'Of course, we did,' was her husband's abrupt reply. Stiffening up a little, he added, 'We have nothing to reproach ourselves for.' Then, banging his right fist on the table, he raised his voice. 'There was work to be done so the business could grow and we did it. Babies or no babies, it had to be done.'

'Yes, Sanjay,' his wife went on, 'it had to be done. But what if we worked just a bit *too* hard? Maybe we weren't around the girls enough. I don't know. When there was no time to feed them myself, we left them with your mother or mine. Maybe we were just too preoccupied with the shops. We just didn't think about it. Maybe we *should* have thought about it. Spent a little more time with them.'

'Nonsense,' said Sanjay, walking towards the window and turning his back on everyone. 'You were fine, Gurinder, we were both fine.' There was a marked note of irritation in his voice. Staring out on to the paved front garden, he said, 'I didn't want my children growing up soft and weak. Always being picked up every time they cried.'

Mira and Parminder looked at one another. Neither of them recalled much physical contact with either of their parents while they were growing up. They seemed to spend most of their time with their grandmothers since Sanjay and Gurinder had been far too busy running the shops. Even now, demonstrative affection between parents and children was not much in evidence.

'When Kalpana cried,' said Gurinder, 'she used to scream at the top of her voice. You said we should just leave her or she'd scream even more. Because she was just trying to get attention.'

'Yes,' said Sanjay, still looking out of the window. 'And she's still doing it, isn't she? Screaming out for attention.'

'She was such a nervous little baby,' continued Gurinder, reminiscing. 'She'd get over-wrought at the slightest thing. But you said we should ignore her.' The accusation in her voice was unmistakable.

'Over-sensitive,' said Sanjay, 'that's what she was.' And, after a pause, 'She never was a favourite of mine.'

'I know,' said Gurinder softly.

Parminder and Mira looked at each other again. They had never heard their parents have a discussion of this kind before. It scared them.

'And now look at her,' said Sanjay, ignoring the accusation in his wife's last remark, 'going from one extreme to another.'

Ashok couldn't wait any longer. He felt he was beginning to lose his authority over the proceedings, so he stood up and announced his plan:

'I would be happy to go to the hospital and see Kalpana. Tell her that her family is deeply ashamed of her but, if she comes home, she will be forgiven. Provided, that is, she lets herself be guided by her family.'

'Yes,' agreed Sanjay, turning away from the window to face his son-in-law. With his hands behind his back like a Victorian patriarch, he said, 'Yes, tell her she has done great wrong, but all will be well if she comes home and submits to my will. All this living in a flat on her own, it's not right.'

Gurinder had the last word. 'And tell her,' she said, a smile coming to her lips, 'that I will find her a good Indian husband. A good Hindu. She can get married here at home, too. Tell her we will go out and find the finest material for the dresses. It will be such a wedding, the like of which will not have been seen in the whole of India. Ah, just wait till I tell my friends.'

A week later Kalpana was back in front of her counsellor, her hair wet and her small pink notebook resting on her lap. The medication was beginning to have an impact and her mood swings were far less prevalent. At last she felt like talking.

There's no Hindi word for depression Therefore, it doesn't exist

That's what her brother-in-law said when he came to visit her the other day. He was a doctor, so he should know. But so was Dr Chaudhry, and he said it *did* exist. To say she was confused would be putting it mildly. Kalpana couldn't think straight in her condition anyway, so there was no point trying to figure it out.

You've let your family down You've dishonoured them

That much was true, though. She couldn't argue with any of it. She'd let her parents down. She'd let her family down. Her religion. Her boyfriend. Everyone. Even herself.

Marisa asked Kalpana to explain. 'How exactly have you done that, Kalpana? What is it that's so bad about you?'

'I…I've not done what my family wanted me to do. I've moved out of their house. I've bought my own flat. I've had boyfriends. And I can't... I mean, I won't, marry someone they try to force on me.'

'Why exactly is that bad? Isn't that you just trying to assert yourself? Trying to do what you need to do to be you?'

You've disgraced your family

'But I'm not supposed to be me. I'm supposed to conform. To give way. To the family.'

'That's why you've been seriously depressed, Kalpana,' said Marisa. 'Because you feel guilty for being yourself. Deep-down you feel it's wrong, but you can't stop doing it.'

There's no Hindi word for depression Therefore, it doesn't exist

'My brother-in-law says that depression doesn't exist. He says...'

'And you're brother-in-law's a doctor?' said Marisa, shaking her head almost in disbelief. 'Why don't you give him a book about depression? One written by another doctor.'

Marisa was taking a chance here. Gambling. She had a hunch it might work.

'What!' exclaimed Kalpana.

'Challenge him using his own ammunition. Give him indisputable medical facts.'

The patient still looked puzzled.

'Kalpana, you don't believe him, do you? Look, you are seriously ill. You have a recognised biological illness which has been diagnosed by one of the top psychiatrists in the land, who happens to be Indian. What more is there to say? You know, if you like, we can get Dr Chaudhry to speak to him…'

Marisa paused to gauge the patient's reaction. Kalpana was wrinkling her forehead and fiddling with her hair. It was obvious she was trying to think it through. But her brain-power was not at its best and her ability to concentrate limited.

'At the end of the day, Kalpana,' continued Marisa, 'we have to accept that we can't change people. The way they feel or think about something. No matter how hard we try. We can only change ourselves. The way *we* feel, the way *we* react. We have to accept that because if we don't we'll drive ourselves mad. We won't be able to move on.'

'But I can't move on. I can't!' cried Kalpana, closing her small pink notebook with a bang. 'That's how I've been brought up. To put my family first. You see, they wanted me to marry Ashok…they gave me a photograph and a horoscope and introduced us to each other. As far as my parents were concerned, he had everything. Right down to the last details. The right profession, the right family background, the right height, the right fucking inside leg measurement.'

'And you refused?'

'Yes…which is why he's so angry with me. He can't forgive me.'

'You rejected him, Kalpana. That was your right. But that's his problem, his hang-up. He has to deal with it, not you. You can't be responsible for other people's problems.

You can only be responsible for yourself.'

You've disgraced your family

'But you don't understand. He's the one who keeps telling me…keeps reminding me that I've let them all down. And he's right.'

'Kalpana, learning to put yourself first and lose the guilt—it's not easy. You're someone who takes family responsibility seriously. So, these changes, they won't happen overnight. You need to give yourself time to learn not to be hard on yourself. But now you're aware that's what's making you ill, that's a great start. It'll be easier to achieve a kind of distance. A kind of acceptance of what you are and who you are.'

'But, I don't feel like I'm achieving anything. What I'm doing to my family feels like rebellion. Defiance. Betrayal, even. And it hurts so much. I hear what you're saying. That I've got to put myself first, but that just makes me feel bad. Inadequate. Not good enough. Like I need to do everything over and over until I get it right.'

'Yes, that's part of the illness. An insistence on being perfect. But no one's perfect, Kalpana. It isn't possible. Tell me something. Is that why you keep washing your hair? Because you're never satisfied it's perfect enough? Meaning, you don't think *you're* perfect enough? For your family?'

You're a disgrace to your family

'My hair?' said Kalpana, letting out a long, deep sigh. 'I wash my hair because…because…oh, I don't know…

because…because it's never enough. Nothing I do ever feels like it's enough.'

'And changing your clothes? Is that to get reassurance? A reaction? Approval?'

Kalpana pursed her lips together and closed her eyes momentarily. 'Maybe.' Winding a lock of her hair through the fingers of her right hand, she repeated, 'Maybe.'

'Kalpana,' said Marisa, smiling at her patient, 'let's leave it there. I can see you're really tired and that you need to rest. We can talk tomorrow if you like.' Then, stroking her chin with her right hand, she added, 'Will you do something for me in the meantime?'

'Do something?' Kalpana asked suspiciously.

'Will you write me out a list?'

'A list?' asked the patient, greatly perplexed.

'Yes, a list with all your good qualities on it. All the good things about Kalpana. Just one word for each quality. Put down as many as you can think of.'

'You must be joking,' sneered Kalpana.

'No, I'm not joking. Look, I'll start you off. Now, if I were you, I think the first one I'd put down is, er, let me see, I know, LOYALTY.'

'Loyalty!' exclaimed Kalpana. 'How d'you make that out?'

'Easy,' replied Marisa. 'The way you feel so responsible for letting down your family. Anyone who wasn't loyal or dependable wouldn't feel like that, would they? Or, perhaps, you might call it INTEGRITY. Well, maybe it would be an idea to jot both down. But it's your call. *You've* got to come up with the words. Right?'

Kalpana was remembering the last time she saw her family. It was her cousin Monu's wedding. At the Mehndi—a kind of hen night when all the female relatives hang out together and get their arms painted with henna tattoos—Monu went crazy and even had her legs done. As she sat on the sofa, her arms and legs splayed out, waiting for the dye to set, Kalpana's mother fed her tikki and dosai. Gurinder hardly spoke to her daughter. Nor did Kalpana's sisters attempt much contact with their older sister. Except Yasmin, and even she was nervous of the others seeing her talk to the enemy. Kalpana watched this in deep sorrow—this was her family. At the wedding ceremony and the festivities that followed, her father completely cut her. She had to go through the proceedings as if she didn't know him and had never set eyes on him before. Yet she was his flesh and blood. Didn't he feel anything for her at all? Ashok was even worse. He went out of his way to make her feel small and excluded. People had obviously been primed. Few of her relatives spent much time with her. As far as most of them were concerned, Kalpana Prasad was an outcast.

Kalpana has been moved out of the Observation Unit into one of the pretty yellow rooms. She still has Grace with her, but the move has been made to show Kalpana she is relied on to behave responsibly towards herself. The gesture has not gone unnoticed by the patient—the medication and the therapy are working hand-in-hand to make her begin to notice things like that. She sits at her dressing table trying to compile her list. Her list of qualities. It's not the kind of list she usually draws up at home.

KALPANA PRASAD'S QUALITIES
Loyalty
Integrity

It looks very strange, not right, somehow. She'd like to add some more nouns, but she can't think of any. The only thing that comes into her mind is:

You make me sick

Dominic must have thought she had qualities at one time but, for now, all she can remember is him saying:

You make me sick

Towards the end that was all he could come up with. Why had it all gone so pear-shaped?

To begin with it had been great. Hot. Passionate. Fun. They'd be at it all the time. Laughing and fucking. Fucking and laughing. But then, after the heat had cooled down, they discovered they had nothing in common. Well, except for a shared taste in expensive living and exotic travel.

Dominic tried so hard to understand about Kalpana's problems with her family. He really tried. But what he found really difficult was coping with his girlfriend's moods. Especially after she'd been having a conversation with her father or her brother-in-law. That was definitely the worst possible time to catch her.

'How many times do I have to tell you, Dominic? I'm depressed. And I don't mean down, low, flat. Right? I mean DEPRESSED. Really DEPRESSED. OK?'

'Don't tell me, you've just been speaking to Ashok.'

'No, my dad.'

'Ohmygod, that's even worse.'

'Can't you just try and understand? For my sake?'

'Oh, *I* understand all right. *They're* the ones who don't understand. *They're* the ones with the problem. You're an English woman, born, brought up and living in England, and you have an English boyfriend. While they're living in the fucking Dark Ages and haven't noticed the world's moved on. They're stuck in a fucking time warp, for God's sake. Christ, what would they have done if you'd been a lesbian? Make you commit suttee? Burn you to death?' Dominic laughs, though he's not really amused.

'Dominic, you're not helping. I feel guilty. That's what's making me depressed.'

'Well, then, let's go out. There's that restaurant that's just opened in the high street. Why don't we give it a whirl? It'll make you forget about all that crap.'

'Dominic, you're just not listening. I'm depressed. I don't feel like going out and I'm shattered. I feel more like taking an overdose, if you really want to know.'

But Dominic had had enough. 'We've been over this, Kalpana. You're getting things way out of proportion. Calm down, will you? Pull yourself together. Either put on your fucking sari, go home, sit at your father's knee and tell him you've been a bad, bad girl. Or get on with your life and tell them to fuck off out of it.'

Kalpana had had enough, too. 'For fuck's sake, Dominic. You never understand. Just leave me alone, will you?'

And, he did. Well, except for a few messages.

Kalpana, I want to apologise for what I said the other night. I'm sorry, I just get so frustrated with the situation, sometimes. Your bloody family. I feel like I'm always competing with them for attention. Well, no, not them. With the fact of them. Oh, you know what I mean. Ohmygod, I'm really making a pig's ear of this. Fucksake, Kalpana. I love you, you crazy bitch. But all this is making me sick—it's doing my head in. God knows what it's doing to yours... You're never going to please your parents, your family. You're just going to have to accept it or it'll fuck your head up...

Beep, beep, beep...

Kalpana, that bloody machine of yours. Why don't you reprogram it to give people more time to leave a message? Anyway, as I was saying, you need to sort your head out. Maybe, you should see someone, if you know what I mean. Someone professional.

Beep, beep, beep...

Oh, hell...

Dominic didn't call again after that. Kalpana spent the next week in bed, and the following week, and the week after that. Then, she lost count. She lost her appetite and all the energy drained out of her, leaving her thin, weak and sallow-skinned. She closed the curtains and buried herself under her duvet. She didn't open her mail. She didn't answer the phone or look at her messages. She didn't bathe or take a shower. Her bedclothes remained unwashed, as did her pyjamas which—after about four days—started to give off a really cheesy odour. She didn't wash her hair for weeks, either, there didn't seem any point—the whole thing seemed POINT LESS. She just slept and slept, and when she wasn't sleeping, she just gazed out in front of her at the curtains— multi-coloured butterflies dancing on a pale green background. She studied every part of their blue-pink wings until she could close her eyes and reproduce them faithfully in her mind.

Kalpana lost track of time as the days merged one into the other, each one filled with the repetitive pattern of sleeping and gazing. As she looked infinity in the face, the future lay before her like a vast desert with no oasis in sight. From now on every day would be like this—sleeping and gazing, gazing and sleeping. There was nothing to look forward to, nothing at all, just butterflies. The thought of getting up was enough to make her stay where she was— in bed. Sleep meant being unconscious. Unconscious meant not having to think about the future that lay before her. Unconscious was good. But she couldn't sleep—not all the time, and often not at night, anyway. Her thoughts wouldn't let her, her thoughts about that vast desert that lay before her. If she did manage to drop off, she would wake early and find herself unable to get back to sleep again. By late morning she'd be so worn out she'd sleep the rest of the day and into the early part of the evening.

Eventually, her mood picked up, but it picked up way too much and she went from utter despair to utter elation. Unable to sleep more than two or three hours a day, she'd get up, plagued by bouts of endless energy and stampeding thoughts. Sometimes she'd wash her hair. Other times she'd make lists—lists, lists and more lists—or she'd tidy and clean. All the time, she chanted to herself or sang, unable to stop running round herself in ever-decreasing circles. For days she yo-yoed between ultimate highs and ultimate lows, moving from desolation to jubilation in a matter of hours or even minutes. Then, one day her highs hit an all-time high when frenetic activity became the order of the day, but this time with one specific objective in mind.

The first thing she did was to call the florist and order six dozen marigolds. There was a bit of trouble about this. Marigolds weren't readily available and certainly not in those kinds of quantities. But, eventually, after a lot of shouting down the phone, she got seventy-two marigolds delivered to the flat. Then, she lit some candles. Kalpana had a lot of candles—mostly Egyptian Jasmine and Orange Blossom. She placed six of them on the bedside table in her bedroom and one in the table in the sitting room.

She ran her fingers through her hair to check if it was dry. It was, so she went into the shower to wash it. Afterwards, she rubbed it with a towel, then pushed her hair behind her ears and combed it through till it reached halfway down her back.

She went to her wardrobe and took out her favourite sari and shalwar. Both the tunic and the loose trousers were breathtakingly beautiful—delicate, pale blue silk, edged in ribbon and sequins. She put them on in front of the mirror, making sure that everything was done properly. This took some time—it was a complicated procedure. When it was finally done, she removed a beaded necklace from her jewellery box and placed it round her neck. Then, she dabbed some sandalwood oil on her neck and her wrists and sprinkled some over her bed. From a small bottle of vermilion, she took the applicator and painted a crimson bindi dot on the centre of her forehead.

The flowers arrived. Sitting cross-legged on the cream carpet in the sitting room, the marigolds in front of her, she proceed to cut most of the stalks off, leaving a few intact. These she tied into a garland which she placed round her neck. Then, she walked into the bedroom and scattered marigold heads on the bed, strewing others over the rug.

She walked into the bathroom, took out the entire contents of her medicine cabinet and emptied them onto the bath mat. She grabbed two large bottles of paracetamol and about six strips of anti-depressants, put the rest of the medicine back in the cabinet and walked back to the sitting room. She placed all the tablets in the middle of the floor.

Then she went to the fridge, took out a magnum of champagne and helped herself to a flute from one of the units. She walked into the sitting room and sat cross-legged on the thick cream carpet. The cork flew off the bottle and hit the television on the other side of the room. She poured out a glass. Next, she removed all the tablets from their containers and sorted them out into two different piles. Everything was ready so she began mixing her cocktail. This consisted of popping a pill, then swallowing a sip until all was consumed and nothing remained.

It wasn't long before she started to feel extremely woozy. Somehow, she managed to lift herself up off the floor, her legs wobbling like jelly beneath her gaunt frame. She didn't want to leave a mess on the carpet, so she staggered to the table with the bottles and containers, shaking all the way. She tottered into the bedroom, finding just enough strength to climb on to the bed. Her hands took some of the marigold heads and threw them up in the air. Some of the petals came to rest on top of her like soft snowflakes landing on a graveyard. Kalpana placed her hands together and raised them up to her chin, resting her fingertips just below her lips. Within minutes she was asleep.

The next thing she knew she was lying in a hospital bed having what felt like the coiled tube of a vacuum cleaner rammed down her throat.

The nurse pushed the flap back and looked through the glass. Kalpana was tossing and turning. She was in the middle of a nightmare. One she'd not had before. She was standing on a circular platform made of large, roughly hewn blocks of ice. Running round the edge was a thick band of hot coals. The platform was raised about five feet off the ground and round the perimeter of the circle stood every member of her family—and Dominic. Either she scalded her feet over the burning coals or froze to agonising numbness over the ice blocks. If she tried to get off the platform, her family and Dominic would push her back on to the fire. None of them would let her climb down, forcing her to choose between tiptoeing over the fire and the ice. However you looked at it, it was a bummer.

She woke with a start and bolted upright in her bed. She wasn't sure which was worse—being unconscious to the world but having dreams like that, or being wide awake and having to face her life. It was her birthday today, too, and she hadn't received anything from her family. Nor, for that matter, from Dominic. The post had come and gone bringing nothing. They knew where she was and if they didn't have the address, all they had to do was ring Ashok or Directory Enquiries. How difficult was that?

There were no phone calls either. Just the following text from Ashok:

OLDER BUT NO WISER!!
HAPPY BIRTHDAY, LOSER

She had a father, a mother, three sisters and a brother-in-law, but they might as well be dead. Or perhaps it was the other way round—maybe she was the one who was dead. They were certainly treating her like a dead person. Why were they so ready to throw away their own child when she was finding it so hard to give them up? Marisa had tried to get her to see that there was nothing wrong with her or the way she lived her life. It was her life, after all, and she was free to live it the way she wanted, without feeling guilty. Only she wasn't. Kalpana believed she must have done something terribly wrong to merit being written off by her entire family.

Kalpana grabbed her small pink notebook and opened the page entitled *KALPANA PRASAD'S QUALITIES*. She stared hard at the words *LOYALTY* and *INTEGRITY*. As she did so, she shook her head, questioning her right to apply them to her—Kalpana. But why would Marisa make it all up? It didn't make any sense. She tried to remember exactly what Marisa had said. Something about being loyal because she felt so bad about letting her family down. If she was really bad she wouldn't have given a fig about it, would she? Well, maybe, but when she started thinking like that, her family would come marching into her mind. As she visualised each and every one of them, she found it impossible to pursue any rational line of thinking. The image of her family wagging their fingers at her or shaking their heads invaded her brain and took it over.

What was the other thing Marisa had said? Something about the fact that once Kalpana realised what was happening and why it was happening, she would be on her way. There was a long way to go, yes, but it was a start. And what was happening was that her family, and all it meant in terms of her cultural background and religion, was controlling her. They had always controlled her. Even when she stepped out and claimed a life, a path for herself, the family still controlled her by controlling her reactions. When looked at like that, Kalpana's guilt was inevitable.

Perhaps the only solution, Marisa suggested, was—only when and if she felt ready—to let her family go. Not pretend that they didn't exist or act aggressively towards them, but, since their acceptance was not on the cards, create space between her and them. To expect nothing, hope for nothing—just let it be.

They had called her selfish, heartless and a grave disappointment. She couldn't do anything to change their minds and it was pointless trying. To accept that their judgement didn't matter was no mean feat. But to learn to feel good about herself was something she could work on—a positive way forward. Kalpana looked at the incomplete list. Marisa hadn't shown she was disappointed when Kalpana had failed to add any words. She didn't give Kalpana the impression that she had let anyone, even herself, down by not coming up with any more nouns. Marisa told her not to be hard on herself, not to judge herself too harshly, to be more forgiving.

Kalpana's pen moved and she wrote STRENGTH OF CHARACTER under INTEGRITY. Whatever any one said about her, nobody could say she was weak. If she had been weak, she wouldn't have got sick. Her illness was 'the curse of the strong'—someone had told her that, or maybe she'd read it somewhere. Weak people didn't get this sickness.

And then another word came into her mind: SENSITIVITY. She was on a roll now. Mind you, thought Kalpana, that often felt more like a curse than a blessing. After all, if she hadn't been so sensitive in the first place, she wouldn't be in this bloody mess. When she thought about it, most of the people in the Cloisters were there because they were just too fucking sensitive for their own good.

Marisa and Kalpana climb into the taxi and sit down. Marisa tells the driver where they are going and then sits back.

She turns to Kalpana and says with a concerned expression on her face: 'Are you absolutely sure about this, Kalpana? I'm not criticising you, I'm only wondering if it isn't a little bit drastic.'

'Yes,' replies Kalpana, looking out of the window. Then she smiles at Marisa and says, 'Yes, I'm quite sure and thank you for coming with me.'

'We've got two and a half hours so that should be enough. I've got a three-thirty I need to be back for and you mustn't be late, or we'll both get into trouble.'

It was unorthodox, this trip, but Marisa had spoken to Dr Chaudhry and explained how important it was for Kalpana to do it. He had thought about it and then agreed to the plan. It's a lot of responsibility for Marisa—Kalpana hasn't been allowed out since she was admitted four weeks ago—and she's nervous. She knows it's risky but, on the other hand, there have been definite signs of improvement in Kalpana and allowing her to do this might make a huge difference. Kalpana's responding well to the medication and the therapy. The manic aspects of her manic depression seem to be slowly but surely ebbing away. She's abandoned her proneness to aggressiveness and violent feelings of desire and rage, and is a lot calmer. Her mood swings appear to be under control. She still has severe depressive episodes when her guilt takes her over, but the suicidal thoughts have abated and her OCD is much less frequent. She doesn't get as agitated as she used to.

Kalpana is convinced that what she is about to do is right, and that she won't regret the trip. Dressed in a pair of jeans and a white T-shirt, her hair is dry and unkempt. She hasn't washed it for a day or so but the fact doesn't bug her. The red, flaky patches on her scalp caused by constant scourings are beginning to heal.

Marisa and Kalpana spend the rest of the journey in silence. Kalpana seems to prefer it that way, sitting back in her seat looking out of the window at real people and real life, safe in the knowledge that they can't get at her.

They arrive at their destination. Marisa pays the cabbie and the two of them get out. Marisa turns to Kalpana and asks, 'Are you ready?'

'Yes,' answers Kalpana resolutely. 'Yes, I'm ready.' And the two of them walk in through the door.

Kalpana is shown to a seat and is told that André will be with her in a few minutes. Marisa takes the seat next to her charge, who is looking at herself in the mirror, and holding on to the arm rests tightly. The two women are offered refreshments and they both opt for a cappuccino. André arrives, his skinny, bony body swathed in a pink silk shirt and black leather pants. His feet are covered in fake leopard skin and his hair is fashionably coiffed, coloured and cut—a good advertisement for his craft. The grin on his permatanned face stretches from one ear to the other. He introduces himself, then runs his fingers through his client's long locks.

'Darling,' he enthuses loudly, 'what gorgeous hair. Don't tell me you want me to cut it all off? Please don't tell me that. It's so...'

'Yes,' interrupts Kalpana, looking straight at herself in the mirror, 'I want it short.'

André looks at Marisa with a troubled expression on his face. He is dismayed that an Asian babe with such beautiful, radiant hair would want to rob herself of the jewel in her crown. Marisa shrugs her shoulders and nods. André, looking thoroughly dejected, turns his back on his client and summons one of the juniors to take Kalpana to the basin and wash her hair. He walks off in a huff.

Marisa flicks through a magazine as she watches Kalpana having her hair washed. Soon she is back at her seat with wet hair and a towel round her shoulders. André returns to his client and, without looking at Kalpana or Marisa, takes numerous pairs of scissors from his black bag of tools and performs the operation, sniffing occasionally to express his dissent. Kalpana watches the small tufts of black hair fall to the floor and, as they leave her head, something that has been with her forever departs never to return. Not just hair—but a way of life.

André refuses to go any further than her ears. 'Sorry, darling,' he apologises with a deep sigh. 'This is far as I'm prepared to go.' Deeply hurt, he puts his scissors back in the bag. 'Shazza,' he shouts languidly, addressing a junior by the basins, 'where's my drier?'

Twenty minutes later Kalpana studies herself in the mirror. She looks different and she feels different, too. She smiles. She likes it. It's exciting, it's new and it enthrals her. She looks at Marisa who smiles back, nodding her head with approval.

They take a taxi back to the hospital and Marisa arrives in good time for her counselling session. Kalpana signs herself back in, then goes and sits on the grass with Cat, Marianne and Lynette. They are pleased to see her and think the new hair cut is ace. Grace is no longer with her. She has been assigned to a new patient since Dr Chaudhry feels Kalpana no longer needs someone with her. Kalpana notices Grace sitting with her new charge on one of the benches. She smiles at Grace and Grace smiles back, giving the patient's reinvention a resounding thumbs-up.

JAMES

*When you tell people you're in hospital
for depression, what really scares
them is (i) could it happen to
them and (ii) can they catch it off you?*

James is stretched out on a cold metal slab in the Electroconvulsive Therapy Room. His body is sweating, his heart is beating ten to the dozen and his hands are shaking. His mind is tormented by recurring nightmares of the past and his eyes are pink with fear. To one side of him stands Dr Chaudhry; to the other the Shock Doc. What kind of a person gets a kick out of inflicting torture on defenceless human beings, he asks himself, *and* gets paid for it? James screws up his eyes to get a better look at the man. A character in a movie comes into his mind. He can see the guy in his head, he just can't remember the name of the film. James is having difficulty with his thoughts, which seem blurred and mixed up in scary, confusing mists inside his brain. Wait a minute, he's got it now: the Nazi dentist in *Marathon Man* played by Lawrence Olivier. *Is it safe? Is it safe?* That's what Olivier keeps saying to Dustin Hoffman just before he sticks something sharp in his mouth and extracts one of his teeth or pulls out a filling. Unlike the Dustin Hoffman character, James will be given an anaesthetic and a muscle relaxer before the heavy stuff begins and a few hundred volts are shot through his brain. According to Dr Chaudhry, ECT's no worse than a visit to the dentist. If *Marathon Man*'s anything to go by, that isn't exactly reassuring. And has Dr Chaudhry ever had ECT? James thinks probably not.

He looks round at the chrome and white torture chamber and its star attraction—the ECT machine. He finds it hard to believe that something so barbaric, with its reputation for dodgy side effects, can still be considered humane. Some countries like Italy—whose Fascist regime introduced it in 1938 to subdue pigs—and Holland have outlawed it. Despite this, Dr Chaudhry assures James it's very effective in serious cases like his where the depression's so entrenched, it's simply inhuman to wait weeks for the anti-depressants to kick in. Dr Chaudhry is conscious that a man like James— with his sharp intellect and impressive academic record— might appreciate a little history. So, he's fed him some gems about ECT—like the fact that it goes back to the first century AD, when a Roman emperor strapped an electric eel to his temples to cure his headache. Couldn't they have come up with something a little less drastic, James wonders?

The thing that frightens James is not the treatment itself— the experience of it. No, he can stomach that or, at least, he thinks he can. What really scares him is what it might do to his memory. It would be great if all the depressive memories could be wiped out just by passing a few electric currents through his skull, but that's not going to happen. That's just a myth, according to Doctor Chaudhry. No, if anything's going to go, it'll be the nice memories—the ones he'd quite like to keep. Doctor Chaudhry has admitted that ECT *can* damage memory, but the effect is usually short-term, and if it can stop the agony and the apathy as well as the dark thoughts, then it will be well worth it. They say you can also get brain damage but Dr Chaudhry doesn't buy that one either. And he says there's minimal risk of heart failure. What's most likely to happen, he tells James, is that he'll get a really bad headache. Anyway, it's too late for all this should-I-shouldn't-I business. James has made his decision. What he's going through right now is so bad, he'll try anything which stands a half-decent chance of putting him out of his misery.

'James,' says Dr Chaudhry, gesturing to the man facing him, 'this is Dr Latimer. He will explain what the treatment will entail. You're in very safe hands. Dr Latimer is a specialist in his field.'

James places a shaky hand on Dr Chaudhry's arm and says, 'You're not leaving?'

'James,' replies Dr Chaudhry, 'everything will be OK, I promise you, and I will be there when you wake up.'

As James watches Dr Chaudhry leave, Dr Latimer starts to speak. A man of average height with sloping shoulders and short, greying hair combed neatly over the top of his head, he has thick lips, brown-black eyes and a warm smile. In short, he looks nothing like Lawrence Olivier. 'James, let me run you through what we're gonna do. First, we're gonna give you a general anaesthetic so you don't feel anything, and then, once you're out of it, something to relax your muscles. That's just to protect you against the effects of any violent spasms. Fractured bones, that sort of thing.' Dr Latimer's narrow, long fingers produce what looks like a headband with two blue earplugs attached to it. James stares at it, swallows and starts to shudder—he looks like he's already receiving shock treatment. 'When that's done, I'll place an electrode on each side of your forehead.'

'Now,' continues the Doctor, who leans over his patient and begins to explain the intricate details of his instrument of torture, 'all I do to start the procedure is to turn the dial on the machine and flick the on switch. A current will flow through your brain. It won't hurt a bit, though you might experience some kind of jolt. And that's it. It'll only take a few seconds.' Rubbing his hands together, he asks, 'Are we all set, then?'

James looks straight ahead, clenches his teeth, making the muscles around his mouth tighten. He blinks and then nods.

'OK, then,' says Dr Latimer, 'let's go.' He summons a plump, grey-haired nurse to administer the anaesthetic and then an injection to paralyse his muscles. James notices her matronly chest leaning over him and the mentholated smell of her breath as she proceeds to apply cold jelly to his temples. He shivers briefly before succumbing to oblivion.

The nurse nods to Dr Latimer and drops James's wrist. The electrodes are attached to his forehead. Dr Latimer puts on a pair of tortoise-shell glasses and turns to the machine beside him. He flicks the switch and turns one of the knobs clockwise. For about thirty seconds James's body convulses while his eyebrows flicker and his hands and feet twitch. To the untrained eye he looks like he's experiencing an epileptic fit or a heart attack.

The bad news is James will need to have a whole series of seizures if they're to do him any good—twice a week for at least a fortnight. When it comes to ECT, once is never enough.

James is sitting at the desk in his glass-walled office. An enormous figure the size of a hippopotamus is coming towards him. Actually, it *is* a hippopotamus—a hippopotamus weighing half a ton dressed in an ill-fitting pinstripe suit. At least seven foot tall, its body is thick and rubbery, its face plump and bulky, and its huge, flabby muzzle awesome. Through the gold-rimmed spectacles James can see its bug eyes popping out of their sockets and the bulgy lids above and below. James begins to feel very small as an audience gathers outside his office and the mammal waddles closer and closer towards its prey. He feels like he's getting tinier and tinier and that the beast's inflated torso is getting larger and larger. Soon it's towering over James like a colossus. The hippopotamus bends over James's chair. As he does so, James becomes aware of an overpowering smell—the animal seems to have drenched itself in a whole bottle of sickly-sweet aftershave, and is now so close that James can feel the odd bristle protruding from its nostrils, almost tickling him on the cheek. The animal's muzzle moves up and down to reveal a gargantuan mouth and tusk-like teeth. Producing an outsize megaphone, the hippopotamus holds it up to its mouth and places the other end against James's ear. The creature starts shouting at the top of its voice, but James hears nothing. It's like he's in a silent movie or a film with the sound turned off. The whole thing's happening in slow motion, dragging out James's humiliation. He knows the hippopotamus well. It's Attila the Brum, alias Sir Vince

Spacey, James's boss and the chairman of the bank. The chairman tugs at his arm furiously. James resists, screaming, 'Leave me alone, leave me alone.' And he begins to cry. But, it's not the chairman—it's Dr Chaudhry trying to rouse his patient from a nightmare.

'It's OK, James, it's OK.'

'Where am I?' asks James, looking rather shell-shocked as he glances round his yellow room. He rubs his eyes and tries to sit up in his bed, but it hurts too much. His body feels like it's been dragged through a forest backwards. His face is wet and clammy and his hair lies matted against the sides of his head.

'No, don't get up, James. Just rest. You're at the Cloisters and you've had electroconvulsive therapy. You must be very tired, so I won't talk to you for long, but tell me, how do you feel?'

'What?' says James, looking as confused as he feels, stroking the back of his neck.

'I'm Dr Chaudhry, your doctor.'

Eventually James remembers where he is. 'I feel like I've been asleep for a week.' Squirming a bit, he adds, 'My muscles ache. I feel kind of woozy and I've got a terrible headache.'

'You've been sleeping for about twelve hours. Don't worry, though, it's nothing unusual. You need to sleep whenever you feel the need. Don't resist it. The muscle ache is normal and so is the headache. We'll give you something to stop the pain at once.'

'OK,' says James, blinking. His brain feels like stew bubbling away inside a pressure cooker.

'Tell me something,' asks Dr Chaudhry, 'When I woke you just now, what were you dreaming about?'

Any colour left in James's face begins to disappear, while the frown lines on his forehead become more pronounced. Finding it hard to breathe, he says, 'I...I can't talk about it right now.'

'OK, James. That's fine. Just get some rest. We'll talk later.'

James—overcome with exhaustion—is asleep in ten minutes.

James was sitting in the Day Patients' Lounge waiting to go swimming. Some chap called Damien was supposed to be taking him and a few others for a bit of gentle therapy. As patients popped in between sessions to get a coffee, James didn't look up. He just sat on the faded green sofa, his right arm close to his side, his left arm resting on his lap. James followed the minute hand on his watch going round, as he listened to the music blaring out of the radio:

Sometimes the system goes on the blink
And the whole thing turns out wrong
You might not make it back and you know
That you could be well oh that strong

He knew all about going 'on the blink'. He'd been 'on the blink' for quite some time, now. But the last two lines bugged him—they just didn't seem to make any sense. As he silently repeated the mysterious lyrics over and over, a girl came in and helped herself to a cup of water from the machine. Tall, red-haired with freckles, she wore faded blue jeans and a crumpled pink shirt. She sank on to the sofa opposite him and let out an elongated groan. Her forehead was damp with sweat, her eyes bloodshot and wet from crying, and her hair lanky and stringy. Not that James saw any of this, of course—he just kept on looking down. Eye to eye contact was beyond him.

'Boy, that was shit,' said the girl, shaking her head and pulling her nose.

James did not reply—conversation was much too daunting a prospect for him. He'd been at the Cloisters for over a week and undergone three ECT sessions, as well as a number of difficult one-to-ones with Dr Chaudhry. All he could manage was to twitch his shoulders and shuffle his feet from side to side.

If it hadn't been for his wife, James might never have made it to the hospital. That awful day, he came back from work and just sat on the floor in a dark corner of the study sobbing his eyes out. All he'd allowed her to do was watch. He wouldn't let her in and that's how he remained—desperately lonely but utterly unreachable. The next day she dragged him off to their GP who had no hesitation in signing him off for three months, telling James he was completely burnt out. That if he didn't have a complete break, he'd have a breakdown (if he hadn't had one already). He also gave him something 'to calm him down'. James spent the next three weeks mooching around the house like a zombie, unable to do the simplest things like playing with the kids, watching TV or emptying the dustbin. All he wanted to do was squat silently in a corner. Helen didn't know what was happening to her husband and she couldn't get him to talk about it. He refused to talk about anything. She guessed it had something to do with that ogre—Vince Spacey. Since he'd arrived to take up the helm of Gussington International, things had taken a turn for the worse and she'd watched her husband change from a confident, outgoing man into a reclusive, gibbering wreck. Whatever world James had inhabited before, it had thrown him out and slammed the door in his face. He just didn't belong in it any more.

The pressure this put on Helen was immeasurable. James would spend hours in bed just staring into space or studying his watch face. The sound of the doorbell or the phone would make him jump, as would the delivery of the day's post. He'd immediately start to quiver, pull the bedclothes up over his eyes and retreat under the safety of the duvet. He'd lie there as still and as stiff as a stone—except for his pounding heart—taking the tiniest, shallowest breaths, terrified to disturb the dark silence. Any mention of the words Gussington International, or the sight of the company name brandished on an envelope, and beads of perspiration would appear on his forehead, his body would shake and—clutching a retching stomach—he'd disappear to the bathroom to be sick, or to succumb to now regular bouts of diarrhoea. When he managed to close his eyes, his sleep was fitful, marred by anguish-ridden nightmares from which he would wake screaming and crying. James had been reduced to a terrified child.

The final straw came one afternoon when they went to the supermarket. Helen didn't feel like she could leave him at home—she was too frightened of what she might find when she got back. She was driving them home when, all of a sudden, she remembered she'd forgotten the bread.

She stopped on the opposite side of the road to the bakers, gave James a pound coin and asked him to buy a loaf while she waited on a double yellow line. She watched him anxiously as he staggered out in front of the cars, oblivious to the discordant symphony of hoots that accosted him as he failed to wait for the right moment. He looked out of sync—as if he was having trouble balancing himself. The drivers stared at him, no doubt thinking the dishevelled man dressed in khaki combat trousers and a white baggy T-shirt was drunk, drugged or out of his mind. Or all three. James seemed completely unaware of the danger—he didn't appear to know where he was or what he was doing. Helen rushed out of the car, gestured assertively with a flat palm for the drivers to wait while she pulled him back to the safety of their Range Rover. He sat in the passenger seat and cried all the way home. Helen felt like joining in but she knew she couldn't. She had to stay strong and in control.

She took him home and put him to bed like a sick child, taking his clothes off and removing his trainers. She rearranged the pillows and, wiping his forehead with a damp flannel, combed back the knotted hair. He slept for hours while she watched him breathing slowly. He looked so peaceful lying there. She reached out to touch his forehead gently, but pulled her hand back suddenly in case she woke him. His face seemed so fragile and his cheeks soft and delicate. Nine years ago she'd married the sweetest, loveliest man. Tall, curly dark hair—now with increasingly grey streaks—warm, brown eyes, a sexy smile and a wicked sense of humour. He'd always been such a snappy dresser, too. This new unkempt look—including the four-day growth of beard—was unfamiliar to her. He lay there quietly snoring, insignificant, vulnerable and withered, looking like he'd been gobbled up by the bed. This wasn't the man she'd married almost a decade ago—the father of her children. She hadn't wanted them to witness him like this so she'd packed them off to her mother. In any case, he wasn't much of a father right now. He couldn't play with them like he used to. He no longer seemed interested in what they got up to at school or on the sports field. She had to face it—he no longer seemed interested in her. To be honest, he no longer seemed interested in anything.

The morning after the bread incident Helen wheeled James back to the surgery. The same afternoon she and her husband were sitting in Dr Chaudhry's office at the Cloisters. Dr Chaudhry told Helen this was going to be a long, painful business—getting him back to the land of the living. He was suffering from severe clinical depression and PTSD. All she could think was 'Why is this happening to us? Why is this happening to me?' James knew what he was putting her through. He knew. And what made it worse was there was absolutely nothing he could do about it.

James was having a one-to-one with Dr Chaudhry in the consultant's office. Whenever James went to see Dr Chaudhry he would sit in the same seat—a high-backed green armchair, standing in the darkest corner of the room opposite a large mahogany desk. He looked tiny and shrunken, settled deep into what seemed like an extraordinarily wide chair. In reality, there was nothing odd about the chair; it's just that James had lost weight in the past six weeks, maybe as much as twenty pounds. Dr Chaudhry studied the grey man before him. James's skin had turned a kind of ghostly grey, strings of greasy, greyish-black hair hung over his eyes and a mass of grey stubble had taken up residence on his chin. His face seemed swollen and his lips were cracked at the corners. His grey clothes were crumpled and creased. Placing his hands together beneath his chin, Dr Chaudhry adjusted his glasses and asked James how he was feeling.

'I…I'm OK,' he mumbled, fidgeting. As usual, he sat studying the minute hand on his watch face, finding it difficult to talk.

'Are you eating properly? I see that you're continuing to lose weight.'

'Am I? Oh.'

'It's important that you eat and sleep regularly, James. When it comes to healing the mind, we can't afford to neglect the body.'

'No,' said James, vaguely, keeping his eyes down.

'James, in order for us to help you, we need to know a bit more about what happened.' Dr Chaudhry coughed and then said, 'I know this is very painful, but we need to speak about what took place at…er…at work.'

James wriggled uncomfortably in his loose T-shirt. Beads of sweat had collected on his temples and his head was shaking. He rubbed his eyes. He felt breathless, that he needed to escape. He could taste his saliva and he began to dribble. He tried to twist his shoulders round so he could bend his head and wipe his mouth, but he couldn't make it. He got up and said:

'I have to go…I feel sick…' and he left.

After about fifteen minutes, James returned. 'Sorry,' he

said. Then, squirming in his seat, he added, 'Yes, OK. I'll try.' He cupped his head in his right hand as his mind began to travel back in time.

James Maraschino had been Head of European Corporate Finance at Gussington Bank for five years before it was taken over by INTERNATIONAL—an American group specialising in just about everything in the financial services sphere. James's name was respected both at home and abroad as a key player in the mergers and acquisitions game, and he lived and breathed it. Although he was a tough negotiator and an aggressive opponent, he played fair and by the book.

James was a family man with a wife he loved and three children he adored—Amber, ten, Sadie, eight, and Freddie, six. When he wasn't playing with the kids, or having a quiet dinner out with Helen, he'd have his nose in some biography. He loved reading—especially history—which he'd studied at Oxford. James had been unfaithful only once which—given the salacious goings-on in the department—was no mean feat. Secretaries in Corporate Finance were frequently hired for their sexual allurements and willingness to participate in the rather risqué entertainments put on after work. It was not unheard of for girls to be asked to photocopy their private parts, and for the machine's outpourings to be distributed to the department in the form of an office memo. Sometimes, girls dressed in short mini skirts and breast-hugging tops would bend over to pick up a screwed-up bit of paper that some mischievous buck had thrown on the floor to amuse himself and his playmates. The girls themselves were compliant. They egged the men on and were certainly not averse to the odd shag—even when it meant having the lurid details emailed round the department. Given this background, James's self-restraint was remarkable. He and his team had been on a business trip in Italy celebrating a deal. His colleagues had plied him with drink and the next thing he knew he found himself in bed with a dusky Roman signorina. He vowed it would never happen again and he kept his word.

James had watched his world, the City, turn into a global community run by yobs—power-crazed wheeler-dealers and money men who would kill rather than let anyone come between them and winning. Animalistic bullies, they enjoyed ruining other people's lives. James loathed what the City has become, but he was stuck. It was a culture in which he prospered.

Throughout his career as a corporate financier, James had never taken a day's sick leave, and depression was something he'd neither experienced nor thought about. He worked a punishing schedule of ridiculous hours, frequent long-haul travel—often at the drop of a hat—and tight deadlines. He was popular amongst his team and highly valued by Gussington's senior management. But, then came the takeover. James was involved in the negotiations from an early stage, and the acquisition worried him. INTERNATIONAL were notorious for their gratuitously thuggish approach to business, and for not taking any prisoners. James knew how to be ruthless, and he was good at it, but there was such a thing as being too greedy. James could see that, the hostile way INTERNATIONAL were playing the acquisition, there'd be a mass bloodletting. The aggressor was determined to eat Gussington for breakfast.

Record numbers of casualties did not bother them—they were acceptable sacrifices on the altar of Profit.

James also questioned the choice of the new chairman, to whom he would have to report directly. He didn't have to read the press cuttings to know what this would mean for the organisation—and him.

CITY DIARY
APPOINTMENT OF CHAIRMAN, GUSSINGTON INTERNATIONAL

Following the announcement of what promises to be one of the bloodiest and most controversial takeovers in history—in which Britain's biggest banking group is being devoured by the number one US conglomerate—the appointment of the Chairman to the newly-formed Gussington International has today been named. Birmingham-born Sir Vincent Spacey—known unaffectionately in the City as Attila the Brum, because of his unorthodox approach to dealmaking—will assume leadership of Gussington International with effect from 1 March. Spacey masterminded the £40 million management buy-out of retail giants Woolmingtons and MDR back in the 1980s during his Chairmanship of Chaplins Bank—one of the first institutions to be involved in the development capital and private equity markets. When Spacey invested his own money in the deal to emerge with a personal profit of over £15 million, he was labelled the greediest man in the City. A former lawyer and Oxford graduate, tennis fanatic Spacey (62) is married with three grown-up children and has houses

in Chelsea and Oxfordshire. When he was knighted in
1998, it was for his services to the financial services
sector—not, as he had hoped, in recognition of his
contribution to charitable causes. Spacey has friends in
high places—amongst them the current occupant of
Number 10 Downing Street and his immediate
predecessor. Given his aspirations to join the House of
Lords, his choice of chums is auspicious, to say the least.
Though, in the current climate, he won't be able to rely
on a loan to guarantee his peerage. As Chairman of
Gussington International, Spacey is expected to behave
true to form and instigate a major downsizing programme.
Analysts anticipate heads will roll from a very great
height—and for a very long time to come.

There was no getting away from it; Vince Spacey was a
living legend. The brainy son of a Brummie brickie—and
proud of it—Vincent had won a scholarship to Oxford from
his local grammar school and come out with a first in politics.
From there he trained as a lawyer, practised for a couple
of years as a corporate finance solicitor, then went straight
into banking, determined to screw all those toffee-nosed
snobs who had put him down as a youngster. A meteoric
rise to the upper echelons of investment banking saw him
Chairman of Chaplins Bank by the age of thirty-nine. He'd
only been there five minutes when he decided to sack the
entire board—provoking a twenty-five per cent hike in the
share price overnight. With just one click of his fingers,
Spacey replaced the entire board with his own 'yes' men.
    Vince did nothing to lose his broad Birmingham accent.
If anything, he milked it. When combined with a carefully

chosen array of obscenities, it would be used to great effect to bawl out those who failed to conform to the chairman's school of banking: *Fuck the bastards before they fuck you.* Machiavelli would have been proud of Vince—like the Italian civil servant, he believed that the end always justified the means. Every one of Vince's foot-soldiers was expected to work like a dog and put the bank's interests before anything else. *An evening spent at home with the wife and family is a wasted marketing opportunity* was his mantra and he insisted everyone working for him stick to it—except him. Spacey had been happily married to his childhood sweetheart for over thirty years and they were a devoted couple.

Early on in the negotiations, before news of the takeover broke, Sir Vince telephoned James in his office. His PA, Chloe, took the call—James was out. Spacey lost his temper when he discovered James had taken the afternoon off to go to his daughter's sports day. The mantra was regurgitated with characteristically blue language down the phone. Chloe's ears were left ringing from the volume and tone of the chairman's admonishment. She passed the message on to James verbatim as tears streamed down her face.

Having been spat out by the outside world, James now belonged to one in which he didn't have to make any decisions, even simple ones like when and where to take his medication. Every morning at nine-thirty he would line up patiently at the nurses' station. When he arrived at the front of the queue, a nurse would locate his file, check the allocation, measure out the dose and hand it to him. Then he'd swallow his pills under her beady eye. Once the nurse was satisfied the medicine had gone down, she would make the necessary entries in his file and replace it in the cabinet. James felt comfortable in his new home where he was looked after twenty-four/seven. Nothing was expected of him so he couldn't disappoint anybody. Nobody screamed at him, stared menacingly at him or threatened him. Nobody there tried to frighten the living daylights out of him. James began to feel the outside world didn't exist, and he much preferred it that way. Like the majority of patients, his centre of gravity had changed from 'out there' to 'in here'. Helen came to see him regularly—though, in many ways he wished she wouldn't. She reminded him of his failures, his inability to cope with what life had thrown at him. He still loved his wife and children but, without intending to, they made him feel guilty for messing up his responsibilities as a husband and a father. Helen wasn't part of his new world and she couldn't be expected to sympathise with his wish to leave the old one behind and sink into oblivion. As for the children, how could they understand? His family belonged to a future he didn't want to think about—a time yet to come when he'd be discharged. He didn't recognise the concept of a future right now—even thinking about what he was going to do in five minutes was too much of an effort. The word 'discharged' sent shivers up and down his spine. It meant having to face a death sentence, for he knew he wouldn't be able to survive. The thought that he might have to go back to Gussington petrified him. It made him shrink back deeper and deeper into himself.

Dr Chaudhry had recommended James attend assertiveness classes to help him re-establish his confidence and remind him how to stand up for himself. He had let someone encroach on his territory with catastrophic repercussions for his self-esteem and his dignity—not to mention his mental health. The therapist leading today's group was talking about aggressives—people who invaded other people's space to scare them into submission. This was how they dealt with their fears and insecurities. They violated others' rights by putting them down, seeking out the one vulnerable spot in their armoury and exposing it. Before others did the same thing to them. And that was the point, they thought everyone was out to get them, so they'd always shoot first. As Sarah, the therapist, went into more detail about the type of character that would qualify for this description, James felt himself getting hotter and hotter. Aggressives were fundamentally yobs—control freaks who flourished in environments that encouraged struggle, competition and hostility. Thugs who thrived on inducing fear in their subordinates. Loud bells were ringing in James's ears. Aggressive types tended to be paranoid because their behaviour creates enemies. They'd always be watching their backs, unable to trust or be trusted by others. The clanging in James's ears was getting louder and louder. Why were they like this? Normally, it was because they were jealous of others more popular or capable who showed up their inadequacies. That's why they always blamed others for their own cock-ups.

James recognised this for what it was: a character analysis of Sir Vince Spacey. When he first met the new chairman, it was in James's office—the takeover was at an embryonic stage and the appointment was still under wraps. As Spacey walked into James's glass-walled office, James was immediately struck by the arrogant, larger-than-life figure who dominated his surroundings. Dressed in a shiny dark blue suit which ill-fitted his bulky, awkward figure, he reeked of nauseatingly sweet aftershave. His penetrating eyes, topped and tailed by flabby lids, stared straight at James through the gold-rimmed lenses. His wispy grey hair was a little long for his age, reaching just below the nape of his neck, and his moustache made him look cocky, slightly jaunty. His double chins wobbled as he spoke. Sir Vince was at least six-foot-four—about six inches taller than James— and he bent over him to accentuate the difference. James welcomed him warmly and attempted to shake his hand. Spacey gripped James's hand tightly with his fist and before he could say, 'Please, come in,' Sir Vince strutted over to the desk and made himself comfortable in a large red armchair. He crossed his legs, opened his jacket button and leaned back, his arms resting on the sides, revealing diamond cuff links shaped like miniature tennis rackets. It was quite clear who was running the show. James opened his mouth to speak but his new boss was there first.

'So, here we are,' said Sir Vince in his trademark Birmingham twang. Rubbing his hands together and clearing his throat loudly, he asked, 'Whattya got for me, then?'

James looked at Sir Vince, puzzled. 'Er...sorry?'

'WIP, mate,' Sir Vince replied condescendingly, fiddling with his tie. 'Need to take a butchers.'

'Oh, right,' said James, nodding. 'Yes, of course. Chloe can print out the Work-in-Progress list for you and we can go through it.'

'Great,' said Sir Vince, barely smiling. His features were menacing and he knew it. He seemed to get a kick out of the fact that his looks scared people and that he carried around with him a real aura of fear. 'Need to make sure it's all OK, you know?'

'If you'd like to work on some of the projects with…'

'I'll be the judge of that,' interrupted Spacey. His tone was intimidating and impatient. He continued to stare at James in the eye while pointing a chubby finger at him. His grin had turned into a sneer. 'And, I'll want daily updates so I know what's going on. Can't afford any fuck-ups…'

It was James's turn to interject this time. 'Sir Vince, my team will be delighted to let you have any information you need. But, as I am sure you will understand, it would greatly undermine their confidence if they felt they lacked your trust, or weren't able to do their jobs to the best of their very considerable abilities. They're an impressive bunch and…'

Spacey, who didn't know the meaning of the word 'patience' had had enough. 'James,' he said, getting up and walking over to his chair, then leaning over him, 'you're an intelligent man so I'm not going to pussyfoot around. If you don't cooperate with me and give me what I want, you'll be a lot stupider than I've given you credit for. You've got to be kidding if you think I'm going to let a load of fucking cowboys run my business into the ground.' Raising himself up to his full height and walking towards the door, he turned round and pointed his fat index finger at James. 'Just a friendly warning, James. All those things you read about me in the papers? They're true.' Opening the doors with his back to James, he gave him a wave, saying, 'Have those spreadsheets on my desk by close of play.'

That night James had a huge row with his wife. They hadn't argued in months but he was in a foul mood. He didn't feel like talking to the children either and when Amber kept going on about her tennis lesson, he got very irritable and told her to leave him be. Although neither he nor Helen realised it, their lives were about to be torn apart by the antics of a psychopathic bully who would stop at nothing to gain control. And if he made people miserable, wrecked marriages, broke up families and made them ill in the process—that was a bonus. As Lynette would have said, had she known, Vince Spacey should have been admitted to the Cloisters—not James. Yet it was Spacey who was responsible for sending him there.

For the next six months James's life was a living hell full of incidents like the first that left him belittled and demeaned, and in a constant state of panic. Sir Vince would bellow and pick away, criticising him for the way he dealt with clients. With his hands in his pockets and his jacket off, he'd pace up and down his office berating him for being too soft. James was a well-liked, personable chap who got on with all his clients, but Spacey's taunts and disparaging rebukes were making him lose his confidence. The chairman would undermine him in the presence of his team, ignore his advice and exclude him from major deals on which James had been working for ages. Despite any evidence for it, Sir Vince raised doubts in James's mind about his competency and his performance. And all this was hurled at James in electric blue vocabulary, with the volume turned up to maximum. Spacey would give James ridiculous goals and targets that couldn't be met. He'd change them halfway through or push deadlines forward unrealistically without any notice. James was overburdened with work, yet his authority had been taken away. When he came up with ideas, they'd be laughed at. The next thing he knew, they'd be presented to the client as one of the chairman's brainwaves. Refusing to make direct communication, Spacey got Brenda, his PA, to send James emails, leave post-it notes on his desk setting him menial tasks. The Head of European Corporate Finance was commanded to report direct to the chairman's PA on a regular basis. Sometimes she'd even stand over him looking at her watch, timing how long it took him to complete a particular task, not leaving until he'd finished.

When he was at home—which became increasingly rare because of the longer hours he was forced to work—he and Helen would be pestered by call after call, instructing James to have something on the chairman's desk the following morning. This naturally put intolerable stress on the marriage. James was tense all the time, repeatedly ill and constantly tired from having difficulty sleeping. And so it went on. James never thought of going to Human Resources and never considered resigning. James loved his job and he was bloody good at it. He liked his clients and he was devoted to his team who respected him. It was not the job that was the problem, just the thug who'd come crawling out of the woodwork, making his life unbearable. He didn't see why should he allow himself to be pushed out. Anyway, he knew what people would say. They'd accuse him of being weak.

After all, that's what James would have said to anyone in the same boat had he not known the inside story. Get a life. If you're working in a highly competitive, pressurised environment like corporate finance, the management style's gonna be tough, isn't it? Stands to reason—it's the nature of the industry. Anyway, you know what they say, if you can't stand the heat... . Be a man, for fucksake, and take it. If you can't there's plenty who will for that kind of money.

The problem was that, while everyone outside the organisation knew Spacey was a hard taskmaster, not everyone knew what a sadistic bastard he was to work for— just the sad sods who'd been put through the mill and didn't dare spill the beans. Those inside the bank who observed what was going on kept quiet. Like James, most of them had a wife, children and a socking-great mortgage. They didn't want to become a target. Fear is a powerful thing and—being the king of thugs—Spacey lived off it.

If James hadn't experienced this kind of behaviour himself, he'd never have believed it possible. He'd never seen or heard of anything like this before and he didn't know anyone who had. The thought that this might be bullying never occurred to him. Bullying was something that went on in schools. It had certainly gone on at his. At the end of the day, though, he couldn't go to HR. They'd never take his side against the chairman. They'd probably make him redundant for being a trouble-maker, and then how would he get another job? He could just imagine telling the headhunters he'd left because he'd been put under unbearable stress by the chairman of Gussington International. They'd laugh and tell him to bugger off. As for suing the bank for bullying and depression—a concept which never even came into his mind—his City chums would have told him that was another no-no. After a harrowing, drawn-out court case full of personal attacks, he'd be told he was off his rocker. Bottom line, his career would be up the swanny because of the stigma. James knew only too well the predicament he was in and that, in reality, it's easier for an ex-con to get a job than it is for someone with a breakdown on their employment record—even when it's the employer's fault. How crazy it all was, he thought. You get screwed by your boss, end up sick, too sick to work, too sick to live, then you lose your job and can't get another one because of the fucking label that's stuck on your forehead. When, all the time, it's your boss who should have a health warning brandished across his skull in big capital letters. Fortunately for Spacey and the bank, James was way too ill to get litigious—or even think about it—so, for the time being at least, they were safe.

After six months of being treated like a football, James was severely, profoundly traumatised—though he didn't know at the time he was suffering from depression or that he'd been bullied. He was in no state to reason things out. He couldn't concentrate for long and his ability to think straight was behind him—a long way behind him. He was making mistakes and his self-confidence was all but destroyed. His stomach was being gnawed away by nerves so much he was worried he was haemorrhaging inside. He wasn't sleeping, he'd lost his appetite and he was having panic attacks. Anxiety and fatigue dogged him twenty-four/seven and he became withdrawn. He was dressing without care and looked worn and torn. It was only a matter of time before he completely succumbed to meltdown. Just one more push—that was all it would take. And it came one afternoon following a client strategy meeting at Gussington International attended by James, the chairman and two members of his team.

The client was a German telecoms group that had set

its sights on an Italian target. James's team had given an impressive presentation which was well received by the client, though there was one aspect they didn't like. Sir Vince had slipped in a controversial clause in the interests of the bank without warning James or his team before the meeting. In James's book it was unethical, though he didn't say so. He was as diplomatic as possible and didn't make Sir Vince look stupid, but he couldn't let it pass. That old familiar blob of anxiety was beginning to form in his stomach and he felt very frightened. With great difficulty and in a halting, stammering voice, he articulated his concerns. Sir Vince stared at him furiously and bit his gum. He was mouthing silently to James, 'Just you wait.' James found it difficult to concentrate after that—he was exhausted and drained. He felt a panic attack coming on and prayed for the meeting to end.

Half an hour after the close of the meeting Chloe got a call from Brenda summoning James to the chairman's office. James knew what was coming and he was trembling. His shoulders were hunched, his body tightened, and his stomach churning. A wave of panic shot through him. His breathing quickened and his heart pounded away as he knocked nervously and walked in. There was Spacey sitting at his oak desk in an enormous gold recliner, his big feet propped up on a velvet footrest, on top of a thick gold carpet. The huge desk was littered with papers, evidence of Spacey's obsession with control—his need to have his finger on the pulse of everything that was going on. Photographs of Sir Vince with the great and the good cluttered up every inch of available wall. There were several pictures of Spacey with the Prime Minister. Even one of him shaking Nelson Mandela's hand. There were photos of the chairman posing with a number of tennis champions at his Oxfordshire home. The floor-to-ceiling bookcases were crowded with trophies celebrating deals the ex-chairman of Chaplins Bank had pulled off. James closed the door behind him, his heart quaking as it clicked shut. Then, the fireworks began. The chairman slammed his fists on the table, got up and started calling James every name he could think of, then proceeded to throw things at him.

'You fucking bastard. You fucked me over back there. You show me up like that again and I'll fucking have you.'

Sir Vince strode up to James who was pinned against the door. His feet were rooted to the spot. He had no strength left either to fight the monster or to run away. There was no escape. Waves of nausea ran through him. He felt like he was having heart tremors. Spacey leant over him, playing his usual trick of intimidating James with his height. He whispered in James's ear, 'I mean it, Maraschino. You think you're such a hotshot, don't you? Well, I'm telling you, mate, you're nothing. You're nothing but a snivelling idiot.'

James was paralysed with fear. He felt as if his body was made of tissue paper, not flesh. His rubbery legs collapsed beneath him and he fell to the floor in a heap. He sat there shaking and sobbing with his arms in front of his face shielding him from further attacks. Then he started whimpering like a frightened child: 'Leave me alone, leave me alone. For Christ sake, leave me alone.'

But Spacey wouldn't oblige. 'You're fucking burned, Maraschino. You're just not up to it, are you, mate? You fucking wanker. Get out of my sight.'

James eyed up his meal. Dr Chaudhry had told him to eat, but he wasn't hungry. Why on earth had he picked toad-in-the-hole? The smell of greasy sausages and batter was really getting up his nose and making him queasy. He didn't remember making a conscious decision to eat it, but—thanks to the ECT—his memory wasn't good. He had managed to find a table with no one else on it—he wasn't up to chatting—so he could be by himself. And then something made him look up. His face had become hot—he could feel someone's eyes on him. He glanced up furtively, cupping his stubbly chin with his right hand in an effort not to draw attention to himself.

It was a woman. She was talking to two other girls who sat opposite each other. The one with her back to James was wearing a white baseball cap. The second one was heavily built with bright eyes and rosy cheeks. She sat to the right of the girl who'd been looking at him. So, why *had* this girl been watching him? Did she think he looked like a loser, a bit of a weirdo? He studied her briefly. She wore a white T-shirt with a sweetheart neckline, and had auburney-gold, shoulder-length hair. Her large eyes were hazel and her olive skin made her look a bit continental. Italian, maybe. Pretty. Occasionally, she'd flick her hair back away from her face as she chatted. James thought he'd seen her before, but he didn't know where. His memory was all to pot. James dropped his head back down and carried on playing with his food.

Kalpana was irritated. The pieces didn't fit and she was making a lot of noise about it. James sighed heavily but kept his head down. All he wanted to do was carry on with his jigsaw puzzle in silence, but it was impossible to concentrate with the racket Kalpana was making. Tilly walked over to her and asked her what the matter was. 'These bloody pieces, they don't fit. Look, I'll show you.' Kalpana tried inserting a piece in several different places without thinking about where it was likely to go, slamming it down so brutally, she didn't give herself a chance to find the right niche. James was getting increasingly agitated. His mouth curled down at the sides and his breathing became more rapid. Kalpana was behaving aggressively, violently even, and it unnerved him—it made him tense. The lines on his brow stiffened and he felt nauseous. His hands were shaking, making it difficult to carry on with the jigsaw.

'Right, that's it,' Kalpana announced, slamming her fist on the half-finished picture of Van Gogh's *Sunflowers*. She hurled the pieces back into the box as quickly as she could, but the lid wouldn't shut, and she started swearing. She removed the cover and shook the box, but that didn't work either. She smashed the lid back down. Tilly tried to pacify Kalpana but she wouldn't be calmed down. She raised the box above her head and shook it vigorously. She lifted the lid up and peered inside to see if she could identify the guilty pieces causing the bumps. When that didn't solve the problem, she threw the whole thing up in the air and walked out.

James staggered over to the darkest corner of the Art Room and slumped down onto the floor. Shielding his arms and his head with his arms, he started shaking like a terrified rabbit. Tilly went over to him and hugged him.

Helen had decided to bring the children in to see James. She'd told them he was ill and had to stay in hospital. When they asked her what was wrong with Daddy, she said he'd been working much too hard at the bank and was very, very tired. They seemed to accept that explanation, though they didn't really understand why he couldn't be tired at home. She explained he needed complete rest and that the best place to get that was in the hospital. James found the visit exhausting. The children were lively and talkative and he wasn't up to it. The visit was cut short. They had a row. Helen had every right to feel exasperated, tense, exhausted. Given everything she'd been through, she was a good candidate for the Cloisters herself. Dr Chaudhry had said as much at their last meeting and advised her to consult her GP. It would undoubtedly do her good to have a rest. With what she had to contend with, nobody could blame her. But what about the kids and the house? Someone had to mind the shop, hold everything together. Dr Chaudhry was convinced she was heading for her own breakdown. She was exactly the kind of person who was vulnerable. Responsible, strong and ultra-sensitive, the row had been about fear—her fear of losing him. James had withdrawn from her through no fault of hers or his. It was work that had done the damage. That bastard Spacey and his bullying. But whoever's fault it was, she took it personally. It made her feel like shit and it hurt like nothing she had ever known. She went in to see him one afternoon before collecting the children from school. 'How are you feeling, darling?' she asked him. What she was really asking him—though she couldn't articulate it—was 'Are you going to come back to me? Ever? I need to know. I don't want to live without you.' She felt like she was pushing him, but she couldn't help it, she had to know. She knew she should have let him be, but she just couldn't.

'OK,' he replied, keeping his head down as usual. Sensing what she really wanted to know, he added, 'Just need some time to myself for a while.' Yes, he knew what she was asking him, though she couldn't say it, but he couldn't give her an answer. At least, not the one she needed to hear.

Helen tensed up. Her stomach was churning and her heart was pounding away. 'Are you going to come back to me? To us?' she asked pitifully.

He sat there twitching, checking his watch face. He couldn't or wouldn't look at her. Although he knew exactly what she was driving at, he said, 'What d'you mean?'

'James, for God's sake,' she continued, the tears streaming down her face. This was the point of no return. She stood up and everything that had been piling up inside her came tumbling out. And, as soon as she heard the words fall out of her mouth, she knew she had gone too far.

'I feel...I feel like I'm married to...to...oh, I don't know...God, I know it's not your fault, James, but this is hard for me too. I feel like I'm losing you...like I've lost you forever. I can't bear it, James, I can't. I've had to be strong but if, at the end of it all, I'm going to lose you, because of that bastard at your office...for God's sake, James, why don't we sue him? The bank? I've been talking to some of our friends...they think we could sue them... . We shouldn't let them get away with this, James. We can't let them ruin our marriage, for God's sake. James, there's the children…James, please.'

James had clamped his hands over his ears. He couldn't take it any more. Her outburst had been childish and hysterical, she knew that, but she was desperate. Whatever it took to get him back from this deep, dark place he had retreated into, she would try. She sniffed, rubbed her eyes and kissed him softly on the cheek. He didn't recoil but he didn't say anything either. He took his hands away from his ears and adjusted his watch face.

Helen flicked her hair behind her ears, rubbed her eyes and sighed. She whispered, 'Goodbye,' and left, tears running down her face.

James needed some air. He went out into the garden and crouched down against the wall. He fumbled in his trouser pocket for his Benson and Hedges and took one out. His hands were trembling as he placed a cigarette in his mouth, found his lighter in the other pocket and lit up. Funny, he thought, he'd never smoked before. He used to think it was a disgusting habit, but over the past months it had become something of a comfort. If such a thing were possible. It was something to focus on, something to give his hands to do to instead of shaking. He could see Helen's car just before it disappeared from the end of the drive. He hated himself for what he was putting her through. The way he was making her feel had to be his fault—he saw no other explanation. But he couldn't help it. He just couldn't and that made him feel worse. He was a helpless, useless, pointless heap of shit. No good as husband. No good as a father. No good as a man in a suit in an office looking after his family like he ought to be doing. Was he ever going to snap out of it? The idea of returning to the old world, to his marriage, to his family, and his job was beyond him.

James looked up at the sky. The sun had popped out of nowhere. It had been dark and grey and cloudy—yet, suddenly, he felt its warmth spreading over him like a blanket. Calming him a little. Then he saw her. The auburny-gold girl from the dining room was walking past in a pink T-shirt and jeans. He heard her sigh as she overtook him, heading straight for the lawns ahead. As she walked her hands played with something. An iPod. She placed the plugs in her ears and switched it on. When she got to the grass, she lay down on her back and looked straight up at the sun. She had a spiral notebook with her that she placed on the grass.

James studied her. He now realised he'd not only seen her in the dining room, but also in some of the classes. There was that one, he remembered, where Susan, the Irish girl, had broken down. It wasn't that he fancied this girl— he wasn't capable of fancying anyone at the moment. At least, he wasn't capable of doing anything about it—following it through. There was just something about her. Which was stupid, really. He'd never even exchanged one word with her. Before he knew what he was doing, James had stood up, stubbed out his cigarette and walked over to where she lay. He knelt down and sat cross-legged next to the notebook, then started playing with the grass. The girl had obviously sensed him. She sat up and, taking the plugs out of her ears, said, 'Hi.' She seemed to know who he was. That didn't really surprise him. Everybody seemed to know who he was. For all he knew he probably got pointed out to visitors as the hospital's resident freak. He liked her voice. There was something soothing about it. It didn't ask anything of him. It didn't have any expectations of him. It didn't confront him or try to push him. It made relaxing listening as he played with the grass between his fingers. They had some crazy conversation about four-leaf clovers, of all things. Where had that come from? Then he remembered as a child going on long walks in the country with his mother. They used to look for butterflies and birds' eggs. Since he felt like a helpless child, it seemed appropriate to be reverting to childish things. She made him laugh too. God, when was the last time he'd done that? He had to ask her name. Marianne. Mar…i…anne. He liked it. She'd let him listen to some music on her iPod. James Taylor. Christ, he hadn't heard that song for years. It felt good—just for a few moments, anyway. In the end he just sat there quietly with her. It felt OK. There didn't seem any need to talk and it felt OK. Really OK. No awkwardness, no unanswered questions hovering in the air. Just peace and quiet. For however long it would last. Their eyes had met. Once. For about three seconds. It felt like a long time. He'd wanted to look at her but he'd been too scared. What of, though? Of her judging him? Of her thinking he was useless? He wasn't sure. He may have been wrong but he didn't think he saw anything like that in her eyes. But he wasn't going to risk it. He looked away quickly. Why should she be any different from the rest?

It's James's first time at Drama Therapy. He doesn't know what to expect but he's not looking forward to it. It's in the Stables and, as usual, everyone starts off sitting in a circle on brightly coloured cushions. Sarah's taking the group which is good news. James likes Sarah. She listens to him and she never judges him or tells him to snap out of it. James is feeling a tiny bit better. He can look up occasionally. He scans round the room. Everyone of these poor sods looks stoned, like their souls are dead. There's Susan with her head so far down it almost reaches her chest, her hair hanging down over it in limp, oily strands. James empathises with her. Like him, she seems beyond help, plunged deep into some dark cavern of despair which no one can access and from which there is no way out. He continues going round the circle of shadowy figures with numb faces, lost in some other world. Sarah asks the class to stand and hold hands. Then she gives them different things to do. They move round the Stables pretending to be a giraffe or an octopus. When they meet someone they greet them with a smile. Sometimes, there's music. When it stops, patients clap, stamp their feet or crouch down. Zombiefied bodies waltz round unable to keep time with the music. It's too much to expect them to do otherwise. James doesn't know what it's all in aid of but, in a weird kind of way, it feels sort of OK. Kind of liberating. It makes them all let go. A little.

And—right out of nowhere—it's given James an idea.

Typus melancholicus.
Melan being the Greek for black,
chole meaning bile

James wished he could read Ancient Greek but, since he couldn't, he'd have to make do with this translation of Hippocrates. He looked through the hefty volume on his lap. It was taking him a long time to get through it—his ability to concentrate was limited—but he was fascinated. Helen had also got him a copy of Robert Burton's *Anatomy of Melancholy* and he was trying to read it at the same time. Basically, the Greeks believed that melancholy—which they defined as excessive fear and sadness—was made up of a surfeit of black bile in the body. Hippocrates, one of the world's first doctors, thought you got rid of the black stuff by bleeding the patient in order to release it. You'd probably kill the poor bugger, but at least you'd get rid of the bile and there'd be no more melancholy. During the Middle Ages, Catholics believed that an excess of black bile in the bloodstream signified demonic possession and could lead to acedia—one of the Seven Deadly Sins. Nowadays we'd call it Sloth but it's better described as a kind of spiritual apathy. Bottom line was if you were depressed, you were one of Satan's slaves and way beyond redemption. Through time, melancholy metamorphosed into depression, with treatment moving on from purging to Prozac. James was only at the beginning but he was determined to get to grips with the whole story. He wanted to know more about his illness. Where it came from. Why so many people suffered from it. How it could be treated successfully. Why sufferers had been stigmatised and mistreated throughout history. At the Cloisters he'd seen so many lost souls in agonising pain and he wanted to do something to help. He just wasn't sure what or how.

James looks at Dr Chaudhry, not able to believe what he's being told. For the first time in days, no, months, he feels some kind of peace.

'Could…could you please repeat that, Dr Chaudhry? Please?'

'It is impossible for you ever to go back to your current employer,' Dr Chaudhry reiterated. His palms are raised to just below his chin and he blinks through his silver-rimmed glasses. 'To do so,' he continues, 'would only jeopardise your return to full health. As your psychiatrist, I cannot allow that to happen.'

James still can't believe it. He's breathing rapidly and his heart is pounding. 'You mean never? Really, never?'

'Never, James,' says Dr Chaudhry, leaning back in his chair, moving his spectacles up and down. 'I realise this presents a problem with regard to your employment, but I am acting in the best interests of your mental health, which I have to put first. The problem of finding alternative work is not something you are fit to address now, either. You are not up to it. The matter will have to wait until you are well enough. Now is not a good time for you to make any important, far-reaching decisions. I have to tell you, James, that you may never be fit for work—well, not the kind of work you've been doing in the City. The effects of what you have undergone may last a long, long time. At present, however, you are obviously still employed and I will need to write to the company doctor with an update. They have been pressing me for one. Once I tell them you are not fit to return to work, both in the short-term and the long-term, they will make a decision as to your future, though I doubt they will do this in a hurry without taking legal advice. You may wish to speak to a lawyer, but you are still very fragile and I do not want you placed under additional stress. Perhaps if you discuss this with your wife, a good friend or relative could help take the responsibility and stress away from both of you.'

But James wasn't really listening. All he could think about was the fact he would never have to face that bastard again. He would never, ever have to set foot within a mile of the place where he had been reduced to humiliation and desperation. To hell with Gussington. Let them sack him, let them make him redundant. He didn't care. He just wanted to be free of them—and he was. At last. He walked out on to the lawns. He needed to speak to Helen, tell her what was happening. He couldn't think properly, though he knew this would mean changes. There'd be no salary—though there was bound to be a package of some kind. Maybe they'd have to sell the house. The children might have to be taken out of school. Just thinking about it made him feel tired. Exhausted. But still relieved.

Marianne was in her usual spot lying on the grass, so he went to tell her the news. After about an hour it began to get a bit chilly, so they carried on the conversation…in bed.

'What on earth d'you mean, James?' shouted Helen down the phone. 'We have to sue them. Or, at least, threaten them. They've landed you…us in this hole. We have to. Otherwise, what are we going to do about money? Think of the children. If you don't give a fuck for me, what about them?'

'Helen, I'm tired.'

'You're always tired. Too tired to care about what's going on with me, with the children. Since you got ill, since you've been at the Cloisters, you just don't seem to give a shit for your family. How are we going to live? I can't go out to work, can I, not with the children? We've got three of them, in case you'd forgotten.'

Silence.

'James, James, are you there? James? Listen, I've been to see an employment lawyer. They say she's the best. Jo Kerman, that's her name. Anyway, she reckons we can get a really good settlement if we sue the bank for negligence. For failing to stop you being harassed by that bullying psychopath and landing you with a psychiatric illness. And if you've been declared unfit for work, then they'd have to compensate you for that. You're only forty-five, for God's sake—that's twenty years they'd have to pay you. You'd never have to work again…we'd never have to worry. The children…'

'James, are you there?'

But the line had gone dead. James had switched off his mobile.

James and Marianne lay side by side in bed looking up at the ceiling. He stroked the inside of her thigh while she placed her hand on his knee and proceeded to run her finger up his leg. She sighed, then rolled on to her side with her back to him. He moved up closer until she could feel his chest in line with her back and his legs in line with hers. He put his arm round her waist and began caressing her right breast, then her nipple. His penis slipped inside her buttocks. After about a minute, he climbed over the top of her till his body was on the other side and his eyes were staring into hers.

'What?' she asked, smiling.

'I want to look at your eyes.'

Marianne laughed. 'That's nice.'

Marianne's auburny-gold hair lay sprawled across her face. James pushed it back softly and started to stroke her head. She looked like a little girl. Childlike, helpless, vulnerable. He felt so tender towards her, not wanting to let her out of his sight for a moment.

'I'm sorry,' he whispered, kissing her ear.

'What for?' she whispered back, opening her eyes.

'You know. For just now, not being able to…you know?'

'Ssh, James, it's OK.' She kissed his eyelid, and then said, 'There's no rush. Just feeling your warmth next to me…that's enough for me right now. I used to be so hung-up about the future. But now…I don't know, I'm trying to enjoy the moment.'

James's finger ran up and down her arm, then he took her small hand in his, studying each one of her fingers in turn. Noticing cracks and cuts on the front of her thumb and her index finger, he asked her what these were.

'Eczema. I was born with it. It just doesn't seem to go away. It was much worse when I was a child, though. At school I'd be teased mercilessly. No one would hold my hand—they laughed at me and said I was infectious.'

James began to caress her hand, taking care to kiss every crack and cut he could find.

'Hold me, James.'

James moved up closer and put his arm round her. He

kissed her on the lips, a long, passionate kiss, his tongue devouring her mouth deep and hard.

Afterwards, she said: 'James, d'you mind me asking what you're going to do? About the bank, I mean.'

James opened his eyes and rubbed his top lip. He looked nervous. 'I…er…I don't know. It's all so shitty, the whole thing. Having to face it all.'

'I know,' said Marianne. 'I don't think I'd be able to deal with all that. It's enough to…to put you in the Cloisters.'

And they laughed nervously.

Marianne went on. 'There's a time limit, isn't there?'

'What d'you mean?'

'Don't you have to present your case to the Tribunal within a fixed period?'

'How come you're so clue…?'

'Oh,' interrupted Marianne, 'a friend of mine had a problem at work. Nothing as bad as yours, but she was being bullied too. By a colleague. Anyway, it's a lot for you to take on while you've got all this shit here to deal with. So,' she said, kissing him, 'if I can help at all…I don't know…do some research or something, you only have to ask.'

James kissed her on the lips again and said, 'Thank you, Marianne. You're so lovely.'

'You see, I understand where Helen's coming from. She's worried about the kids and what's going to happen in the future. And I s'pose I agree with her there's no way that bastard should be able to get away with what he's done to you. I hope you don't mind my saying that. Maybe I spoke out of turn.'

James was looking a bit agitated. Not only was the

207

thought of suing the bank terrifying, Marianne had mentioned Helen and reminded him that was really where he belonged. Not with her. Marianne spoke sense and he knew it. She was fair-minded and appreciated Helen's point of view. He knew it must hurt that she was in bed with a man who belonged to someone else.

Holding her face in his hands, he said, 'Marianne, look, I need to say something. I will always love Helen. She's been such a wonderful partner, wife, mother…but it's too late for us. What I've been through the past few months… I can't go back. I just can't. My children will always be my children and I adore them. I'll always want to be with them. Look, I don't know what's going to happen in the future. I don't know if I'm capable of ever being a father, a husband, a breadwinner again. I've cocked all of that up. I've lost my confidence in my ability to do even the simplest of things. I've hardly got anything to offer myself, let alone another member of the human race. But,' he continued, drinking in her tearful hazel eyes, 'I think I'm falling in love with you, Marianne. I mean, I…I have fallen in love with you.'

James hardly dared look at Marianne.

'D'you mean that, James?'

James wiped a tear from her face and they kissed. 'Just look at us. Enough panic attacks to start a nationwide epidemic, the last thing we need is a relationship. So frightened and insecure, we're like children.'

'Oooh er, what would Dr Chaudhry say?' laughed Marianne. 'I love you in spite of all that, James. I can't help it.'

James grimaced as he read. Bleeding people was one thing, but boring holes into their skulls in order to serve an eviction notice on the Devil was a bit much. Known as *trepanning*, it was used in ancient cultures that believed supernatural forces could get hold of a man and make him mad. The idea of mental illness being caused by evil spirits lasted for a long time—mental disease was tied up with satanic worship and regarded as a sin. It wasn't till you got to Burton and his *Anatomy of Melancholy* that you got anywhere near the idea that emotions like fear could be a possible trigger for depression. But how were the mentally ill treated back then—when they weren't being bled or drilled into? James turned the page. Mental hospitals originated back in the late Middle Ages when they provided a refuse tip for those who could not or would not conform to the conventions of the day. Inmates were paraded before the public like zoo animals. Restrained by chains, kept in dirty, dank, rat-infested cells like prisoners—which, of course, they were—the poor sods had a miserable existence. It wasn't until the eighteenth century that these disgraceful asylums began to be reformed. Although not much was being done to advance people's understanding of the illness and its roots, in certain camps things like fear, sadness, guilt and a genetic disposition to depression were mooted as possible causes. It was the mid-nineteenth century before people began to believe that depression and mental illness originated in the brain. And then along came Freud and Jung. Just as James was about to get his teeth into the fathers of modern psychiatry, his mobile went.

'James, hi.' It was Jo Kerman, his lawyer.

'Hi.'

'I just wanted to let you know that I'll be with you by two tomorrow so we can go through everything. Will you be OK if we do an hour? Have you told your consultant?'

'Yeah, yeah, that's fine.'

'Look, James, if you get tired we can call it a day. And once I get a full account of what happened from you, I won't need to bother you again. Helen and I can handle things from then on.'

'Yeah.'

'James, I won't pretend it's going to be easy, any of this. But, as both you and Helen know, you've got a really strong case. And excellent witnesses. Chloe, some of your team. And we've discussed your chances of getting another job in the City after the case. At the same level, salary scale, that sort of thing. It will be very difficult. That's why we've put such a high figure on the claim. If it all works out, as I believe it will, you will never have to work again.'

'Actually,' said James, 'I do want to work again.'

'But James, we've talked about this. Your employer must be made to realise you will never be fit to work, so he can compensate you accordingly.'

'No,' interrupted James,' I mean…look, I want to help other poor buggers like me. I want to train to become a counsellor.'

'You think I'm bonkers, don't you?'

James was sitting in Dr Chaudhry's office in his usual seat. He didn't look as tiny in it as he used to. He'd put on weight and filled out a bit.

Dr Chaudhry raised his palms to his chin and remained silent for a few seconds. He pursed his lips and looked at James thoughtfully. 'I think your wanting to train as a psychotherapist an excellent idea. Your experience and your temperament make you well qualified for the role. That's not what concerns me. You have decided to sue your employer and I cannot overestimate how hard that is going to be for you. You have made progress here. The electroconvulsive treatments have had a positive impression, as have the psychological counselling and group therapy. But this case is going to be brutal. The stress it will place on you may become intolerable—it may make you vulnerable to another breakdown. Vivid memories of your experiences will be re-triggered and the combined impact may be devastating. That is what worries me. They are not going to let you walk away with their money without a fight, even if right is on your side. The whole thing is likely to get extremely bloody. As your psychiatrist, I do not think it is in your best interests.'

'I know, I know,' said James, rubbing his neck. 'I've agonised over it but I've talked it over with Marianne.... There's a time problem. You see...'

'Marianne? Marianne Evans?' asked Dr Chaudhry, looking at James quizzically.

'Yeah. Yeah, I'm...I'm. Yeah, I'm seeing her. Kind of.' James read the concerned look that appeared in his consultant's eyes. Raising his hands, he said, 'I know, I know, I'm taking on too much. But, it just happened. We're not doing anything rash. We're not rushing into anything. I'm trying to do one thing at a time. She...she understands me. What I'm going through.'

Dr Chaudhry listened to James without interrupting him, whilst studying carefully what his patient was saying.

'Look, I don't know what's going to happen. Yeah, it's messy, but it feels right. You know? It feels like *me*. That's what you've been teaching me, isn't it? To be myself, do what makes me happy? As far as the case is concerned, I'm doing it for Helen and the children. If anything happens, if I don't go back to her, I want her to have enough, more than enough, to have a good life. Without me. If that's what it comes down to. She's been brilliant and I still love her but…I've changed. I don't recognise myself. Since all this shit happened, since I've been here. It's made me re-question what I want out of life. I'm just going with what feels right. That's all I can do.'

Edna had invited James to tea. She liked James a lot and often asked him to visit her. While he sat in one of her green velvet chairs, holding a delicate china teacup in his hand, he was thinking about what Dr Chaudhry had said. He knew he was taking on too much. Helen's two solicitor brothers might be handling the case—he didn't want his wife shouldering the responsibility—but he knew it could last a long time, and he was bound to be dragged into it from time to time. If Gussington didn't settle out of court, and things went as far as the tribunal (God forbid), he would have to give evidence. How would he survive that? There was no guarantee of a win, though the barrister had reiterated Jo's belief that the case was practically watertight, and that the bank would be bound to settle out of court—though they'd probably do so on the steps of the court-house at the eleventh hour. James tried to put it out of his mind.

Edna had invited Helen and the children too. But Helen declined, so it was just James, Amber, Sadie and Freddie. He was seeing a lot of his kids now and enjoyed listening to their stories about school and their friends. It made him feel half-human again, that he wasn't a complete failure as a dad. It was helping him to become reconnected to the family he thought he'd lost. He still got panic attacks and his dreams continued to feature the horrific events that had landed him in hospital. The difference was when he woke up sweating, he'd tell himself he might be able to have some influence on the ending. The final outcome. Perhaps it was more true to say he couldn't control the outcome, but he could control his response to it. But what was he going to do about Marianne?

When he first came to the Cloisters his life became amazingly simple. Literally overnight he had submitted to those who were stronger than him—Helen and the clinic—relinquishing control of every facet of his life. Suddenly, he was robbed of all his responsibilities and the need to make any decisions. But now things were beginning to get complicated. How, he wondered, was it possible to love two women at the same time? He felt he was being dishonest to both. He knew he could never go back to his wife. Not in the way she wanted or needed. Helen had been with him for over a decade of his life. She had loved him, stood by him through all the shit and given him three perfect children. He couldn't tell her about Marianne. Not yet. The thought of hurting her crucified him. And he'd hurt her so much already. The way he saw it, everybody was going to end up a loser. That was a given. But that, as he had learned, was part of life. Loss and pain. It was how you dealt with it that counted. That made the difference. He also felt guilty towards Marianne. He couldn't offer her anything more permanent, more sure than the fact that he loved her. As far as the future was concerned. But the thought of having to let her go troubled him much more than the thought of losing his wife. Marianne never pressed him. She did nothing to make him feel guilty, inadequate. She was just there. Warm, loving and accepting. And that was what he needed. She didn't mind if he lost or won the case, except that to lose it might demolish him. There were no conditions to her love. No asking for anything in return.

James knew that if Gussington dug their heels in, as they most probably would, the dispute could go on for over a year. That was going to be tough on all three of them. He might not be involved in the day-to-day details, the ins and outs, but it was always there in the background—the 'what ifs' niggling away at this brain. What if they wouldn't settle out of court? What if he had to go into the witness box and give evidence? What if, having gone through a protracted and bloody fight, the money wasn't enough? What if there was no money at all? And, worst of all, what if the experience—however it panned out in the end—took him back to square one and he reverted to squatting in dark corners trembling with fear?

Certain things kept him sane. His treatment, discovering yoga and meditation, his kids and Marianne. It all helped him to relax his muscles and his brain, to be more accepting, calmer. He had done all he could and was left to play a waiting game. As he did so, he tried to focus on his choice of new career. He had enrolled on a counselling course the following autumn. It excited and scared him at the same time. Before all the Spacey crap had started he'd been passionate about things. He'd had energy, drive. Now, something of his old self had come back to him. He was on the threshold of a new life. If only...

CAT

Pain is the touchstone of all spiritual progress.
That's what they say in Alcoholics Anonymous.
Bollocks to that—I'm sticking with the drugs

She sits cross-legged on the bed surrounded by tabloids. Dr Chaudhry suggested she give the papers a miss but curiosity—and a stubborn, self-destructive streak—have got the better of her. Curiosity killed the cat and it's certainly doing its best to kill this one. Tears are streaming down her face as her raw, bloodshot eyes scan the evidence. In the photos she's doing what she's always denied doing, with the man she's always denied doing it with. The one who led her into it in the first place, and who has now abandoned her to face the music. Everyone said he'd bugger off as soon as the shit hit the fan. And they were right. She drags deeply on a burnt-down stub held up to her mouth with her thumb and index finger, and blows a cloud of smoke up towards the ceiling. She twitches her nose and rubs her nostrils several times. She's been chain-smoking for over an hour and the ceiling's beginning to show the effects as a yellow-brown patch forms in the centre. Smoking isn't like doing a line, Christ knows, but all that's out of the window now she's in rehab undergoing her first week of detox. Doing without the white stuff's no picnic. The memories of the euphoria she used to experience are alive and kicking. The withdrawal symptoms are killing her and her craving to snort is unbearably strong. Not being able to use makes her feel irritable, exhausted and severely depressed. At night she's so restless she can't sleep. It's ironic because once upon a time people like Freud used to prescribe cocaine to relieve the symptoms of depression.

Coke's the only thing that stops her from feeling worthless—without it there's nothing to come between her and the furious self-loathing that has dogged her for so long. In just a few minutes all the insecurities, the torment and the guilt have withered away, and with them the fear that everyone including her thinks she's a fake. On the downside, it's wreaked its devastation and jeopardised her career on more than one occasion. Arriving late for shoots, she'd turn up wasted, totally out of it. Once she even collapsed in the studio. She fell down the stairs and passed out. She's been living on a diet of alcohol, cigarette and coke for a long time now. It may have kept her thin (a prerequisite for a model) but there's such a thing as being too thin. Even for a model. Those who get to see all six and a half stone of her naked are able to count every bone in her ribcage and her spine. Her arms and legs are nothing short of scrawny. Her eyes are raw and vapid—there are scary things behind them. Her skin's turning greeny-grey and her lips are almost blue. Since she's started the detox she's taken to throwing up a lot. Afterwards she looks in the mirror to find her face and body splattered with vomit, her nose swollen, the ends of her nostrils soiled with mucus, her hair dripping with sweat.

Not being able to snort makes her want to cut, though there's nothing she can do about it at the Cloisters. In some bizarre kind of way, cutting brings relief to the chaotic darkness within her, making her feel real, connected, shocked back into something she needs to feel a part of. To feel warm blood oozing out of her is infinitely preferable to feeling the anguish of her soul going AWOL, never to make a comeback. Cutting seems to stop the tension. It makes her feel more able to endure the overpowering feelings of misery, loneliness and despair that have become squatters inside her brain. Once she cuts, the tension fades away to be replaced by a numbness which goes hand-in-hand with the physical pain. Sometimes weeks—even months—can pass between sessions, or she'll harm herself several times the same day. Cutting makes her believe she still has some control over her life. Over her body. That she isn't dead. The pain of cutting is so much more bearable than the pain inside her head. The empty pain that lies deep inside her. If she forgets about it for a split second, it will force its way back into her brain, expelling any other thoughts that may have temporarily dislodged it.

The last time she cut herself, she'd just found out about Dave and that slag. After the row, waves of anxiety rushed over her, leaving her fragile, helpless, unable to cope. His hostility frightened her, made her feel rejected, unwanted, abandoned. Panic-stricken—she was fearful of something she couldn't explain, and remained convinced that nothing would ever go right for her again. A passionate, almost sensual throbbing had taken over every fibre of her body, making her desperate to cut. As she sat on the bathroom floor just minutes after he left, she felt submerged in an ocean of self-loathing. She just wasn't enough—whatever that was. That's why he had gone off with that tart. It was her fault. She made him do it and it made her want to punish herself. Breathing quickly, almost panting, she took the knife in her hands. Her fingers were shaking, causing the blade to pulse up and down, shining, almost blinding her. Confronting her left wrist, she made the first cut, then another, then another. Smooth, swift motions glided seamlessly over the top of her skin. Sharp, searing pains lay siege to her flesh as she sat watching a pool of blood redden the gleaming white tiles beneath her. She took the bloodied razor in her left hand and began to cut the other wrist. She dug hard, downward incisions into the flesh, deeper than ever before. Submerged in rage, she wanted to slice and slice until there was nothing left of her but strips of blood-soaked Cat lying on the floor.

She examined herself in the bathroom mirror, mesmerised by this surreal image of catwalk queen Cat Green surrounded by flowing, unstoppable blood. Terrified, yet hypnotised by this vision of herself causing harm to herself, she held up her arms, now stinging with pain. The blood was beginning to congeal and she felt increasingly weak and nauseous. The river of crimson velvet beneath her was getting larger and larger. She dipped the index finger of her right hand into the rich liquid and let it wade from side to side. She raised her hand to the lid of the toilet seat and wrote the letters 'DAVE'.

Now, weeks later, Cat sits up in her hospital bed, her arms supporting her. She raises her hands to her face and studies her impeccably manicured nails. Why the fuck does she bother when she has such an obsession with hacking her arms to pieces? What's the point? No one, including her, is going to notice a French manicure when only a few inches away her skin's covered with rows and rows of brown scars which even the make-up can't camouflage.

She discards her umpteenth stub and lights up another one. The fact that you're not allowed to smoke inside the clinic doesn't register with Cat. Inhaling deeply, her stomach feels like it's turning inside out. She's still staring hard at the pictures. Some lowlife—someone from her inner sanctum—is responsible for leaking them to the media, and she has no idea who the toe-rag is. She'll get to the bottom of it, though, and they won't know what's hit them. It's hard to believe that the girl in the photographs and the girl on the bed are one and the same. Cat always insists every shot of her is meticulously cropped and air-brushed. Yet, here she is looking bleary-eyed and hollow-faced as she kneels on the floor, the centre-piece in this cocaine-fuelled orgy, crushing up crack on a toilet seat with a credit card. Her companions hover like vultures, impatient for her to finish so they can get their fix. In another shot she's snorting a joint through a tightly rolled fifty-pound note. In another she's devouring a line straight off the carpet. Others show the effects of her partying as she rocks back on her haunches and laughs uninhibitedly. The white stuff has obviously begun to kick in.

The photos jog her memory and she tries to piece the night together. They had booked a suite at Claridges. She was wearing black velvet hot pants, a low-cut pink top and thigh-high boots with killer heels. Her long blonde hair flowed loose, hanging messily around her shoulders. The evening had started off with shots of vodka and tequila swiftly followed by gargantuan glasses of wine and countless cigarettes. Dave had brought a couple of crackheads with him and Cat was accompanied by her pals Sophie and Nell. Cat and Dave had decided to use the occasion to pilot a song they were collaborating on. Cat was convinced she could make it as a pop singer but her friends didn't look so sure when they heard the results. Her voice was on the high-pitched side and Dave was so stoned nobody could make out the lyrics. In any case, the party—most of whom were so out of it they'd stripped off—had other things on their minds. Some were shooting up grams of cocaine straight off the carpet. Others were applying it to themselves and others as liberally as if it were talcum powder.

It's unlikely that anyone present that night could recall exactly who had sex with whom or how many times. Cat thinks she remembers getting into bed with Dave, then with both Dave and Nell. Or maybe it was Soph, not Nell. What the hell. By that time Cat was so fucked she wasn't sure what was going down. Or was that *up*? She can't recollect anyone taking photographs, though people were definitely fiddling about with mobiles. She does remember going into the bathroom at some point. The coffee table had become overcrowded with empty bottles and cigarette packets, and the soft, deep-pile carpet wasn't the best place to rack up the powder into neat little rows, even on the back of a plastic CD cover. So, she went into the bathroom to do it on the toilet seat lid. Realising the white stuff was still in the bedroom, she went back to get it. When she got there, she found it had all gone, and an order was despatched for more supplies. It's not the kind of thing you can get by dialling room service, so a call was made to one of Dave's friends. Stan the Man turned up flanked by some of the dodgiest individuals Cat had ever seen, out to have a good time at someone else's expense. Cat handed over four thousand pounds in crisp new fifty-pound notes without asking anyone to chip in and without anyone offering, then stashed the wraps in her handbag. Cocaine's got to be one of the costliest ways of killing yourself—she must have forked out about fifty thousand pounds over the past six months.

Night is fast approaching. The blackness of her room is converging with the blackness inside her brain. She stubs out her cigarette and pulls the bed covers over her head. Curled up small and tight like a discarded foetus, she feels utterly alone. Nobody wants to be with Cat Green. Not one of her friends—Nell, Soph, Jade—has offered to help her get out of this shit. Dave has gone off to do a gig. Her mother is furious with her for not giving the bastard the elbow and has left her to her own devices. The fashion houses have all but dropped her and her agency is disgusted with the self-destructive way in which she has behaved, leaving them to pick up the pieces.

Sometimes she feels tough and defiant. Like it's Cat against the whole fucking world. Her jaw hardens, she clenches her fists and she's ready to climb into the ring and take on all comers. The next second she collapses into a heap and feels desperate, unable to cope. Her head's all over the shop. Despite everything he's done to her, she misses Dave. Even though he's refused to go into rehab with her, though she begged and begged, she won't finish with him. If anyone tells her Dave's the reason she's in rehab, or that he's only sticking to her because he's knee-high in debt, she won't listen. Her addiction to him is far more toxic than her addiction to coke. She won't do *anything* that might mean losing him, so if getting clean means she definitely *will* lose him, then she'll just stay dirty. At least, that's how she feels right now.

Cat's crying so hard she can be heard in the corridor. A plump West Indian nurse knocks on the door and sticks her head round. A short, cheery woman dressed in a pink floral skirt and a purple baggy top, she walks up to the bed and tries to comfort Cat. Putting her sagging arm over the lump in the covers, she says:

'You poor love. There, there, I know how you're feeling. It's OK, it's OK.'

Cat doesn't want anyone's pity. She lashes out with her arm and kicks the duvet with her foot. Her face emerges from under the covers puce with rage.

'You have no fucking idea how I feel,' she snarls. 'None of you do. How could you?' Her tear-stained face is swollen and red. Her lips are parched and beginning to crack. 'I don't want anyone—least of all you—to talk to me about my shit.'

The nurse shrugs her shoulders, then beats a hasty retreat, Cat decides to go outside. She grabs her fags and puts on a white baseball cap to hide her face. It's not exactly looking its best. Not cover material anyway. She opens the door and slams it behind her. She doesn't register the West Indian nurse sitting at the desk in front of her.

On the lawn-side of the Quad there's a small, secluded garden. You go through a tiny, out-of-the way door to face a narrow lane. After you've walked down the lane about a minute and a half you come to a miniscule patch of grass near the main gates that not everyone knows about. Laid claim to by a group of hardened addicts who are very fussy about new recruits to their private club, they do their best to keep its existence a secret. The staff don't seem to know about the garden. Or if they do, they turn a blind eye. Cat walks into the garden and lights up. She sits on the bench and rubs her eyes. A few patients are milling around but she doesn't really notice them. A bloke saunters up to her and asks if he can cadge a cigarette. His body is thin. His angular, bandy legs—shoved down a pair of drainpipe jeans— look like a couple of extended pipe cleaners, at the end of which are a pair of dirty green trainers. His face is lined and coarse, his dry, lifeless black hair is long and straggly, except for the bits that stick up on the top of his head. He reeks of fags and is scruffy enough to pass for a dosser. He can't see Cat properly because her cap's pulled down over her eyes. But she can see him and he's no stranger.

'Christ, Rick,' she says, lifting her cap up, 'what the fuck you doin' here?'

'Charmin,' replies the old rock guitarist, now he's clocked her. 'Dryin' out, of course. Takin' stock. That kind of shit. You know.' He sits down next to the model and, seeing she's not about to offer him a cigarette, snarls, 'Give us a fag, then, you old tart.'

Cat chucks him her packet of Marlboro' Lights and her lighter. Rick's long fingers take one out of the packet. He lights up, inhales deeply and blows a cloud of smoke up towards the sky. 'Read about your shit, Cat. That Dave's bad news, babe. Even by your standards.'

'Yeah, OK, Rick,' says Cat, rubbing her top lip with the

bottom one. 'Don't need a lecture from you too, you old git. Anyway, how long you been here?'

'Week Two. Detox. And it's bleeding shit. Don't think I can put up with this abstinence lark much more. It's doin' my head in.'

Cat grabs back her cigs and helps herself to one. While she's lighting up, Rick carries on gassing.

'Jya know Keef's in here, too?'

Cat chokes on her fag. 'No way!' she says. 'Christ, we could have a fuckin' good party here, only we got no stuff.'

'Yeah, yeah, right.'

'What's Keef in for, then?'

'You know, the tour and everythin.' Mac told him if he didn't clean up there'd be trouble. The last time we did a gig, wanker forgot his bloody chords.'

'Yeah, I know. I was there, remember?'

'Na, not really.'

'No, you wouldn't, would-ya? You probably don't recall beating the shit out of him when he ballsed up on stage, either?'

'Oh, yeah, remember that OK,' Rick chuckles half-heartedly to himself.

'Tough being without a drink, or the other stuff, isnit?'

'Yep,' sighs Rick, 'fucking shit. Mind you, me and drink's no fuckin' good either. Christ, I got so wasted one time, I jumped out of a car while it was still moving. Jesus,' continued Rick, 'I broke my fuckin' legs.'

'Yeah,' says Cat, nodding. 'I was there.'

'Oh,' says Rick, rubbing his forehead and looking a bit confused.

'You don't remember, do you?'

'No.'

'Funny that,' says Cat, throwing the stub down on the grass and treading it in with the toe of her foot. 'Don't s'pose you remember that time you, Soph and me were at the Ivy. Fuck, you were so rat-arsed you crawled under the table and started touching up that old woman's legs.'

'No,' says Rick quietly, shaking his head and looking blankly into the distance. Suddenly, he turns to face her and they both laugh their heads off. Perhaps he has remembered, after all.

Cat's made her stay at the Cloisters conditional upon her not having to discuss her 'shit'—as she likes to call it—with other patients. Although it's all over the tabloids, and any attempt to keep her dignity seems a bit academic, she can't bear the idea of going over it all with complete strangers and being treated like some kind of test tube specimen in a laboratory. She'll go to group therapy sessions—even the clinic's newest invention, Self-injury Recovery classes. She'll sit there, but she won't join in. And if she wants to plug her iPod in, she will. Cat feels that just checking into the Cloisters should be enough to conciliate the fashion houses and convince the agency she's toeing the line. She doesn't feel there's any need to actually *do* the therapy. That's probably Dave's influence. He's checked into the clinic a number of times and checked himself out after only a few days. There's no coke here and there are too many rules and regulations. The routine doesn't suit him. Dave doesn't do routine. He probably doesn't know what routine is. Anyway, Cat's determined to keep herself to herself. Or, rather, she was, but the other night something happened on the ward which has made all that a bit difficult.

She was in her room, her nose pressed up against the window pane. Being thin, she'd managed to climb up and perch on the ledge. She couldn't sit on it properly, it was too narrow. The only way she could stay up there was to squat on her haunches, balancing herself on her two bare feet. It wasn't comfortable, but she felt claustrophobic and needed to get some air. She helped herself to a fag from the pack in her pocket, then opened the window. She couldn't see much—it was about eleven o'clock and pitch black. In the stillness she was thinking about Dave, her life and Os when, suddenly, a deafening, piercing scream came from down the hall. She threw her cigarette out of the window and jumped off the ledge on to the floor. She ran to the door and opened it to find nurses and patients rushing up the corridor towards Kalpana's room. That was the crazy Asian bitch that kept washing her hair every five minutes.

Cat stood in the doorway watching the drama. She didn't feel the need to join in. She didn't want to be involved. She preferred to stay on the sidelines observing the fracas. For once, it wasn't her who was causing the trouble. She wasn't the centre of attention. Although the commotion was almost deafening, Cat didn't really hear it. She felt like she was in a cinema watching a silent movie. But instead of every one rushing around frenetically, the figures running up and down the hall looked like they were travelling in slow motion.

In what seemed like just a few minutes, Kalpana's body was brought out of her room in the Observation Unit and taken away on a stretcher, flanked by three nurses and the duty doctor—a kind of mock funeral procession. And it could have been a funeral. At that stage nobody knew whether Kalpana was dead or alive. After the body was removed, Cat watched a woman emerge from Kalpana's room with blood on her hand, a ghostly, numb expression in her eyes. The woman staggered into the kitchen, put her hands in the sink and turned on the taps. She proceeded to wash her fingers, paying close attention to every tiny bloodstain she could find. There wasn't any soap, so she used washing-up liquid instead. After a few minutes she grabbed the tea towel and rubbed her hands dry. She didn't seem to notice Cat or the woman in the pink dressing gown in the kitchen—she was too preoccupied with what she was doing. When the woman in the pink dressing gown said, 'Hi. You OK?', she nearly jumped out of her skin.

Putting her hands up to her chest, she said, 'God, I didn't see you standing there. You scared the life out of me.'

'Sorry, I was a bit phased. You know, all that...all that...'

'Yeah,' said the girl, putting the tea towel down. 'I know. Um, by the way, I'm Marianne.'

'Lynette.'

Cat examined her two fellow residents as they chatted. The one on the left was rather plump. Shame, though Cat, because she was really quite pretty. If she slimmed down a bit...mind you, no good going to the opposite extreme like her. Not much over six stone and more like superscrag than supermodel. The other girl was supposed to be a writer. Novels, apparently. So she'd been told. Cat had never heard of her, but then Cat never read anything. Well, except maybe the labels on her designer clothes. Most of the time she was just too out of it. Much too out of it to do anything remotely serious. Except when it came to Os, of course. She was serious about him all right. She loved him with a vengeance. She'd do anything for them not to be separated. It looked like she might have to resign herself to it, though. In the aftermath of the publicity surrounding the photos, Os's father had instigated legal action to have his ex-lover declared unfit to be the mother of her own child so he could get custody. He was terrified of Os being around wasters like Dave and his drug-dealer mates, and was sure they smoked in front of him.

Cat was fed up of watching, she was ready for a gossip. She walked towards the kitchen and introduced herself.

Dr Chaudhry saw Cat three times a week while she was undergoing detox. Today was her third session.

As she lay on her bed looking up at the yellow-brown patch on the ceiling, she had to face it—her life was one unholy mess. She might be worth millions but so what? She was separated from her child. The man she loved was a louse and didn't appear to care two pins for her. She hated herself. She felt worthless. What was there to live for? What, for fucksake, could Dr Chaudhry and his team at the Cloisters do about all of that? Cat knew there were no certainties, no guarantees, and that this was probably her last shot. If this didn't work…well, there was always coke.

Dr Chaudhry looked round Cat's room, which was fast resembling a pigsty. In other words, she was making herself at home. Her stuff covered up every inch of the place. Plastic jars and bottles stood or lay on their sides on every available surface, their lids off. Cigarette butts were stacked up in small mountains wherever you looked. Clothes and shoes were strewn in messy piles on chairs, tables and on the carpet, while the insides of wardrobes and drawers lay empty and unused.

Dr Chaudhry was sitting in a chair at the foot of the bed. 'When was the last time you saw or spoke to your father, Cat?' he asked.

'My dad?' asked Cat with a nervous look on her face as she stared up at the ceiling. 'Christ, do I have to talk about him?'

'No,' said Dr Chaudhry, massaging his chin, 'but it might help.'

'My dad and I don't get on. He...he's a bully.'

Cat got up from the bed and walked up to the window. She helped herself to a cigarette, lit up and started to inhale.

'What sort of bully, Cat?'

'Look, he left home when I was very young,' she sighed impatiently. 'He went to live abroad. He wasn't around much. Well, he did come back when I was about twelve but...look, I really don't see where...fuck...'

The tears started to run down Cat's face as she squatted on the floor under the window. She was beginning to open up. 'He had an affair. He remarried. Look, my father's always made me feel like shit. He criticises every little thing I do. He always has. He thinks I'm a complete waste of space. He's never given me any attention. My mother was no better, either. I despised her for letting it happen, for letting him go. She was weak.'

Cat paused to inhale, and to catch her breath, then went on talking. 'Every fucking holiday I'd be sent abroad to spend time with him and that bitch of his. Three times a

230

year, for fuck's sake. He was always so bad tempered, so impatient. He still is. His wife made me sick. They were all over each other. They didn't want me there, so why did they fucking make me go? Why?' Cat was sobbing her heart out now, wiping the tears away with her sleeve, and then sniffing. 'That was when I started to cut myself. I told him about it once but he just laughed and said it was all a lot of nonsense. That I was being childish and melodramatic. I was so upset I started cutting myself more and more. To shock him into responding to me. To punish him for abandoning me. For his total lack of interest.

'I took an overdose once. I was fourteen. I wasn't trying to do myself in, Christ no. I just wanted to get his attention. That's why as soon as I did it I dialled 999, told them what I'd done. I took a whole bottle of aspirin. Or, maybe it was paracetamol. I dunno. Anyway, I swallowed a bloody great pile of them, washed down with a couple of bottles of cider. My friend had been pissing me off big-time, she'd been trying to get off with my boyfriend. But it didn't have anything to do with them, not really. It was about him—my dad. The school went ballistic. The head tried to get me thrown out. But when Mum explained it was cos of the divorce, she soon changed her tune. Only just gone through a divorce herself, Mum reckoned. Anyway, there I was lying in my hospital bed...' And then Cat laughed. 'Great fucking view, too. I was taken to that hospital on the river. You know the one I mean,' she said, turning to Dr Chaudhry. 'The one opposite Westminster. St Something or other. I could see Big Ben if I yanked my head round a bit. Christ, it's all coming back now. Yeah, my dad came over. I felt triumphant for about five minutes only to hear him say I'd been a complete fucking idiot and he was going straight back to Europe. And I had, hadn't I? I mean, nothing changed, did it? He went back to his life and to her. And that was that.'

Lynette, Marianne and Cat were in the Day Patients' Lounge. The radio was on loud as usual. There were ten minutes to go before the next class and the girls had come in to grab a coffee. Suddenly, a short, slim girl with light brown hair reaching down to her waist rushed in. Her hazel-green eyes looked furtive, her face was covered with spots. She was just a kid, no more than about nineteen. She'd obviously been running—she was out of breath and her chest was heaving.

'You'll never guess what's happened,' said the girl. 'They've found them. Talia and Noreen, they're back.'

The girls exchanged excited glances.

Noreen and Talia were about seventeen. They'd been at the Cloisters just ten days. As soon as they clapped eyes on each other they hit it off. Their circumstances were similar. Both had a problem with alcohol and food. They consumed way too much of the first and far too little of the second. Unbelievably thin, super-bright with wild, secretive eyes and long, unkempt hair (one blonde, the other brunette), they were shipwrecked souls looking for emotional rescue. One had lost her mother recently, the other her father. Life held no attractions for Noreen and Talia, so they decided to escape. One morning they walked out of the Cloisters arm in arm. They went missing for about five hours.

'Where did they go?' asked Cat, agog for the gossip. 'Are they all right?'

'Yeah, they're OK,' said the girl, after helping herself to a cup of water to quench her thirst and collapsing on to one of the sofas, 'God, you'll never believe this.'

'So you keep saying,' said Lynette, sidling up to the radio and flicking the off switch. It was difficult to hear with the din. 'Just tell us, will you?'

'Well,' said the girl, swallowing to clear her throat. 'First, they stole some money. Don't know who from but, anyway, they got some and they went to the off-licence to buy some wine. Then they climbed to the top of one of those tower-rise council block thingies. Down the road, not very far from here.'

'Bloody hell!' exclaimed Marianne. 'What happened then?'

'I'll tell you if you give me half a chance,' replied the girl, still slightly breathless. 'They got to the top of the block when they realised they didn't have a corkscrew. So, they smashed the bottles against the wall to get the wine out.'

'Oh, my God!' said Cat, covering her ears. 'I know what's coming. I just know what's coming.'

'Well,' the girl went on, 'when Noreen saw the jagged edge she went mad and started cutting herself. That's in between the two of them getting absolutely trashed. Apparently, they made a suicide pact right there on the roof. It's a miracle they didn't throw themselves off.'

'That's a relief, at least,' said Marianne.

'Yeah,' agreed the girl. 'Something made them climb back down again. When they got down to the street they were still pissed so they decided to play a game.'

'What kind of game?' asked Lynette.

'The one where you lie down in the middle of the road next to the traffic lights and wait for them to turn green. As soon as you see them change, you get up and run.' The way she explained the rules made it sound like maybe she played the game herself.

The three girls stared at each other in horror. They'd done some crazy things in their time, but that was just plain nuts.

Cat looked at her mobile for the hundredth time that day. The message had zapped through about three-thirty that morning When she saw it her heart started racing and her stomach dropped to her feet. She found it impossible to get back to sleep. The text read:

WHAT THE FUCK YOU
STILL DOING THERE!

She glanced at the clock. It was about four in the afternoon. She was sitting in Dr Chaudhry's office. He was at his desk writing. The lead in his pencil broke and he reached for his sharpener. Cat watched him as he placed the tip of the pencil inside the black drum and swivelled it round and round. Cat found the movement slightly hypnotic. It made her feel drowsy as the words of Dave's text kept whizzing round and round in her head. Eventually, Dr Chaudhry removed the pencil, unscrewed the top of the drum and emptied the shavings into the metal bin under the desk.

Cat wasn't interested in anything Dr Chaudhry had to

say to her. The truth was she wasn't really interested in her recovery, as everybody—her agent, the fashion houses, and even the clinic—seemed to refer to this ephemeral, nebulous thing that didn't exist and stood very little chance of ever doing so. This imagined penance they wanted her to achieve. For their sakes. Not hers. They didn't care about her, she knew that. If they tried to force her to choose between Dave and anything else, she'd choose Dave. No matter what she might say or do in the interests of appeasing the agency or the fashion houses—her paymasters. They played games with her, so she was playing right back. By her rules.

As Cat waited for her consultant to complete his notes, she thought about Os. She was scared she had lost him already, and that was enough to make her want to reach for the coke. If, in the end, she did lose the custody battle, she knew she wouldn't be able to do anything to overturn it—not now the photos had come out. Earlier she'd broken down in front of the girls. The pressure had got to her— the fear she might never see Os again was just too much. It made her feel...it made her feel like killing herself. Part of her felt completely responsible. The photos had made everything much worse, she couldn't deny that. To everyone who saw them she must look like such a crap mother. But, at the same time, part of her felt belligerent and bolshy, and a number of questions began to besiege her brain. Why shouldn't she smoke crack if she wanted to? It was her fucking life, wasn't it? Why couldn't she see who the hell she liked? But she knew the answer to all these questions. The fact was it *wasn't* her life anymore—not while it was being controlled by others. The agency, the fashion houses and, though she refused to admit it, Dave himself. They all had her in thrall and competed with each other for control over her. The agency had hired people to keep trouble like Dave away from her, fearful of what impact this connection would undoubtedly have on its investment. In theory, no, they couldn't stop her seeing Dave, but, in practice, yes, they could. By giving her ultimatums. By pressurising her. By threatening her with the reprisals of non-compliance. If Cat responded to the text, she'd open up the floodgates and a dialogue would ensue. She'd discharge herself, go back to Dave and all hell would break loose. The agency would jump on her back again and what about the media? Christ, it didn't bear thinking about. On the other hand, if she didn't reply to the message, she risked losing him. Whether Dave was really in love with Cat—or just her willingness and ability to fund his expensive drug-taking habits—Cat wasn't really sure. She was too scared to wander down that particular avenue so she blocked it off.

Dr Chaudhry put down his pencil, apologised to his patient for keeping her waiting and got up. Ensconced in his favourite red armchair, he began to study her. Cat was looking pale and hollow-faced, her yellow-grey skin splattered with spots. The detoxing was having its effects, though the chain-smoking wasn't helping the process. Raising his hands to just below his chin, he said, 'Last time, Cat, you were telling me about your father. I'd like to move on to something else today. Tell me, how important is fame to you? Would you admit, for example, that you have an addiction to it?'

Cat glared at Dr Chaudhry. Was he trying to provoke her by implying she was a spoilt, rich brat who loved being treated like royalty, who thought anything she did was OK because she was a Class A celeb? That she could have anything she wanted and do anything she wanted? Just because she was famous? Of course she was addicted. Everybody was hooked, not just her. It was all the peripheral stuff, the perks. The stuff that tried to make up for all the shit. Of having to face yourself in the cold light of day. Despite what anyone might think, Cat found it hard to like herself. The fame thing helped her to forget that most of the time she just didn't feel good enough. But the problem was it never lasted. Obviously, or she wouldn't be addicted to smack to keep her high. She wouldn't be cutting herself. If the fame thing suddenly disappeared, who or what would Cat Green be? She'd never given herself the chance to really find out. Truth is, she was too scared to take that leap. Everyone around her propped her up because it was in their interests to do so. She wasn't stupid. She could see that was how things were. She'd fallen off her pedestal and they were trying desperately to hoik her back up. Her failure meant their failure. She was hooked all right and just thinking about it made her feel small, insignificant, inconsequential. Used. She hated that word. USED. How could such a small word have the power to make her feel so bad?

'Of course I'm addicted,' she replied aggressively, 'You get used to the lifestyle. It gives you a buzz. Everyone gets hooked. Not just me.'

'And,' said her consultant, 'you rely heavily upon the people around you, don't you? The people who are responsible for your celebrity? Do you think you could manage without them?'

Cat was fuming. How did this short, ugly little man with

spectacles—she guessed he was Pakistani or Indian—know what she was thinking, what was going through her mind? How to get straight to the shit which kept piling up on top of her? He was telling her that her celebrity had been created—worse, manufactured—not by her, but by others. He was implying that it had nothing to do with her really—it was those around her manipulating their product to maximise sales. Not for her, for them. Dr Chaudhry wanted her to really, really think about it so she could get some control back in her life. Some real, sane control. And he did make her think about it. She was only fifteen when she'd been discovered. Almost immediately she'd been branded, made-over, packaged into a commodity—something crafted, moulded and engineered to be sold at a premium to the highest bidder. 'Yes,' she thought, 'he's right. I don't control my life—not the way it is now. They do. That bunch of sycophantic arse-lickers protecting their precious investment. Their product. Me.' During a split-second flash of enlightenment, her anger made her feel motivated, empowered: 'I have to do something to get back control,' she thought. 'But what if I haven't got the courage? What if I'm just too weak?'

Cat plopped herself down on one of the cushions in the Stables. Neither Lynette nor Marianne attended this session, so Cat was on her own. Most of the group were staring at her, some making it more obvious than the rest. They'd never seen a supermodel in the flesh before and they were curious. Cat was deeply conscious of it. She felt like shouting at the top of her voice, 'Look, you bunch of weirdoes, stop staring at me, will you? Haven't you got anything better to do? Why don't you go off and have a panic attack or slash your wrists?' But she managed to keep a lid on it as she pulled her baseball cap over her eyes, hung down her head and folded her arms defensively. Considering this was the Anger Management class, she was definitely feeling angry. Fucking angry. So fucking angry she was about to give the therapist in charge a real run for her money.

Sarah, who was taking the class, asked all nine of them to stand. Then she invited them to introduce themselves and tell the group how they were feeling. Cat looked round at the circle of misery surrounding her. She was particularly struck by the trembling figure of a young woman with long black hair who had previously been sitting on her hands. Everything from the woman's head down to her feet twitched nervously. Her hair hung in a fuzzed-up maze of knots and tangles. The corners of her mouth were pulled down into deep ruts, while her dark eyes looked terrified and furtive. It was her turn to speak. She opened her mouth and the words came tumbling out. 'I'm Stella,' she stuttered. 'A few weeks ago I woke up one morning to discover that my husband had hanged himself in our kitchen. I came down to find him dangling from the ceiling. He must have spent all bloody night rigging it up while I lay sleeping peacefully in my bed. I'm...I'm so fucking angry. How could he do that to me?' she demanded, sobbing. 'How could he coldly and calmly knock a nail into the wall, tie a rope round it, put his neck inside and fucking hang himself? Knowing that I...his wife...I'd discover him hanging there...like that? How could he do that to me? I just don't understand.'

Stella fell back onto her cushion and began to weep hysterically, almost violently. They were tears of rage, as well as of loss and grieving. She was mad with her husband for what he was putting her through. 'The power of the dead over the living,' thought Cat. A wife turned into a widow by her dead husband's selfishness, unable to forgive him. As the woman's anger poured out of her in torrents, the rest of the class gathered round and tried to comfort her. In a matter of moments Cat felt the attention shift from her to the poor young girl. Her celebrity was powerless now—it had no influence whatsoever. Part of her felt relieved. The other part felt helpless, useless, not enough. A feeling she knew only too well, like an old friend.

Sarah was quick to act. She asked the group to turn towards the wall and place their palms against it. 'Imagine you're trying to break it down. Lean on it as hard as you can. Put all your strength into it. Push and push. Throw all your weight into breaking that wall down. Concentrate every part of your brain on it. Focus on it to the exclusion of all else.'

Cat was sceptical. How the fuck was that going to help with all the rage inside her? She was furious with Dave for letting her down. For buggering off when the chips were down. She was livid with her agency for treating her like a piece of meat. She was incensed with the fashion houses for trying to control her. Most of all, she was enraged with her father. For screwing her up in the first place. As Cat pushed and pushed, and threw herself into bringing down the wall, it began to touch something inside her. Something knotted, twisted deep within, started to unwind. She wasn't sure what, but it felt liberating. It made her feel tired, too. When the session ended she staggered out onto the lawn. She knelt down, then fell onto her back and stretched out, opening herself up to the warm sunshine and the four winds. Some of the anger had dissipated, leaving her drained, weak. But how long would it last? A wave of panic shot through her as she became aware of her vulnerability in all its intensity. She lay there shivering as a fly flitted across her arm. She felt bitterly cold. The sound of sudden laughter interrupted her thoughts. She looked up to see the little West Indian nurse chuckling with another member of staff by the entrance. She was always cheerful, that one. Maybe that's what she needed to get her through working in a place so drenched in pain. Perhaps it was her way of distancing herself from it.

Cat lies in bed looking at the moon through the window. As usual, she can't sleep. With a sigh Cat glides her hand under her T-shirt towards her breasts. Taking each one in turn, she massages and caresses it with her fingertips, paying particular attention to the nipple. She's beginning to feel wet, so she slides her right hand down inside her thong. She starts stroking the insides of her thighs, then moves her hand towards her moistness, rubbing gently up and down. Slowly and softly she moves her index finger back and forth until she comes close to that precious moment of release. She delays it, wanting to intensify the sensation. Finally, she can't bear it any longer and explodes in a succession of peaks, one after the other. It's all over in a matter of seconds. And then come the tears. Slow, silent droplets of water dampening her pillow. She usually cries afterwards.

Cat can hardly bear to look into the future. Of what it might hold for her. Mostly she's terrified of herself. Of the cavalier way in which she treats what is, after all, her special self. Only, she doesn't think she's special. She starts to wonder how and when it all went wrong. What it was that wormed its way into her life and caused it to come unstuck. She wonders whether all that stuff about her father is really legit. Was it really that which put her in this mess, or was it the fame? The overwhelming suddenness of it. The totality of it.

'I am an addict. I am an addict,' she repeats over and over out loud. But it has no effect. She just feels numb. Untouched. There's no shame or guilt and, anyway, she thinks, why should she feel bad or wrong about what she's done? Why should she be singled out for doing what everyone else does?

But, even if there's no guilt, there's plenty of misery and that's bad enough. That's why she's can't stop crying. Her face is wet and she feels icy cold. Her body's trembling, her stomach's nauseous and her hands are clammy. That'll be the withdrawal symptoms. And the detox. And the meds. The terror's getting to her now. Maybe she's having a panic attack. The space she sees stretching out in front of her between now and the end of her life seems vast, empty, petrifying. She lies frozen in pain, disconnected in her loneliness from everyone and everything around her. She refuses to dim the light. She's too scared to face the darkness. She looks around in search of the objects she has brought with her from home to make her sentence more bearable. The giant teddy bear Dave bought her with her money sits at the end of the bed. Cuddling it usually makes her feel cosy and warm but now, in the midst of her deep despair, she distrusts even the familiar and the reassuring. Such things have lost whatever power they once had to bring solace. Dr Chaudhry has advised Cat to keep a thought diary. He says it would be a good idea for her to record her feelings and thoughts. It's bad enough having the thoughts and feelings in the first place, she reckons, without having to write them down. She recalls the conversation she'd had with Lynette earlier on. The chat they'd had about Dave. Nobody understood what she saw in him. And it was nothing she could ever explain to anyone. Logically. With any degree of clarity. He was a crackhead, he was wasting his life. But, she was the same. That was the point. They were exactly the same. In a twisted, depraved kind of way they were soulmates destined to destroy one another.

Cat's sitting on the window ledge in her room. She's figured out a more comfortable position. The window is split up into two large panes divided by a central pillar. If she sits with her stomach up against the stone support, and dangles one leg out of each open window, she can stay up there for ages. If anyone sees her from the gardens, they might get the wrong idea and think maybe she was about to jump. But, at three a.m., it's unlikely that anyone's out there. Cat can sit there puffing away to her heart's content. Technically speaking, as far as smoking's concerned, she's not breaking any rules. Though most of her body's still inside the building, her mouth—which is doing the smoking—is not.

Yesterday, Cat had some bad news, and it's rocked her to the core. Her lawyer called to tell her that the way things are going, she might as well forget about winning the custody war. Now, it can only go against her. Os is staying with his paternal grandparents. He has been since the photograph debacle erupted. She hasn't seen her son for weeks. She misses him so much it's like part of her has got up and walked away, never to return, leaving a huge hole and a barren, grieving heart.

Cat's still there on the window ledge at nine-thirty. She can't be bothered to go down for breakfast, though she climbs down from time to time to go to the loo and replenish her fag store. Staring out of the window, which overlooks a small, neo-Gothic courtyard, a fine morning is coming into shape. She blows up a cloud of smoke into the air and watches it disperse into the sky. She gazes down at the patients gathering on the lawns below her. Some are walking slowly up and down. Others are laid out on the ground worshipping the early sun peaking through the clouds, smoking and listening to iPods. Many are making calls or texting from their mobiles. Cat can make out rotating mouths engaged in the monotonous chewing of gum.

The other day Dr Chaudhry gave Cat a glimpse of the courage she would need in order even to begin her recovery. Momentarily, she had experienced a flash of exhilaration at the thought of regaining control over her life. But it was all too fleeting. And even while it persisted, she felt an underlying mistrust in her ability to hang on to it. And the doubt is still there, festering away. In any case, making an effort was conditional upon hanging on to her son. Since Os is now as good as gone, there's no longer any point. Given Cat's distorted logic, everything now points towards one course of action. Going back to Dave. And, of course, that means going back to coke since the two are inseparable. Dave plus coke equals oblivion which is exactly what she wants. And as quickly as possible. It's the only sure way to dull the pain, numb the feelings. If the Cloisters had been able to come up with their own version of oblivion, they'd really be pulling in the punters. Well, people like her, anyway. If the oblivion finally kills her, what does it all matter, anyway? Especially if she can take her agent and the fashion houses—not to mention the bastards who shopped her to the media—down with her. Then there'll be something to celebrate. It will all have been worth it. Even if she's dead.

Cat stares out into the day. Something down below catches her eye. She blinks several times. She squints. She screws up her eyes. She wonders if she's hallucinating. But she isn't dreaming and she's so shocked she nearly falls off the window ledge back into her room. There he is, getting out of a black cab on the forecourt. It's him all right. Unmistakably him. It's the black hat. His trilby. Only he wears a hat like that. Too big for his head, he wears it back, revealing his high, white forehead. The casual way he's standing, too, as he pays the driver and tilts his hat, it can only be him. He's wearing a pair of faded denims and a white short-sleeved shirt, open at the neck. As he puts his hands in his pocket and is about to go inside, something makes him look up towards her. He spots her at once. She feels his titanium white eyes boring into hers. They remain locked in each other's gaze for what seems an age.

He dashes inside.

Cat jumps down off the ledge and starts pacing the floor. She's excited and petrified at the same time; intoxicated by the thought of being with him again. Terrified of what this might mean for her. Within a matter of minutes he has found her. She stands there amidst the topsy-turvyness of her room, rooted to the spot, shaking and sweating. Her heart is pounding ten to the dozen and she's on fire. In a frenzy of high spirits he bursts into the room. He crashes into the furniture and starts shouting and throwing things around. He's high, of course. Though, on what, it's not immediately apparent. It could be any combination of things. Wearing his trademark white vest under his white shirt, his arms display an array of tattoos and jab marks that co-habit the same bare flesh.

He walks up to Cat, gets behind her and marches her towards the door. Slamming it back, it jolts against the wall.

EPILOGUE

If you're on your own in this life, the days and nights are long,
when you think you've had too much of this life to hang on
...Don't throw your hand.

© *Berry/Buck/Mills/Stipe, Everybody Hurts, 1992*

BBC NEWS FLASH

This morning Cat Green was found dead at her home
in Notting Hill Gate. The 33-year-old international
model is believed to have died from an overdose of drugs
and alcohol. Two months ago Cat Green discharged herself
from controversial rehabilitation clinic, the Cloisters, after
only a few weeks. She checked into the clinic after
photographs of her snorting cocaine at a party with rock
star Dave Hackett were published in a national newspaper.
The former model leaves behind a two-year-old son. No
announcement has yet been made about the funeral
arrangements.

To: marianne.evans@swiftel.co.uk
From: lbf@hello.co.uk

Dear Marianne

I heard the news for the first time this morning. About seven a.m. I was feeding Lily in the kitchen. Pete was fiddling with some papers and his briefcase. Taking something out. Putting something in. Oh, I don't know. It doesn't matter, does it? I just can't believe she's gone. That day she discharged herself. When Dave came marching in to get her, swanning past everybody, crashing into everything. As high as a kite. I didn't realise I'd never see her again. I was going to call you, but I knew if I did, I'd break down. I'm still crying now. I know we didn't really know her that well, but…she was one of us. She was in just as much pain as you and me. I know she was. I just can't believe it…

    Lynette
       xxx

From: marianne.evans@swiftel.co.uk
To: lbf@hello.co.uk

Dear Lynette

I was going to ring you, too. But I didn't know what to say either. James and I are devastated. It seems like only yesterday we were all doing the Salsa together with that lunatic Damien and his yellow silk shorts. D'you remember the day we went out shopping? That chap, Kevin. I hadn't laughed so much in years. Cat. She was such a one-off. I just can't believe it. Killing herself. I never thought she'd do it. Kalpana, yes, but Cat. I just can't get my head round it.

> God bless you, Pete and Lily
> M xxx

To: marianne.evans@swiftel.co.uk
From: lbf@hello.co.uk

M
Don't s'pose anyone will think to invite us to the funeral?! Silly thought. How's it all going with J?

> xxx

From: marianne.evans@swiftel.co.uk
To: lbf@hello.co.uk

No, but we could do our own thing. A sort of memorial thingamajig with music, candles, that kind of thing. We could contact Kalpana. See if she's up for it. Have you got her number or, maybe, her email address?

J has moved in actually. Scary for both of us! He still feels v guilty about Helen. It's going to take time but he's getting ready for his course while they prepare for the case to get to court. He still gets black spells when all the Spacey junk comes back, but Dr Chaudhry's been brilliant.

> M   xxxx

To: marianne.evans@swiftel.co.uk;
              kalpana.prashad@freespirit.co.uk
From: lbf@hello.co.uk

D'you remember that awful song Cat once sang to us? She said Dave had written it for her. I heard on the radio he's going to bring it out as a sort of remembrance thingy. We could light some candles and put it on. I think she'd have appreciated it. What d'you reckon—crazy or what? So happy about you and J.

To: lbf@hello.co.uk; marianne.evans@swiftel.co.uk
From: kalpana.prashad@freespirit.co.uk

Hi M and L
    I'm up for it if you are. And it would be nice to meet up. Talk about old times. Maybe have a drink. When I heard the news, it felt so weird. Not so long ago that could have been me. But, I don't have to tell either of you that. What about having a wake at mine?
               xxxxxxxxxxxxx

The room is in total darkness save for tiny flickerings of light provided by a dozen or so candles casting dark shadows on to the corners and giving off a pungent scent of Egyptian jasmine. Marigold heads are scattered over the soft cream carpet. A hissing noise is coming out of the CD player that sounds like a cross between a laughing hyena and a ewe in labour.

The girls are—to put it objectively—off their heads. Kalpana seems to have ordered in crates of fizz and neither she, Marianne nor Lynette have stinted themselves. Lynette— swathed in a baby pink kaftan edged in gold silk from head to toe—takes up the whole of Kalpana's expansive cream sofa. Her eyelids are heavy and droopy and she's grimacing. The discordant anthem invading her ears is hard to take— even after a magnum of champagne.

Marianne—in jeans and a light green T-shirt—is stretched out on the carpet, her eyes staring up at the ceiling. She's decided to call a halt on the drinking—she probably couldn't say how much she's consumed but it's way over enough. She's mesmerised by the thought that a dear departed friend has been reduced to a disc made of reinforced lead which produces a highly irritating jarring sound when pushed inside a metal box. With one click of the remote control, it can be played and replayed ad nauseam—this hissing and moaning that is in fact Cat.

Kalpana—elaborately dressed in her best blue sari—squats on the carpet, her back resting against the sofa just below Lynette's feet. Her right hand is cupped round a flute half full of lukewarm bubbly. Her eyes remain closed as she shakes her head from side to side, listening to the music. From time to time she opens her eyes and squints.

Suddenly, the CD has a seizure. The caterwauling stops, then starts, then stops, then starts again. The girls are so sozzled they're not immediately aware of it. But eventually they are forced to face the fact that something's just not right. Kalpana struggles to her feet. Given the amount she's knocked back, this is a slow process and does not work at the first attempt. Eventually, she manages to stagger towards the CD player and looks for the off switch. In her drunken stupor it takes her a bit of time to locate it but finally her finger feels the outline of the button and presses it. The effort is too much for her. She falls back onto the carpet next to Marianne's supine body.

In the midst of the silence Marianne's mobile vibrates. James has sent her a text. The plan was that he and Pete would wait in a pub round the corner and take the girls home at the end of the evening. They both sit nervously sipping their lukewarm beer. They're terrified of what might happen tonight. That with Cat's suicide things might go back to how they were.

ARE YOU OK? J xxx

Marianne's left arm stretches out to pick up the phone and she reads the text. She sits up and looks at her friends. They're both crying. So is she. Quickly she starts to type a reply, wiping the tears off the phone so she can see what she's writing:

PLEASE COME AND TAKE ME HOME. I MISS YOU. xxx